THE DUKE MEETS HIS MATCH

OTHER BOOKS AND AUDIOBOOKS
BY KAREN TUFT

Regency

The Earl's Betrothal

The Gentleman's Deception

Wager for a Wife

Kit and Elizabeth

Contemporary

Reality Check

Unexpected

Trouble in Paradise

THE DUKE MEETS HIS MATCH

a regency romance

KAREN TUFT

Covenant Communications, Inc.

Front cover image © Alina Zhidovinova / Trevillion Images
Back cover image Photo by Annie Spratt on Unsplash
Cover design by Michelle Fryer

Published by Covenant Communications, Inc.
American Fork, Utah

Printed in the United States of America
First Printing: December 2020

27 26 25 24 23 22 21 20   10 9 8 7 6 5 4 3 2 1

ISBN 978-1-52441-455-9

To Stephen

I said yes to your marriage proposal after knowing you for three weeks, and it was the best decision I've ever made

Acknowledgments

Thanks to Steve Smith for his pep talks and help in meeting my word count over the course of writing this book and also to Birgit Pullens, who assisted with the German dialogue.

As always, thanks to my editor, Samantha Millburn. I depend greatly on her judgment and insight and consider her a dear friend.

And many thanks to my family and friends, who, this year in particular, offered prayers and words of encouragement and support when I needed them most. You mean the world to me.

REGENCY MAIN CHARACTERS BY FAMILY

Reginald Hargreaves, Marquess of Ashworth *m.* Eleanor

- Alexander *(d.)*
- **Anthony Lord Halford** *m.* **Amelia Clarke-Hammond** — *The Earl's Betrothal*, Book 1
- **Louisa** *m.* **William Barlow Viscount Farleigh** — *Wager for a Wife*, Book 3

Henry Osbourne *(d.)* *m.* Mary *(d.)*

- **Christopher "Kit" Lord Cantwell** *m.* **Elizabeth Spaulding** — *Kit and Elizabeth*, Book 4
- Phillip

Thomas Jennings, Viscount Thurlby *m.* Alice

- Thomas *m.* Isobel
- Martha *m.* Albert Webster
- James
- Isaac *m.* Clara
- **Susan** *m.* **George Kendall The Duke of Aylesham** — *The Duke Meets His Match*, Book 5
- **Lucas** *m.* **Lavinia Fernley** — *The Gentleman's Deception*, Book 2
- Simon
- Rebecca

MAIN CHARACTERS BY BOOK

Character also appears in:

✿The Earl's Betrothal ♥The Gentleman's Deception ♣Wager for a Wife *(prequel)* ◆Kit and Ellizabeth ★The Duke Meets His Match

1 The Earl's Betrothal ✿

- ♣◆ **ANTHONY Hargreaves, Lord Halford**
- ◆ **AMELIA Clarke-Hammond**
- ♣ Louisa Barlow, Lady Farleigh
- ♣ William Barlow, Lord Farleigh
- ♣ Alexander Hargreaves *(d.)*
- ◆★ Lady Walmsley
- ♥ Lucas Jennings
- ♣◆ Elizabeth Spaulding

2 The Gentleman's Deception ♥

- ✿ **LUCAS Jennings**
- **LAVINIA Fernley**
- ★ James Jennings
- ★ Susan Jennings
- ★ Rebecca Jennings

3 Wager for a Wife ♣

- ✿ **WILLIAM Barlow, Viscount Farleigh**
- ✿ **LOUISA Hargeaves**
- ✿ Anthony Hargreaves
- ✿ Alexander Hargreaves, Lord Halford
- ◆★ George Kendall, Lord Kerridge, heir to Duke of Aylesham
- ✿◆ Christopher "Kit" Osbourne, Lord Cantwell
- ✿◆ Elizabeth Spaulding

4 Kit and Elizabeth ◆

- ✿♣ **CHRISTOPHER "KIT" Osbourne, Lord Cantwell**
- ✿♣ **ELIZABETH Spaulding**
- ✿★ Lady Walmsley
- ♣★ George Kendall, Duke of Aylesham

5 The Duke Meets His Match ★

- ♣◆ **GEORGE Kendall, Duke of Aylesham**
- ♥ **SUSAN Jennings**
- ✿◆ Lady Walmsley
- ♥ James Jennings
- ♥ Rebecca Jennings

Chapter 1

July 1813

It was utterly laughable what one did for one's country and monarch at times, George Kendall, the Duke of Aylesham, thought as his traveling coach entered the village of Ashworthy in Oxfordshire. It was still morning, as George had begun his journey well before dawn—arising from his bed even before the cock had crowed and the farmers had risen from theirs.

For, in order to complete the assignment he'd accepted from Lord Castlereagh, the foreign secretary, he must face the woman to whom he'd been betrothed and who had jilted him. He must *also* face the only woman since that unfortunate occurrence whom he'd even briefly considered courting, whose marriage was being celebrated today. And George would be attending the festivities uninvited by either the bride or the groom.

The coach proceeded down the high street of Ashworthy and pulled into the courtyard of the Red Ox Inn. A group of stablehands rushed over to see to the horses, and a man wearing an apron approached the coach while George exited.

"Welcome to the Red Ox, my lord," the man in the apron said, bowing.

"You are addressing the Duke of Aylesham," George's coachman, Bentley, barked.

George fought for patience at Bentley's sharp words. It wasn't as if *every* innkeeper in His Majesty's kingdom could recognize *every* coat of arms on sight.

"My deepest apologies. Welcome to the Red Ox, *Your Grace*," the man said, turning scarlet and bowing several times in succession.

George acknowledged the man with a slight nod. "I need a room for the night and accommodations for my servants," George said. He wanted a brief nap before he had to face the demands of the afternoon, but it was not to be.

He couldn't believe he had actually agreed to this particular assignment.

"Of course, of course!" the innkeeper said, bowing again and gesturing toward the entrance to the inn. "The wife's got a nice breakfast set up, we can have sent to your room, and we can have a bath drawn, and—"

George held up his hand. The innkeeper stopped speaking.

"Breakfast would be appreciated. That is all," George said. "My valet will deal directly with you if there is anything else."

"Yes, Your Grace. Thank you, Your Grace," the man said, bowing repeatedly again.

George nodded and then strode across the courtyard toward the inn, with the owner scurrying over to open the door for him.

Soon enough, he was settled into the best room the inn had to offer—it was devoid of any style, but at least it was clean—and a hot meal of eggs, sausage, beans, and bread arrived soon afterward. George was not particularly hungry, but he ate what was placed before him, as discipline required. He needed his strength today.

It was an utterly ludicrous situation in which to find himself, although it didn't seem particularly humorous at the moment. Perhaps he would find the humor in it at some future date, but not now.

He called for his valet.

Evans stepped into the room from his adjoining one. "Yes, Your Grace?" he asked.

"It's time for me to face the ghosts of my past so that England's future may be assured," he said with not a little sarcasm. Evans would understand; he'd been George's father's valet before becoming George's and was, truth be told, the person who was the closest thing to a father figure George had ever had. Not that Evans was really that much of a father figure.

Actually, George hardly knew what having a father was like, or a mother, for that matter. He barely remembered anything about either of them—only the occasional story or two that he'd been told over the years. George's mother had died giving birth to him, and his father had died when George was still in leading strings. As a result of the latter, George had inherited the honorary title of Earl of Kerridge, Evans as his valet, and his father's solicitor, Mr. Oliver Dutton, Esquire, who'd been designated as George's guardian in his father's will and had remained a pain in George's backside ever since.

"Your mind is wandering again, Your Grace," Evans said.

"My mind never wanders, Evans. It goes precisely where I send it."

"If you say so, Your Grace," Evans replied.

"Hmm," George muttered, removing his ruby stickpin and untying the neckcloth and tossing it aside. "I must endeavor to look better than my usual best today, Evans. You must outdo your always outstanding work."

"Understood, Your Grace," Evans said. "I have already seen to your boots and clothing."

"What would I do without you, Evans?" George said as he unbuttoned his waistcoat.

"You would find someone to replace me," Evans replied. He wrapped a towel around George's neck and lathered his face. "Now, hold still," he said, picking up the razor and flashing it in front of George's face. "I currently wield more power than even the mighty Duke of Aylesham."

George nearly smiled at Evans's attempt at humor. It was the most lighthearted he'd felt since he'd left his London home this morning, although that really wasn't saying much.

Soon enough—all too soon—he was dressed impeccably and descending from his carriage at Cantwell Hall, the estate of Christopher "Kit" Osbourne, Earl of Cantwell, who had married Lady Elizabeth Spaulding this very morning and whose wedding festivities George would be joining at the invitation of Cantwell's brother, Phillip Osbourne.

For George and Phillip had business of the Crown to discuss, and doing it under the guise of a country wedding had been deemed the best approach.

Susan Jennings had attended enough weddings to last her a lifetime—yet, here she was, once again, attending another one. But, really, she had only herself to blame. With her wits entirely intact, she had agreed to travel to Oxfordshire with her brother, Lucas, and his wife, Lavinia, to attend the marriage of Lucas's friend Lord Cantwell to Lady Elizabeth Spaulding.

Susan had grown to love her new sister-in-law, Lavinia, ever since Lucas and Lavinia's own wedding the previous summer. She was clever, and Susan enjoyed their lively conversations. Lavinia was currently expecting the couple's first child, and Lucas had thought Lavinia would appreciate having Susan as a female companion for the long journey. Agreeing to accompany them from their home in Lincolnshire to Oxfordshire had sounded to Susan like an agreeable diversion from the routine of country life.

However, now that Susan had sat through the wedding, which, she conceded, had been lovely, and had sat through the luncheon that had followed, which had been delicious, and had mingled and chatted a bit with the many and varied guests, she was ready for a different type of diversion, one that provided peace and quiet away from the crowds and noise and conversations about nothing and everything.

She liked socializing with people well enough, but she had her limits.

Looking about to make sure she wasn't being observed, she slipped out of the ballroom. She had made a note to herself of where the library was located when she and Lavinia had been taken on a tour of Cantwell Hall after arriving and settling in at Ashworth Park earlier in the week. They had been told by none other than Lord Cantwell himself that he hoped they would make themselves at home during their stay in Oxfordshire and were welcome at Cantwell Hall at any time. Since they'd been in the library when he'd made his pronouncement, she had decided to take Lord Cantwell at his word.

The library was the place Susan would feel most at home anyway.

Its location wasn't far from the ballroom, where all the wedding celebrations were taking place. Susan walked down the corridor, her slippers making no sound on the lush carpets. She eventually reached the library, opened the door, and stepped inside, shutting the door behind her.

She leaned against it and closed her eyes, breathing in the wonderful scent of leather and paper and ink. Her father's library wasn't as large as this one, his collection of books modest by comparison, but it held the same familiar smell she was breathing in right now—one that spoke of years gone by, battles fought, science and mathematics and languages, fantastical tales of heroism and romance all written painstakingly on the pages of the tomes within these walls.

She took in a great lungful of air as though it alone would rejuvenate her and then pushed herself away from the door. It was time to wander the shelves and peruse the titles to find a book or two that would pique her interest for the afternoon, until it was time to return to Ashworth Park.

To her immediate right were four comfortable-looking overstuffed chairs cozily arranged with a few small tables where one might place chosen books. Directly in front of her and to her left were rows of bookshelves placed back to back, creating small aisles between them, and the walls of the library were lined with bookshelves as well. It seemed a veritable feast.

Susan started with the row nearest to her.

The first row held science books, and she quickly learned that the books were arranged alphabetically by topic and title: primarily agriculture and animal husbandry, but alongside those were books on astronomy, botany, physics, physiognomy, and the like. Since those subjects, while interesting, weren't quite what she was in the mood for at present, she continued on.

The next row of shelves dealt with history and appeared to include everything from the Trojan War forward, unless she counted the Bible that she'd spotted sitting on a bookstand near the door, which technically took them all the way back to Adam and Eve. But she had had enough news about the war with the French that she was not inclined to pull any histories from the shelves. And she already studied her Bible on a daily basis.

She continued on through the rows of bookshelves, eventually locating a small section dedicated to literature, which delighted her. After thumbing through several, she eventually decided upon the novel *Evelina*, a delightful discovery, and a book of poetry by William Blake and then settled into a small upholstered chair in a back corner of the room—completely hidden and wonderfully solitary. She removed her spectacles from her pocket and put them on and then allowed the words of Blake to weave a soft, musical rhythm in her head.

George made it past Cantwell's butler merely by handing the man his calling card and glaring at him. From there, it was obvious where the wedding luncheon was being held simply because one needed only to follow the sounds of the guests coming down the main corridor.

He eventually arrived at the ballroom, not surprised to realize he knew many of the people present—the Duke and Duchess of Atherton and Lord Bledsoe and his wife appeared to have made the journey from London. George discreetly avoided the Marquess and Marchioness of Ashworth, who were neighbors of Lord Cantwell and were the parents of Lady Louisa, the woman to whom George had been betrothed eight long years ago. He was well over whatever attachment he had formed to Lady Louisa, but as he had important work to do today, he didn't need the distraction that would come from potentially rehashing events of the past.

Eventually, he spied Phillip Osbourne and subtly caught his attention. Osbourne excused himself from the guests with whom he was speaking and came directly to George.

"You're here," Osbourne said.

"As you see," George replied. "Where do you suggest we talk?" he added in low tones.

"The library," Osbourne said. "It's the first door on the left when you take the corridor that runs parallel to this one."

Before Osbourne could say any more, however, the bride and groom approached them, and George could tell by the expression on the new Lady Cantwell's face that she was surprised to see him—as, of course, she would be, having not invited him herself.

Lady Cantwell was the image of loveliness and gentility. She was undoubtedly the most beautiful woman George had ever seen. Her features were as though painted by a Renaissance master: alabaster skin, shining blonde hair, and eyes of the deepest blue. He doubted there was a man alive who, upon beholding her, would not have become her instant admirer. George certainly had. But alas, she had been off the marriage market since childhood, promised to the Marquess of Ashworth's heir until recently. George had seriously considered marrying Lady Elizabeth when she'd returned to London this Season, despite the disrepute of her father, the Duke of Marwood. But George had taken his eye off the prize—and Cantwell had been the victor.

He nodded to Lord Cantwell and bowed over Lady Cantwell's hand. "Please forgive me for intruding on your special occasion as an uninvited guest," he said to her. Cantwell was studying George a bit too closely for his liking.

"He is not entirely uninvited," Osbourne said in response to his brother's unasked question. "I extended the invitation to him, you see, and as I'm the brother of the groom, I presumed I could invite a guest if I wished."

"Aylesham is always a welcome addition," Lord Cantwell said, still studying George.

George's fingers instinctively sought out his quizzing glass. "Many thanks," he replied. "Lady Cantwell, may I offer my congratulations to you and Lord Cantwell on your nuptials," he said. "However, I would be dishonest if I didn't say that I am disappointed—or perhaps *envious* is a better word. He is an extraordinarily fortunate man. I hope he knows that."

"Thank you," she replied, gazing at George with those soul-deep blue eyes of hers. "I am humbled and grateful for your words."

She truly was the most perfectly beautiful woman, and her graciousness only added to her beauty. He nodded slightly toward her, holding his regret firmly in check, and then excused himself under the pretext of mingling with the other guests.

Instead, he exited the ballroom and went in search of the library.

There had been so few unmarried ladies who'd held George's interest. His granduncle, the former Duke of Aylesham, had encouraged him to find a wife, as male heirs in the Aylesham line were sparse. Worse than sparse. Mr. Dutton had spent a good deal of time researching the family line in search of George's heir. In the meantime, George had spent the past few years subtly reviewing each crop of young ladies making their come-outs, and he'd found no one he could stomach the idea of marrying, and the older he got, the younger and sillier they all seemed.

But enough of such maudlin thoughts, he told himself. Marriage was a business proposition, requiring only that George be able to at least envision himself leading some sort of companionable coexistence with his future wife. He'd held youthful hopes and even the beginnings of love during his brief betrothal to Lady Louisa, and then Lady Elizabeth's near perfection had stirred those hopes again.

It was time to put such romantic foolishness to rest.

The door to the library opened.

Susan looked up from her book.

The door closed with a quiet click.

She waited, her ear straining for any noise. Had someone merely peered into the room and then left? Or was there someone in the library with her now? Ugh, how utterly annoying if her solitude was now to be interrupted. She'd only just set the poetry aside to read *Evelina*. She wanted to continue reading, not deal with the niceties of social conversation. Maybe if she remained quiet . . .

She heard a man sigh, followed by a squeak and swooshing sound that led Susan to conclude—unhappily—that whoever it was had sat in one of the chairs near the door, which meant he intended to be here for a while. Bother. Now what should she do?

She had been here first, she told herself. She would simply ignore the man. Perhaps he would soon leave.

She tried to resume reading—but, honestly, how was one to read under such circumstances, when one's mind was constantly drawn to the awareness of an intruder in the room?

Within a few minutes, the door opened again, and the chair squeaked and swooshed as the man presumably arose to greet whoever had joined him.

Double bother.

"We must make this conversation brief," a male voice said softly.

"Agreed. The less said, the better," another male voice replied. This voice was slightly lower in pitch than the first man's voice. Susan heard the sound of papers rustling. "These are the letters of introduction you will need"—more rustling sounds— "and this is the document from Lord C that will explain our intent."

"Excellent," the first man said.

"This final letter gives instructions to the captain of my yacht."

Susan's forehead knit together. Letters of introduction? A yacht? A document? And who was Lord C? What were these men talking about? Her mind was abuzz with curiosity.

"When can you leave?" the man with the lower-pitched voiced asked.

"As soon as I feel it appropriate, under the circumstances."

"Ah, yes. Family duties. Do you have any questions? If not, it is best that we separate and each return in our own time to the wedding celebration."

"I have no questions at present. I'm fully aware of the gravity of my assignment," the man who'd been given the letters said.

"Excellent. Godspeed."

Susan stayed completely still and waited to hear the door open and close. She didn't have to wait long. The door opened and, after a few moments, shut again.

She let out a breath and stood, closing *Evelina* as she did so. She would put the book of poetry back on the shelf, but she thought she might ask Lord Cantwell if she could borrow the novel and finish reading it before she returned to Lincolnshire—

"Ahem."

She looked up, startled.

A very tall, very haughty-looking, *very angry* gentleman stood at the end of the row of books directly in front of her. He stalked toward her, his mouth in a firm line, his eyes burning like black coals. She disliked him on sight.

"Do you make it a regular practice of eavesdropping on other people's conversations?" he asked her in a surprisingly soft but nonetheless biting tone.

"Do you make it a regular practice of barging into a room that is already occupied and commandeering it?" she replied. It was an overstatement of what he'd done, but she didn't care. He'd provoked her.

He was standing directly in front of her by now. He was much taller than she and looked down at her with disdain, fingering his quizzing glass. "You, ma'am, should have made your presence known, had you any manners at all."

"Perhaps you should have checked the library more carefully if you intended to have a private conversation. Very sloppy on your part, I must say," she retorted.

He raised his quizzing glass halfway to his eye and glared at her.

"If you are trying to intimidate me, you may as well stop right now," she said before he could speak. "I have three older brothers and have dealt with male intimidation in all its varied forms since I was in leading strings. You can have no effect on me."

His quizzing glass was fully at his eye now. He inspected her from the top of her head to her toes. Regardless of her bold words, Susan began to squirm inside. She became acutely aware of her dark, completely unruly hair, her unflattering reading spectacles, and the spray of freckles across the bridge of her nose that she had always detested. Her hand itched to check that her fichu was properly covering her bosom. His eyes, with that awful quizzing glass of his still present, took in their fill and saw everything, she was certain. Every detail. Every flaw. It made her feel little and unworthy.

And *that* made her angry.

"Have you seen enough?" she asked him in a mocking tone. "Would you care to inform me of your conclusions so that I may humbly take them into account and improve myself in future? Or perhaps you would prefer to inspect my ankles first?"

He simply stood there and said nothing, glaring at her with those hot, black eyes of his. It was utterly infuriating.

She smirked and lifted her skirts a few inches, raising one foot as she did so her ankle was in view.

He looked at her ankle and then raised his eyes back to hers, and they locked gazes. His eyes still burned. "I am greatly relieved that we are not acquainted, ma'am, and that there is no one present to make the proper introductions. For you have shown yourself to be utterly without decorum. I can only hope that you have the sense, at least, to treat the conversation you overheard with respect. I pray my hope is not in vain. Good afternoon." He turned on his heel and retraced his steps down the row of books, his back ramrod straight, until he disappeared from sight, and then Susan heard the library door open and close with a bang.

Susan fairly vibrated with anger. It had taken all her self-control not to throw William Blake at him. Despicable man. Boorish, self-important—

She stomped down the row to replace poor William Blake and his poetry back on the shelf. She needed to leave the library. She needed to walk and breathe and not think about what had happened. A walk in the park at Cantwell Hall would be just the thing. A nice, brisk walk where the breeze might blow the thoughts of the horrible man, whoever he was, out of her mind.

She opened the door of the library and looked both ways down the corridor to make sure no one was about, then she returned to the ballroom, her eyes searching to make sure she didn't have a repeat encounter with the man. Fortunately, she didn't see him.

She did spy her brother Lucas, though, and made her way through the ballroom to his side.

"Ah, there you are," he said. "I've been looking for you. Lavinia is tired and would like to return to Ashworth Park. Does that suit you?"

Susan suspected she could walk the entire way to Ashworth Park, rather than ride in the carriage, and it still wouldn't be enough to settle her tumultuous feelings. She smiled at her brother instead. "It does suit me—once I ask Lord Cantwell if I may borrow this book."

Lucas chuckled. "I should have known *you* of all people would disappear into the library. I could have saved myself a great deal of time if I had searched there first. Well, come on; let's go find the groom and beg his indulgence on your behalf so I may take Lavinia back to Ashworth Park. We husbands and soon-to-be fathers must see to the needs of our wives, and I will not have her overexert herself."

They eventually spotted Lord Cantwell, who, Susan observed, was in such great spirits and so enamored of his bride that she could have asked to take the chandelier in the entrance hall and he would have readily agreed.

Lavinia, on the other hand, was too tired for conversation during the carriage ride home, and Lucas was too busy fretting about her to say much of anything, which was entirely fine with Susan. She herself was so preoccupied with her encounter in the library that she stared out the window all the way back to Ashworth Park, the detestable man's words repeating over and over in her mind:

You, ma'am, should have made your presence known, had you any manners at all.

I am greatly relieved that we are not acquainted, ma'am, and that there is no one present to make the proper introductions. For you have shown yourself to be utterly without decorum.

Boorish, self-important, loathsome man, whose dark hair had glinted with burgundy when the light from the window had struck it. Whose intense, dark eyes had stared deeply into her own from their lofty height. Who'd made her shiver when he'd taken in his fill of her. Who'd said such terrible, hurtful words to her. She hated him.

Even worse, she hated that she'd found him attractive even while he'd torn her to bits.

She hoped she never learned who he was.

Chapter 2

April 1814

Susan sat by helplessly and watched as her youngest sister, Rebecca, cried buckets of tears. "It is so unfair," Rebecca sobbed, repeatedly dabbing at her overflowing eyes with her handkerchief. "I've climbed that silly fence stile hundreds—*thousands*—of times! *Why* must I fall *this* time, and not only that but *break my leg* when we are to leave for London in *only two days*!"

This morning, Rebecca had been carried home by a kind, young stranger, her lower left leg slightly askew. Mama had sent for the surgeon, who had arrived not long thereafter and had set and splinted Rebecca's broken bone. Now it was afternoon, and a few minutes ago, Mama had given her another dose of laudanum.

"Never mind that," Susan said. "We are only grateful that someone discovered you lying there and brought you safely home. Otherwise, who knows how long you would have been there." Mr. Arnold, the neighbor whose land was adjacent to their father's property, had died not long ago, and the new owner hadn't arrived to take possession of it yet. "You shouldn't have been attempting to cross a stranger's property anyway."

"I don't see why not. Mr. Arnold always let us." She sniffed and dabbed at her nose again.

"The new owner is not Mr. Arnold, though, is he?" Susan said.

"But it saves *so much time* when walking to the village." Rebecca sighed. "I know, I know. It was wrong of me. And now I'm being divinely punished for my trespass, and I *cannot imagine* a worse punishment when all the news says the French are nearly defeated and the war may end at last. The excitement of being in London at such a time if it all comes to pass! The colors and spectacle of it all! The grand ladies and gentlemen! It was to be rollicking good fun, and now I cannot go!" Her sobbing began anew.

Susan was certainly glad the war might be coming to an end, and she completely understood the English population's desire to celebrate. She was even willing to admit that personally witnessing the historic events unfold was an intriguing prospect. But the bowing and scraping and fanning oneself and holding back one's opinion and smiling demurely in London Society was not something she was particularly looking forward to.

Nor was going to London on her own now at the expense of Rebecca's well-being.

Susan had primarily agreed to Lady Walmsley's invitation to join her in London for the Season because Lady Walmsley had offered to sponsor Rebecca's belated come-out, and for that, Susan had been willing to tolerate Society for a few months.

London held bad memories for her—memories that had nearly broken her heart. Not that she had ever cared to admit such a thing to anyone.

"I have discovered that I adore the company of young people," Lady Walmsley had written in her original letter of invitation. "And when I learned of your brother Lucas's heroic efforts in Spain that saved the life of my dear great-nephew-in-law, I decided I must do something to repay his generosity of spirit."

Both Rebecca *and* Susan had been invited. Susan suspected that her own inclusion in the invitation had been so that Lady Walmsley could reassure their mother, who would undoubtedly have been more agreeable to giving her consent if Rebecca were to be in London with a family member present. They did have a brother currently residing in London, Simon, but as he was sowing quite a few wild oats, he was not a candidate for the job of responsible familial chaperone.

On the off chance that Mama had not been leaning toward giving her permission, she had been entirely convinced after Lady Walmsley's aforementioned great-nephew-in-law himself, the Earl of Halford, had written to vouch for Lady Walmsley and encourage Mama and Papa to give their permission. "Dear Great-Aunt Margaret" thrived when she had lively young people to keep her company, he'd said. So Mama had written to James, Susan and Rebecca's older brother who was a solicitor in the city of Lincoln, to see if he would escort the two of them to London and into the safe hands of Lady Walmsley. James had written back promptly, agreeing to accompany them, and would be arriving later today.

And now Rebecca wouldn't be going to London after all.

"I cannot abandon you after this," Susan said at last, noting that Rebecca was finally beginning to get drowsy from the laudanum. "I shall write to Lady Walmsley and inform her of your accident, and I shall stay with you and keep you company and help nurse you back to health." She leaned across the chaise longue in which Rebecca inclined, Rebecca's splinted leg cushioned by pillows, and patted her sister's hand. "Don't worry. I won't leave you."

"But you must!" Rebecca cried. "How else am I going to hear about anything that happens? You must go and write to me every day! You must attend the parades and the balls and, oh, everything! *Why* did this have to happen?" She dabbed at her eyes again. "My handkerchief is worthless; it's just a sopping rag now."

Susan felt in her pocket for her own handkerchief to give Rebecca, but she didn't have one. She rarely thought about things likes handkerchiefs. "Here now, it's time you rested. I won't have you making yourself ill over this."

"Nor will I," Mama said as she entered the room with a tray holding a fresh pitcher of water. She set it down and poured a small amount into a cup. "Take a sip of water, dearest, and then you must sleep. Resting will help your leg heal faster."

Rebecca handed her soaked handkerchief to Susan and obediently sipped from the cup Mama held to her lips, then she closed her eyes, and Mama set the cup back on the tray. "Come, Susan," Mama whispered.

"Promise me," Rebecca murmured, nearly asleep already. "Promise me, Susan. You must go, and you must tell me everything."

Susan sighed. "Very well, my dear. For you, I will go."

Rebecca gave a tiny nod and slept.

Mama slipped her arm around Susan's shoulders as they walked down the corridor to the front parlor. "It's a sorry state of affairs, to be sure, but she will get over the disappointment."

"I know that," Susan said. "She is a sweet girl with a reasonable temperament and understands that life has its disappointments. But I feel so guilty going to London without her when it is *she* who was so excited about the prospect. Aside from the historical circumstances, the only interest I had in going was to see the expression on her face as she took it all in for the first time."

"You are too jaded by half, Susan," Mama said, patting Susan's hand.

"And I daresay Lady Walmsley will be disappointed when she discovers that she is playing hostess to the old spinster bluestocking and not the blooming debutante," Susan said.

"Nonsense!" Mama exclaimed.

"I shall be thirty this fall, Mama. You know as well as I that I've been on the shelf for so long as to be completely covered in dust."

"I wasn't referring to your age, Susan, and I won't have you making light of yourself. You are my beautiful, clever daughter, and Lady Walmsley will enjoy spending time with you—of that I have no doubt. When I spoke of nonsense,

I was referring to your unmarried state. *You* know as well as I that it has been of your own choosing. You've had suitors—"

"You would like Lady Walmsley," Susan said, cutting Mama off before she could go too far down that particular conversational path. "She has an abundance of vitality for a woman of her years that I find admirable. Much like yourself."

"*None of whom* you gave the slightest encouragement," Mama continued undeterred.

Susan sighed. How many times must they talk about this? "Mama, I know you mean well, and perhaps this invitation from Lady Walmsley has raised your hopes, but, as I have told you on countless occasions, there is nothing that sounds more unappealing to me at present than marriage merely for marriage's sake."

"Can you look upon your brothers' and sisters' happiness and not yearn for what they have?" Mama asked.

"I am exceedingly grateful that my married siblings have found love and happiness. We had the best examples of that growing up, you know," Susan said, giving Mama a hug. Susan herself had yet to meet an honorable man who could hold her interest for longer than five minutes—certainly none of the suitors she'd had during the first years after her come-out had done so, except for—well, she wouldn't think about that single near disaster that had been Lord Frome. How was she to tolerate a lifetime of being shackled to someone who was her intellectual inferior? The answer was simple: she wouldn't. As an unmarried woman, she was still her own person, not some man's property to do with as he pleased. "I cannot help it if all of the gentlemen I have met have left me cold."

An image of fiery dark eyes flashed across her mind and then was gone.

"What's the matter?" Mama asked, looking at her with concern.

Susan shook off her reaction to the image. "Nothing. I'm fine," she said, smiling with what she hoped looked like reassurance. "Now, believe me when I tell you that I am perfectly content to live my life here with you and Papa and play the doting daughter, sister, and aunt."

"I can still hope, for your sake, can't I?" Mama said.

"I cannot stop you, but I'm afraid your bluestocking daughter is only enthusiastic about London because of the history being made. I doubt there is any gentleman in Town who will be able to compete with that."

"I shall pray you are wrong," Mama replied.

Susan chuckled. Mama was such an optimist.

Susan, however, was not.

A slight knock on his library door interrupted the work George was doing with his private secretary, Benjamin Henshaw. "Come," George said, still perusing the documents Henshaw had placed before him.

The door opened. "Mr. Dutton is here to see you, Your Grace," George's butler, Talbot, said.

"Dutton?" George said, finally looking up. "I wasn't expecting him. Did he give a reason for his visit?"

"No, Your Grace," Talbot said.

As annoying as Dutton could be at times, the family solicitor didn't normally show up on George's doorstep willy-nilly like this. He glanced at his secretary. "That'll be all for now, then, Henshaw."

"Very well, Your Grace." Henshaw scooped up the documents, bowed, and left the library.

"Show Dutton in, Talbot," George said.

Talbot bowed and left.

George inhaled deeply and let it out slowly. The past several months had been trying ones, and Dutton's showing up like this portended more of the same.

"Mr. Dutton, Your Grace," Talbot announced, preceding the attorney into the room.

"Have a seat, Dutton," George said, gesturing toward the chair Henshaw had previously occupied. "Apparently, you have something of import to share; otherwise, you would not be here."

"Thank you, Your Grace," Dutton said, sitting as instructed. "And you are correct."

Talbot exited quietly and shut the door.

George watched as the man opened his leather case, removed a folder of documents, and began riffling through them. "I'm waiting," George said in a soft tone not intended to be soothing.

"Beg pardon, Your Grace," Dutton said. "I know your time is valuable." He handed George one of the papers from the file. "As you are aware, for a while now, I have had my clerk researching your family line, in the hopes of locating your heir—your presumptive heir, that is, should you—"

"Never produce an heir of my own," George said, finishing the man's statement. George was only too aware that he'd neglected his duty in that area. But an heir required a *wife*, and George had yet to find a suitable candidate for the role. "And *why* was this search not carried out while my granduncle was still alive?"

"He, uh, held great confidence in your, shall we say, procreative abilities, and whenever I raised the subject, he dismissed it. But—and please forgive me for being blunt—" He paused, apparently waiting for George to object to his warning of the bluntness to follow. When George only stared at him, Dutton continued. "Well, Your Grace, you haven't been as . . . enthusiastic . . . about the matter as I believe your granduncle expected you would be. And after this past month . . ." He trailed off.

This past month.

In addition to a few close calls during his travels to the Continent George would rather not recount at the moment, he'd also been laid up with a serious bout of pneumonia—and truthfully, being that ill had made him take a good, hard look at his own mortality. There had been more than one occasion during his fevered delirium when he had wondered if he'd be meeting his Maker soon. "And so you took it upon yourself to increase your efforts in locating my heir, if there is one to be had."

"Precisely. I have a responsibility to the dukedom, Your Grace, and I take that responsibility seriously." He leaned forward in his chair. "And here I will not apologize for being blunt. I was summoned to Aylesham House on multiple occasions last month when it appeared you were not long for this world. Seeing you at death's door made it imperative that I begin a thorough search for your heir presumptive, yes. Seeing you at death's door more than once convinced me further that I was correct in doing so. That being said, I am greatly relieved—*greatly* relieved—that you are recovered, Your Grace." The man looked grave.

Dash it all, Dutton was right, and George couldn't fault the man for doing his job and anticipating the needs of his employer, now, could he? "Carry on," he said.

"Thank you. If you will look at this document"—he pointed to the paper in George's hand—"you will see that after extensive research, I have diagrammed your line of inheritance, beginning with the first Duke of Aylesham and on down through the male line until we come to you, the fifth Duke."

George looked over the diagram. "None of this is new information." George's father or grandfather before him should have been the fifth Duke of Aylesham, had they not predeceased George's granduncle.

"*This*, however, is new information." Dutton handed George another diagram from the folder. "As you know, the first Duke of Aylesham had two sons; the eldest son, your great-great-grandfather Arthur Charles Kendall, became the second duke. All subsequent dukes have descended from his line. Your line. Since you currently have no heir apparent, I have searched for your heir presumptive following the line of the first duke's second son." He once again leaned over and pointed to a name with his forefinger. "That searching has led me to Roderick Arthur Kendall, your third cousin once removed."

He took a third document from his folder and placed it on George's desk. "I received this just this morning, Your Grace, after making further inquiries."

George scanned the top of the document. "*Penal* transportation?"

Dutton cleared his throat. "Apparently so, Your Grace. Roderick Arthur Kendall, your third cousin once removed and heir presumptive, was transported to a penal colony in Australia for forgery, as you can see by the official record you are holding."

What an odd thing it was, George mused as he read the convict record before him, to feel a sense of elation at finding a blood relative while simultaneously learning said relative was a *criminal*, of all things. "Do we know anything more about this cousin of mine?" he asked.

"Not as yet, Your Grace; although, with your permission, I will see what I can discover."

"You do that," George said, handing the papers back to Dutton in a manner as to inform the man their meeting was concluded.

Dutton looked at him inquiringly.

"Was there something else?" George asked, fingering his quizzing glass impatiently.

"Am I to notify Mr. Kendall of his position as heir presumptive? Should anything happen to you—"

"Nothing will happen," George said, cutting him off. Heaven forbid. "Let us find out what we can about the man and his situation before we go haring off in all directions, shall we?"

"Of course, Your Grace."

"Thank you, Dutton," George said, his tone leaving no question this time that the meeting was over.

Dutton carefully placed the papers in his folder, then slid the folder back in his leather case before rising to his feet. "I shall inform you immediately when I receive any further information."

"Thank you, Dutton," George said again, his tone pitched to suggest boredom. The majority of his associates would have gotten the hint by now, but Dutton was more resistant than most.

The lawyer crossed to the door and opened it. "Your granduncle had high hopes for you, young man. He loved you." And then he disappeared out the door, closing it with a snap. Few people got the last word in with George, but Dutton had managed it, which irritated George—and also impressed him.

His Granduncle Arthur, the fourth Duke of Aylesham, had been a courtly but kind man and a confirmed bachelor, but George knew very well that Granduncle Arthur had expected George to marry. The man had said as much to him on multiple occasions.

George rose from his desk and strode to the window, hoping the view of his gardens would soothe him. It didn't.

Granduncle Arthur had never led the way when it had come to marriage, so George had always returned fire by claiming it was hypocritical for Arthur to browbeat him on the subject. After George's brief betrothal to Lady Louisa Hargreaves had failed nine long years ago, he had become disinclined to marry. Perhaps if Arthur had left well enough alone, George would have been less resistant.

But not only had he been resistant; he'd outright refused. And he *still* refused. He would *not* lower his expectations when it came to marriage, regardless of the fact that his long-lost heir presumptive had been transported halfway across the globe for crimes committed.

He placed a fist on the pane of glass at the window and rested his forehead against it. He couldn't, in all conscience, allow someone with a criminal record to become the sixth Duke of Aylesham. But there'd been those dangerously close calls and that deadly bout of pneumonia . . .

George couldn't imagine a worse possible scenario at the moment than the one he was facing: marry or else.

Heaven help him.

It was a long two-day journey from Lincolnshire to London, and Susan could feel her anxiety increasing with every mile. She'd hugged a brave Rebecca, who'd been fighting back tears and smiling and wishing her well and reminding her to write often. She'd kissed Mama on the cheek; she'd hugged Papa, who had tucked a few pound notes into her hand, and then she and James had set off, waving through the coach windows as the rest of the family had waved back and their nieces and nephews had shouted their farewells.

Two days, Susan was finding, was a great lot of time when one was traveling in a coach by oneself. Almost an eternity. James occasionally rode with her, but most of the time, he was on horseback, enjoying freedom from confinement inside the coach and the brotherly fear of having to converse at length with his sister. But on this particular rare occasion toward the end of the journey, he had braved the carriage and conversation to be with her, for which she was grateful.

"Tell me more about Lady Walmsley," James said when he'd joined her in the carriage.

Susan had deliberately fought her anxiety and had mostly succeeded, but it all came rushing back with James's mention of Lady Walmsley. "She is an elderly lady, a widow, and was recently discovered to be Lady Halford's great-aunt, as you know. She's short, with a fluff of gray hair and twinkling blue eyes that make her seem rather fairylike and delightful. I met her last summer at Lord and Lady Cantwell's wedding. I spoke with her only briefly though, you know, so I'm as surprised as anyone that Rebecca and I received the invitation to spend the Season with her.

"I'll be frank, James. I don't know what to expect. It would have been easier with Rebecca here beside me. How long will you be in London?" she said.

"A week at least—perhaps more," he said. "I have work here in Town. Depending upon how that goes will determine my plans. In the meantime, I promise to escort you and this Lady Walmsley, whom I have yet to meet, to your various balls and routs and such."

"Thank you, James," Susan said. "Having you here for the first week, when everything is new and somewhat awkward, is reassuring. I don't think I could have agreed to come here without Rebecca otherwise."

"Now, *that* I don't believe," James said. "*My* sister Susan? The one who has never looked a challenge in the eye and not dared it to do its worst? The one who ably set every unworthy suitor back on his heels during her come-out? The one—"

"You may stop now—"

"Who insisted on studying with her brothers when they were tutored and always bested them in every subject?" he continued, ignoring her.

"Except you. I rarely bested you. But I take your point. Since I have faced such daunting challenges in the past and survived to speak of them, I supposed I can take on an elderly woman who looks like a forest pixie."

"Perhaps she will turn out to be your fairy godmother."

"Don't be ridiculous, James."

He laughed and then glanced out the carriage window. "We're nearly to Mayfair; I hadn't realized. Time does fly when one is deep in conversation."

Time had truly flown more swiftly with James keeping Susan company. Now she must face what the next few months would entail. Her heart was beating much faster than her pride wished it were.

"I think I see your pixie now," James said.

And he was right. Lady Walmsley was standing on the front doorstep of her townhouse, waving at their coach with her handkerchief in welcome.

Susan straightened in her seat, willed her heart to slow, and took a deep breath when the coach stopped. The coachman opened the door, and James stepped out and offered his hand to Susan.

"Here you are at last!" Lady Walmsley exclaimed, hurrying toward them as Susan exited the carriage. "I have been looking forward to this; what a joy to have young ladies here to join me and brighten the entire household!" She smiled in greeting at them, her eyes searching the inside of the coach at the same time. "But where is this young Rebecca I've heard so much about?"

"Hello, Lady Walmsley," Susan said. "May I introduce my brother, the Honorable Mister James Jennings, Esquire."

"Lady Walmsley," James said, bowing his head in deference.

"I have sad news, I'm afraid," Susan continued. "Rebecca is not able to be with us after all. She had the misfortune of breaking her leg three days ago and couldn't make the journey as planned. I am, as you see, your only guest."

Lady Walmsley's countenance fell. "I'm so sorry to hear about your sister." But then she brightened. "We shall do all we can to enjoy ourselves and send her letters and drawings, shall we? Perhaps it will lift her spirits and help her leg heal more quickly."

James looked over Lady Walmsley's head at Susan. "Fairy godmother," he mouthed.

"You both must be tired and hungry after your travels," Lady Walmsley said. "I have told Foster to have tea set up in the parlor." She waved her handkerchief at them, actually shooing them toward the front door. "Come. Tea awaits. The servants will see to your coachmen."

"I didn't intend to stay, Lady Walmsley. I have lodgings elsewhere," James said.

"I know that, young man," Lady Walmsley said, still shooing him toward the door. "But I daresay your men are as tired and hungry as the two of you after driving that coach all day. Foster will see they have some refreshment. Foster is a complete mother hen, even though he's my butler and not my housekeeper. He thrives on taking care of people." She actually looked a bit grumpy when she described him.

"Thank you, Lady Walmsley," James said. "I am most appreciative."

As they followed the dowager countess into her home, James grinned at Susan. "Fairy godmother," he mouthed again, nodding his head in affirmation.

Susan discreetly swatted his arm and continued on into the house.

Chapter 3

George stared at his appearance in the mirror. "Evans," he said to his valet while moving his face from side to side. "Something seems off, but I can't put my finger on it. Perhaps a different waistcoat?" The one he was wearing was a deep burgundy brocade, which ladies had frequently mentioned brought out the highlights of his hair. Vain thought.

"The waistcoat is fine and is one of your favorites," Evans replied while straightening George's dressing room.

"Hmm," George muttered. He squinted in the mirror. "Perhaps it's the knot in my neckcloth, then."

"The knot is fine; the waistcoat is fine."

Blast the man. If Evans weren't Evans, he would give him the sack for his impudence. He brushed a bit of lint from his shoulder and studied his appearance again. "Nonetheless, something feels wrong."

Evans finally looked up from his puttering. "Perhaps it's your smile, Your Grace."

"I'm not smiling," George said.

"Precisely," Evans said.

George huffed out a breath as Evans's words struck home. "Once again, you have hit the nail on the proverbial head. I am loath to attend Lady Bledsoe's ball this evening. Were she not my mother's particular friend—having told me so on more occasions than I care to count—I would remain at home and do something more pleasant. Certainly, *anything* would be more pleasant than dancing with the latest crop of young ladies making their come-outs. I have tried, Evans. Heaven knows I've tried. But how on earth is one to have a conversation with a young lady when she is gaping at one in awe—or wishes to speak only of fashion or who said what to whom." It was bad enough that no matter what event George attended, or had ever attended, for that matter, the room went silent when he arrived, the crowds seemed to part like the Red Sea, and he could very nearly hear the meddling mamas' conspiratorial words being whispered behind their fans.

"I take it there isn't a particular young lady who has caught your fancy this Season," Evans said, putting George's comb and brush in the vanity and shutting the drawer. "Once again."

"No. I even made an appearance at Almack's, if you can imagine." George waited for Evans's reaction. The man knew George's feelings about Almack's.

Evans said nothing.

"*Blast* it all, Evans, I discovered this week that my heir's a *criminal*, transported to Australia. I cannot bear the idea of leaving the dukedom in such a person's hands. And so, I have been diligently looking for a wife as a result."

"*Have* you, Your Grace?"

Insolence. Nothing but insolence from Evans. "I could only bear Almack's for an hour, I'll admit. *Almost* an hour." George shrugged. "I ventured to dance with a young lady or two—"

"Well done of you, Your Grace—"

"I haven't asked for a second dance from any of them. At Almack's or elsewhere." He was certain all it would take was a second dance or a gentlemanly kiss on a gloved hand for all and sundry to begin announcing his imminent betrothal to whomever the theoretical young lady happened to be.

"The Season is still in its early days, and I hear that dignitaries from all over the Continent will be arriving in Town at any moment. Perhaps your lady wife will be among them."

"I highly doubt it, if history bears itself out. Pray, then, Evans, for my increasing and continued good health." He turned away from the mirror. "I am off to Lady Bledsoe's ball. No doubt you shall see me sooner rather than later this evening."

"Try to have a good time, Your Grace," Evans said.

George only grunted in reply.

Bentley had already arrived with the carriage when George exited the house and stood by the carriage door, waiting to assist him inside.

"Thank you, Bentley," George said, allowing the assistance, even though he didn't need it. Bentley was another servant who'd been around since George's father's day.

George gave him direction, and they were off.

Lady Bledsoe's infernal ball awaited.

"I expected you to be tired, my dear, and I *told* Lady Bledsoe that very thing," Lady Walmsley told Susan as they awaited the return of James, who'd gone to the lodgings he'd previously arranged for during his stay in Town.

"I am a little tired but not so much that you should be concerned," Susan said, tugging on her evening glove to straighten the seam a bit.

"I *do* hate to let Lady Bledsoe down—she's *such* a dear friend," Lady Walmsley continued. "Even so, you are *most* accommodating, Miss Jennings. I told Lady Bledsoe firmly that I would bow to the wishes of my guests. *Guest*, as it turns out."

Susan said nothing, feeling the weight of Lady Walmsley's expectations heavy on her shoulders. Attending a ball on her very first night in Town wasn't precisely what she had anticipated—or hoped for.

"Your gown is . . . how shall I say? . . . *demure*—although quite pretty," Lady Walmsley observed with a kind smile.

If Susan was reading between the lines correctly, Lady Walmsley's words meant she was bound to compliment Susan no matter what Susan was wearing. Susan's gown—the only remaining ball gown she owned after so many years in the country—was well out of fashion. "I think we can be more honest together than that, Lady Walmsley, if we are going to keep each other company for the next several weeks. I suggest a better word to describe my gown might be *plain* or, better yet, *antique*."

Lady Walmsley chuckled, and her eyes twinkled as she patted Susan on the arm. "I do believe we are going to get along famously, Miss Jennings. And tomorrow I am taking you to the best modiste in London."

"I don't expect you to do that," Susan said. "I didn't mean to imply—"

"You didn't imply anything, my dear. I brought up the subject myself. *Such fun* it will be to watch you be pampered—nothing brightens the spirits more than seeing a lovely young lady fitted out as she ought to be while in Town for the Season." She clapped her gloved hands together in seeming delight.

What was Susan to do now? "You are too kind," she said noncommittally. She decided to leave the question of her status as a "young" lady alone at present.

"Nonsense!" Lady Walmsley exclaimed. "You have such exquisite features; they deserve to be shown in their best light, and I am going to take great pleasure in seeing you blossom like the rose you are." She glanced out the window when they heard a carriage approach. "Ah, here is your handsome brother now. How wonderful that he is able to escort us for the next few days! I daresay we can fend for ourselves, but how nice to have a dashing gentleman at our beck and call until then."

Susan had never been described as a rose—or any flower at all, for that matter. She *had* been referred to as a thorn in one's side, which was about as botanical as any description of her had ever been.

Foster, Lady Walmsley's aged butler, opened the door to James. "Thank you, Foster. Good evening, ladies!" James said as he entered, removing his hat and bowing elegantly to them. "You are a vision to behold."

"That's the lawyer in him, I'll wager," Lady Walmsley whispered to Susan. "Very intelligent, with the ability to stretch the truth believably."

Susan laughed.

"Foster!" Lady Walmsley exclaimed. The butler had moved away from the door and was now attempting to place a heavy shawl about Lady Walmsley's shoulders, but Lady Walmsley was having none of it. "You are forever trying to get me to wear a woolen shawl at night. I specifically told you I wanted the *lace* shawl. We've had this conversation *endless* times before. I shall *not* be taking a chill this evening; I can assure you."

"There are clouds accumulating overhead this evening," Foster replied. "I am only looking out for your continued good health, my lady."

Lady Walmsley paused. "Clouds, you say? Very well, I shall use the woolen shawl."

Lady Walmsley's reaction surprised Susan. From what Susan had seen thus far, the older lady wasn't the type to back down swiftly. She and Susan were the same in that regard. Perhaps Lady Walmsley respected Foster's opinion more than she liked to let on.

Woolen shawl now firmly in place, a satisfied-looking Foster backed away, and James offered an arm to each lady.

"I'm doubly blessed this evening," James said.

"Such a charmer, you are," Lady Walmsley said, patting his arm. "I wonder that some young beauty hasn't snatched you up already, Mr. Jennings."

"I attribute it to well-developed survival skills, my lady," James replied.

Lady Walmsley cackled. That was the only word Susan could use to describe it, she thought, smiling to herself. She might possibly get through the evening if she had Lady Walmsley and James to keep her company. In fact, she was feeling an air of excitement she'd not felt for some time now—dressing in one's finest and listening to excellent music and watching elegant couples dance together might be rather agreeable. She'd been absent from Society long enough that she assumed she'd be able to sit with the other spinsters and watch the proceedings unobserved; that would be her preference.

There may be a few of her former acquaintances in attendance whom she'd prefer not to see this evening; it was bound to be inevitable that such would occur, of course. But surely, after the passing of so many years—ten, to be precise—old wounds would be forgotten, and bygones could be bygones. It was optimistic on Susan's part, although she really didn't put much stock in it. She knew from experience what Society could be like.

"Aylesham! I'm *so* delighted you chose to join us this evening," Lady Bledsoe said to George when he arrived at her home. She took his hands in hers and air-kissed both his cheeks. "And how handsome you look! Does he not look handsome, Bledsoe?"

George and Lord Bledsoe exchanged a droll look between them. "A veritable sight to behold," Lord Bledsoe replied dryly.

"I did my best to be presentable," George said.

"Ah, but it seems like only yesterday when your dear mama and I enjoyed our first Season," Lady Bledsoe said. It was the beginning of a reminiscence George had heard countless times over the years. It ought to annoy him, but Lady Bledsoe had cherished her friendship with his mother, so he was inclined to let her have her say. "She was the darling of the *ton*, you know," she continued. "Beautiful, clever—but not one to put on airs."

"So you have said," George said.

"I *wish* you had known her, Aylesham. She was a dear girl, and I miss her every day, as you must surely miss her. But I shan't dwell on that, for we are gathered to enjoy ourselves and mingle with our friends and acquaintances and, hopefully, dance." She looked at him with intent in her eye.

"I shall do as you bid, Lady Bledsoe. I shall mingle, listen to the music, and partake of the refreshments and dance a time or two." Blast, but he still tired too easily these days. The whole business of convalescence was annoying.

"That is all I ask," she said. She stepped closer to him while Bledsoe greeted the next guests to arrive and grasped his hand in both of hers. George's back stiffened reactively. "There is more of your mama in you than merely your eye and hair color, Aylesham," she said softly. "I wish I could explain to you what that means. I hope you reflect on the stories you have heard about her to discover this for yourself. I believe it may bring you the happiness you seek. She would want you to be happy."

"What do you know of my happiness or lack thereof?" George asked with a slight edge to his tone.

She dropped his hand and stepped back. "I speak out of turn, I know, and for that, I apologize. Enjoy yourself this evening." She smiled at him and then turned to greet her next guests, the Earl of Iverson and Lady Iverson, who were currently speaking at length with Lord Bledsoe.

George strode into the ballroom, working to quell the vexation he'd felt at her words. How *dare* she? How dare she judge the state of his life as though she had any right to do so? Looking for happiness was a fool's errand. And how dare she intimate that his *mother*—the mother he'd never known, except from what few stories had been told to him on the rarest of occasions—was the key to unlock this missing happiness? It was foolishness.

Whatever good mood he'd had when entering Bledsoe House—if there'd been a good mood—had entirely fled now. But he had told Lady Bledsoe he would dance once or twice and listen to the music and eat refreshments.

Well, he *would* listen to the music, he thought as he stalked into the ballroom with his trained expression that told those around him to keep their distance. The musicians were bound to be of finer quality than those at many London balls because Lady Bledsoe was a stickler when it came to music. And he would eat refreshments because why ever not? And he would find the two least annoying ladies he could to dance with this evening. Then he would leave, having fulfilled his word to Lady Bledsoe.

He would return home to peace, solitude, and—

He didn't allow himself to finish the thought as he made his way through the crush of people already in attendance.

Chapter 4

Susan had never been the type of person to be overly concerned with people's opinions of her, but being at her first London ball after having been absent for so many years gave her trepidation, if she were to be entirely honest with herself. She was also more tired than she'd been willing to let on to Lady Walmsley. Lady Walmsley had seemed disappointed by Rebecca's absence but had been keen, nonetheless, to shift her attention to Susan. Susan hadn't been willing to disappoint the lady further.

"Margaret, I'm *so glad* you could be here," the hostess of the ball, Lady Bledsoe, exclaimed, taking both of Lady Walmsley's hands into her own. "And I see you have brought your young friends along—but I thought you were to have two young ladies with you?"

"That is true," Lady Walmsley said. "Judith, may I present the Honorable Mister James Jennings and his sister, Miss Susan Jennings? It is their younger sister, Rebecca, who was to join us as well, but she broke her leg, poor girl, and was unable to make the trip after all."

Susan watched the warm exchange between the ladies while she curtsied and James bowed. Susan and Mama had not traveled in the same lofty circles when they had been in London before. She waited for Lady Bledsoe's reaction to her friend's hosting an aging bluestocking of a spinster—who was wearing a gown well out of fashion, to boot.

Lady Bledsoe's eyes took in James's appearance swiftly, and from her welcoming expression, it seemed James had passed muster, which came as no great surprise to Susan. James was tall and fine-looking, especially in his evening clothes. Handsome, even. He looked every bit the successful solicitor and son of a gentleman.

Lady Bledsoe turned her gaze to Susan, her eyes traveling up and down Susan's person with the intensity of a hawk that missed nothing. Susan straightened her back and smiled as serenely as possible, waiting for the results of the assessment.

"I do not believe I am acquainted with you, Miss Jennings, although Lady Walmsley informed me that you had your come-out, when was it? Twelve years ago. Yes, that's it. Twelve. And that you enjoyed two more Seasons after that. I have an excellent memory for faces, yet I cannot find yours among any of my acquaintances."

"That would be correct, Lady Bledsoe," Susan replied, bristling a bit. Lady Bledsoe's remarks seemed intended to point out the obvious: Susan's age and spinsterhood. "Our father is Viscount Thurlby of Lincolnshire, who prefers his home in the country to Town."

"As many do," Lady Bledsoe said. "Well, I'm glad I have made your acquaintance now. You have made a good friend in Lady Walmsley, you know. She is most generous and one of my dearest friends. Welcome back to London, Miss Jennings. I hope you enjoy yourself while you are here."

Susan curtsied again, and the three of them continued down the corridor toward the ballroom. Perhaps she had misjudged Lady Bledsoe's comments. Upon reflection, Lady Bledsoe seemed much like Lady Walmsley in temperament, and they were obviously dear friends. Susan almost began to believe she might begin to feel more at ease, although that belief lasted only for the briefest of moments, for as soon as they left Lady Bledsoe, eyes began to turn her way, and lacy fans rose to cover ladies' mouths.

Susan did her best to ignore them. She walked beside Lady Walmsley, a placid smile on her face, and greeted those people to whom Lady Walmsley presented her and James. James was at his congenial best, for which Susan was grateful—but, then, he had been to London on several occasions the past year or two or three, while Susan had not.

She allowed Lady Walmsley and James to lead the way.

The ballroom was large, with high gilded ceilings painted in shades of pale blue, with ethereal clouds and a bird or two soaring amongst them. The exterior wall was comprised of french doors, a few of which were open to allow fresh air into the room, despite the threat of rain. At the far end of the ballroom, Susan could see the dais upon which the musicians were seated and currently playing a lively country dance. Pots of lilies and roses filled the air with a musky scent, enhanced by the exotic perfumes of the men and women.

As the music soared beneath the gilded clouds, guests danced, their movements weaving tapestries of ever-changing color. Others stood together in small groups chatting, their voices creating a low hum under the music.

These aspects of a London ball were the ones Susan appreciated and felt would be difficult not to like. She had forgotten about them.

She responded politely as Lady Walmsley introduced them to Lady Starr, a lovely older woman whom Lady Walmsley referred to as "her dear friend Adeline." After a brief chat, they continued on, threading their way through the crush of people, Lady Starr now with them at the suggestion of Lady Walmsley.

"For I haven't seen you in an age, Adeline," Lady Walmsley said. "And I must hear all of the latest news from your children and grandchildren."

"I am never reluctant to speak on that subject, as you well know," Lady Starr said, smiling. "I doubt I will do much dancing. But one cannot say no to an invitation from Lady Bledsoe, can one?"

"Indeed not," Lady Walmsley said with a chuckle. "As is plainly obvious by the number of people in attendance this evening."

"If you ladies will excuse me," James said suddenly, "I believe I see an acquaintance with whom I should like to have a word."

Susan surveyed the area in which James had been looking to see if she knew the particular acquaintance, but as she was several inches shorter than James, she was unsuccessful.

"Are we to meet this particular friend of yours, James?" Susan asked while Lady Walmsley and Lady Starr greeted a mutual friend. "And by 'we,' I mean 'me,' naturally. I should enjoy getting to know your friends."

"I suppose I can ask him if he'd like an introduction," James replied. "He's certainly respectable. Extremely so."

"That was cryptic," Susan said. "Be off, then, and I shall puzzle over your elusive answer while I gaze in awe upon the *haut ton* of London."

James laughed. "I shan't leave you for long. In the meantime, try not to scare away those who might wish to join you. You must control your piercing eye and your sharp tongue."

"You are not to worry," she said with a wry grin. "I have already promised Mama I will be on my best behavior while under Lady Walmsley's roof. She exacted it from me under pain of death."

James laughed, as Susan had intended for him to do.

"Be off with you, then, Mr. Jennings," Lady Walmsley said, rejoining their conversation. "Young men will do what they must. Ah, here are three seats together, Adeline. They shall do nicely for the time being."

Susan sat in the chair Lady Walmsley pointed to and watched James melt into the crowds of people and then out of sight. She sat and watched as the music ended and a new dance began, watched as gentlemen escorted their partners to the ballroom floor and, while new partners were invited to dance, watched as new lines formed and the music began again.

Watched it all unfold around her as if from a withdrawn, isolated place. Like a dusty old spinster sitting on a shelf.

It would not do.

She stood abruptly. "May I bring you and Lady Starr refreshments, Lady Walmsley?" Her question interrupted the conversation they were having with the lady seated next to them, whom Susan belatedly recognized as Lady Melton, one of the few people Susan remembered from the wedding the year before. "And you, Lady Melton? Would you care for refreshments?"

"I am feeling a bit parched, I will confess," Lady Walmsley said.

"Are you sure it's no bother?" Lady Starr asked.

"Not at all," Susan assured her. She needed to move, to walk. She needed a purpose. She needed to do more than sit.

Collecting dust.

"None for me—but thank you, Miss Jennings," Lady Melton said.

Susan nodded, rather surprised that Lady Melton remembered her name. "I'll be right back, then, ladies," she said.

The refreshment table was on the opposite end of the room as the dais, and Susan went that direction now, excusing herself as she brushed past people and nodded her head in greeting, intent only on her purpose. She stopped to speak with no one—and no one encouraged her to do otherwise. She remembered now why she had disliked balls. She should have asserted herself with Lady Walmsley and asked for an evening of rest before taking on London Society.

Finally, an eternity later, she reached her goal. Suddenly thirsty herself, she dished herself a cup of punch and began to drink greedily. Too greedily, apparently, for in her zeal to drink, she tipped the cup to her lips at too extreme an angle, and when another guest inadvertently bumped her, the punch sloshed over the rim of the cup and all over the front of her dress—the other person wholly unaware of the mishap he or she had caused. Susan hadn't even seen who it was.

But now the entire bodice of her gown was soaked and slightly pink when it should be white.

How utterly mortifying.

There was nothing to be done but address the problem. She quickly scanned the length of the refreshment table for napkins but could see none. She quickly put her cup down on the table and opened her reticule. Had she remembered to put a handkerchief inside? She'd had other things on her mind when they'd arrived at Lady Walmsley's and couldn't remember.

No handkerchief. Of all the times for her to spill her drink, of all the times to *again* forget a handker—

"Ho! There you are. I was just coming to find you." James's voice was not far behind her.

Susan sighed with relief. Surely, James had a handkerchief—and his height would shield her from the other guests while she set to dabbing her chin and neck and bodice dry.

She turned slightly to greet him and found herself face-to-face . . . not with James, no. But with the *odious boor* she'd encountered in the library at Lord and Lady Cantwell's wedding last summer.

His glinting black eyes narrowed upon seeing her.

"Aylesham, please allow me the pleasure of presenting my sister, Miss Susan Jennings," Susan vaguely heard James say. At present, her ears were ringing, and her eyes were locked with the gentleman's, which were like searing black coals. "Susan, may I present the Duke of Aylesham."

"We meet at last," the duke said.

Had George known that James Jennings's sister was *the harpy* he'd encountered last summer, he never would have agreed to an introduction. But he had. The damage was done. "We meet at last," he'd said—a reply he considered diplomatic since making her official acquaintance hadn't been an objective of his.

She was staring at him now, *the harpy*—her eyes wide, her mouth forming an *O* before it snapped shut.

She quickly curtsied. "How do you do?" she managed to mutter.

"Better than you, I suspect," George said. He pulled his handkerchief from his pocket, snapped it open, and handed it to her.

"Thank you," she said, quickly wiping her chin dry and then dabbing her bodice with the handkerchief to soak up what wetness she could.

Had she been anyone but the harpy, George might have felt sorry for her.

"Are you all right, Susan?" Jennings said. "Shall I escort you to the ladies' retiring room so you can set yourself to rights?"

"No, thank you, James," the harpy—*Miss Jennings*—said. George really needed to think of her as Miss Jennings, but his opinion of her hadn't precisely *risen* thus far in this second encounter. It was difficult to imagine that James Jennings, with whom George had acquainted himself fairly well over the past two years, on the Continent and at home, was the harpy's brother. George admired and appreciated Jennings. He'd been with him in very close quarters a few times over the past several months, and he'd come to see him as a true gentleman and a man of action, with a piercing intellect, to boot. Jennings had mentioned coming from a large family and had shared a few anecdotes about them, but that was all.

"It'll be dry in no time, I'm sure," Miss Jennings added, continuing to dab at her gown. The dampness had soaked in, making the front of her drab gown a splotchy pink-tinged mess. George doubted it would dry as swiftly as Miss Jennings hoped.

"It doesn't look as bad as all that," Jennings said. "If you behave as if nothing has happened, I doubt anyone will notice."

Miss Jennings ignored her brother's words of encouragement and kept on dabbing. George gathered she didn't believe her brother's words any more than George did. Additionally, Miss Jennings's unfortunate mishap very likely would have gone unnoticed had he and Jennings not arrived at her side precisely when they had, for she was standing next to *him*—the Duke of Aylesham, who drew attention wherever he went. He could already feel the eyes of the crowd surrounding them burning into his back.

As much as he disliked Miss Jennings, it would be bad form to allow his friend's sister—regardless of his personal feelings toward her—to suffer from the additional exposure his presence on the scene had unintentionally created. A sinking feeling of doom hit his stomach. "Miss Jennings," he said with great reluctance, "would you care to dance?"

The harpy actually winced. She glanced at her brother.

"The movement will help air out the fabric so it may dry more quickly," Jennings said, nodding encouragingly.

George had no intention of begging the harpy to dance with him; he had no trouble getting dancing partners, despite his reluctance. This was tedious. "You are under no compulsion to dance with me, Miss Jennings," George said, barely moving his lips to utter the words. "It is completely up to you."

"I accept, Your Grace," she said. With no discernible enthusiasm, George noted with no surprise.

She held out his soiled handkerchief to him. "Thank you for the use of your handkerchief," she said.

"You may keep it," George said. The last thing he wanted in his pocket was a damp, used handkerchief that had blotted her bosom. She could burn it, for all he cared.

"Thank you," she said again. She folded it and tucked it into her reticule.

He offered her his hand.

She laid her hand on his—barely. If he hadn't been able to see it atop his own, he wouldn't have known it was there.

He escorted her out onto the ballroom floor and turned to face her, which helped shield her splotchy, damp bodice. The music had come to an end, and people were waiting for the next dance to begin. Miss Jennings dropped her hand from his.

She said nothing. He said nothing.

Her hair, he noted, was dark and thick and was styled as though she'd been attempting to cage a wild beast. Her features, now that he was close enough to observe them better, were fine enough—her brows were dark, like her hair, her eyes a light gray in contrast. He expected to see freckles along the bridge of her nose, owing to the color of her hair, and he was correct—there was the slightest spray of them as to be unique but not so many as to be distracting. Her mouth was set; he did not take the time to consider that particular feature further, and he kept his gaze averted from her bodice. It wouldn't do for the Duke of Aylesham to appear to be ogling a lady's bosom, regardless of the reason.

She wasn't looking at him at all. He'd half expected her to be glaring at him, but instead, she was looking about the room at the other guests. He wondered if she was looking for someone in particular—or simply avoiding looking at him. He couldn't recollect ever having seen her out in society before, except for the one occasion last year. He knew nothing about her other than that she was Jennings's sister—and that she eavesdropped on private conversations and had a sharp tongue.

The music began . . . and George realized with horror that it was a waltz. A *waltz*, during which they must be in each other's arms for the entire duration. Life was ironic at times, so he should have expected something like this to happen.

She looked at him now as though she were preparing to muck out a stable. Obviously, *she'd* just realized it was a waltz also and was as displeased about it as he was.

He raised his arms into position. "I presume you waltz."

"I was going to ask you the same thing," she said.

Touché, harpy, he thought.

He waited, his arms still in position. After a brief moment, she placed her right hand in his left and her left hand on his shoulder. He hoped he wouldn't end up with sticky punch residue on his clothes from her gloves. Evans would not be pleased. He then placed his hand on her waist and began the first steps . . .

She immediately stumbled over his feet, requiring that he catch her in order to keep her upright. "Apparently, you *don't* waltz," he said, feeling a touch smug while she regained her bearing.

"I know how to waltz," she said. "I'm just a bit out of practice, and you took rather large steps."

They began again, and George made an effort to shorten his steps. They would both look like fools if she were to stumble repeatedly. Soon, fortunately, she found the flow of the music, and her feet successfully followed, which was a relief to George.

They danced, not speaking . . . but eventually the silence between them became deafening.

"Perhaps your expression could reflect something more positive than a death march," he said. Blast it all, but this particular waltz was lasting interminably.

Miss Jennings raised the corners of her lips slightly. It was more of a smirk than a smile.

"Ah, now that is *such* an improvement," he drawled. "I doubt I have ever seen such a lovely visage on a lady before. I want to weep with ecstasy."

"Such a compliment you bestow upon me," she replied in the same bored tone as his own, "when all I did was match your own expression."

Touché again, harpy.

Oh, but it felt good to get the last word, Susan thought as the waltz continued on—interminably, to her way of thinking. The Duke of Aylesham was the most arrogant, insensitive, churlish *boor* she had ever had the displeasure of meeting.

This was why she had been perfectly content to remain in Lincolnshire for the past eight years. She'd had her fill of gentlemen like the high and mighty Duke of Aylesham and their assumptions that a lady should swoon with delight at receiving their merest attention.

She thought she might be able to live off the verbal riposte she'd given him for years.

As they danced—not speaking—she tried to look over the crush of people to see if she could spot any recognizable faces in attendance. Anyone to whom she might excuse herself from him and go to upon finishing the waltz.

"Is there someone in particular you are searching for?" he asked.

"No," she said, returning her gaze to his. How was it possible that his eyes could appear as though they took in everything but gave nothing away? "No," she repeated. "But I have remembered I promised to take punch to Lady Walmsley and Lady Starr." Her errand had completely fled her mind upon encountering His Loftiness.

"Then we shall," he said.

Instead of finishing the waltz, he immediately dropped his hold, offered her his arm again, and escorted her to the refreshment table, handing her a cup of punch and picking up two more. "Tell me where they are," he said—no, he *commanded.* Could His Loftiness not even pose his words as a question?

"Follow me," she said in reply—no, she *commanded.*

She weaved through the guests on the side of the dance floor to the area where she'd left Lady Walmsley and Lady Starr. Fortunately, they were still there. Hopefully, the duke would simply hand the ladies their cups of punch and dismiss himself.

"Oh, *look* at who is with your Miss Jennings!" Lady Bledsoe exclaimed, having apparently joined them, as His Loftiness bowed in greeting to all the ladies separately before handing a cup of punch to each. "Aylesham! I'm *so* glad to see you doing as I asked and mingling with the other guests—and that you have found Miss Jennings." She sipped her punch. "Mm, just what I needed after so much chatting. It seems not that long ago when our Aylesham here was a young cub, always serious but so endearing. Do you remember, Margaret?"

"Of course I remember," Lady Walmsley said. "A handsome lad you were too. Tall for your age—it always seemed as though your weight couldn't keep up with your height." She chuckled. "Your granduncle Aylesham was always so proud of you. Such a dear man, he was. My Walmsley was particularly fond of him—a pity he never married. Lost his heart to a young lady who chose another, and he never recovered. You must miss him dreadfully."

"Indeed, Lady Walmsley," the duke said, nodding in deference to her comments. "I do miss him."

Susan waited for him to say more—some stinging retorts to Lady Walmsley for her personal comments about him, for example.

"He was nearly that way again, Margaret," Lady Bledsoe said. "Too thin, I mean. After his close call with death earlier this year, if you'll recall. Pneumonia. I was afraid we were going to lose the boy this time."

"Oh, my dear Judith!" Lady Walmsley exclaimed, giving Lady Bledsoe's hand a quick pat.

Susan looked at His Loftiness with narrowed eyes, searching for any signs of illness she'd previously overlooked but saw none. Perhaps just a tad too thin.

"I am well now, Lady Bledsoe. You have no need for concern," he said.

"I dearly hope so!" Lady Bledsoe began fanning herself furiously. "He is like a son to me, Margaret, as you well know. Like one of my own children."

Was she actually blinking back tears? For *His Loftiness*?

"I do know that, Judith," Lady Walmsley said, patting her knee. "She was very worried, indeed, Your Grace. I can vouch for that. Your letters were, of course, reassuring—"

"But people can say whatever they want in letters," Lady Bledsoe said. "I needed to see the boy to be sure he was being truthful and not trying to paint a rosy picture for my sake. I wanted to go to him to assure myself, but we were told not to come."

"I didn't want your own health put at risk," he said.

"It wasn't until he arrived back in London that I could see for myself that he was well," Lady Bledsoe said. "It was such a relief and a burden lifted from my heart."

"A true burden lifted," Lady Walmsley said, nodding in agreement.

Susan had been struck dumb listening to this conversation. To her, the duke looked impervious to everything. He hadn't even smiled during the conversation; he'd simply responded when he'd deemed it appropriate.

Her loathing of him came down a small notch, however, considering that he'd at least treated the elderly ladies with deference.

"Now that I've returned Miss Jennings to you, you will excuse me," he said, bowing, turning, and striding off into the crowd.

That was more like what Susan had expected to happen when they'd rejoined Lady Walmsley and the others.

The two ladies pointed to the empty chair where Susan had been sitting previously, and when she sat, they beckoned her closer. "You were waylaid by the Duke of Aylesham, were you?" Lady Walmsley said in a low voice, her eyes twinkling. "No wonder we waited so long for our punch! Not that I blame you—he's the catch of the Season, you know."

Susan actually didn't know, but it didn't surprise her. He could weigh twenty-five stone and have the face of a gargoyle and, because he was a duke, would still be the catch of the Season.

"He's been the catch of every Season for at least ten years now," Lady Bledsoe said, still fanning herself.

"That's right," Lady Walmsley said, taking a sip of her punch. "Now that I think about it. I remember something from several years back . . . courting a young lady, something going amiss, that sort of thing. I can't recall the particulars."

"And nothing much to speak of since." Lady Bledsoe shook her head in a resigned manner. "I told him earlier he needed to dance at least twice before taking his leave." She looked at Susan. "He didn't happen to dance with you, did he? Oh, I certainly hope so!"

"He did, actually," Susan said. "More or less."

Both ladies made squeaking sounds that grated on Susan's nerves.

"I wouldn't get too excited about it, if I were you," Susan said. Although it would make an amusing story to share with Rebecca in her first letter.

"But dancing with a *duke*, Miss Jennings, especially the Duke of Aylesham, is just the thing!" Lady Walmsley exclaimed. "People will take note, you know. Aylesham is highly particular about his friends and associates. What a coup! You will be the darling of the Season; I can feel it!" She clasped her hands at her bosom. "We must go shopping for your new wardrobe tomorrow. If it weren't evening, I would take you right now." She glanced down at Susan, reassessing her appearance. "Oh dear. What has happened to your gown?"

"My gown and I had a slight accident with the punch," Susan said. Her bodice was only a bit damp now, but the contrast of color was still noticeable. "The duke was kind enough to lend me his handkerchief." *Kind* was a bit of a stretch in describing his attitude, but she needn't burden the ladies with her opinion of him.

"Well, after tomorrow, this gown will be a thing of the past," Lady Walmsley said. "It has performed its service and will be allowed to retire to the rag bin. And you, my dear, are in for the Season of your life! I am ecstatic!"

Susan certainly hoped not—especially if it was due to having danced only part of a waltz with His Loftiness.

Chapter 5

George awoke later than he was accustomed to the morning following Lady Bledsoe's ball, which got his day off to a poor start. Currently, he sat in his study, drumming his fingers on the top of his desk, reflecting on the previous evening and the dance debacle between him and James Jennings's sister. She had been dripping with punch and had not been inclined to dance—and then on the ballroom floor, she had tripped all over his feet and had looked everywhere but at him. George was glad to be done with the entire business.

He picked up the document before him and attempted to read it before setting it back down with impatience. Concentrating on the task before him was impossible at the moment.

Since Lady Bledsoe had elicited a promise from him to dance twice at her ball and because George had initially concluded that he could hardly claim the half of a waltz he'd danced with Miss Susan Jennings in that number, he'd made the effort to dance twice more before taking his leave. Due to Dutton's concerns over George's lack of an heir apparent and the disappointing results from Dutton's search for George's heir presumptive, George had had Henshaw put together a short list of the most eligible young ladies to consider this Season. During the course of the evening, George had met three of them and had danced with two.

The Season was in its early days yet, so there was no reason for alarm. That was what George told himself. But the three young ladies to whom he'd been introduced at the ball after his encounter with Miss Jennings had been, to put it bluntly, unsatisfactory.

He opened one of the side drawers of his desk and took out the list Henshaw had prepared. Miss Sarah Wentworth, daughter of Sir Joshua Wentworth, baron, and Lady Wentworth, was pretty enough but too quiet. She'd not said a word to George after their initial introduction—her animated mama had provided any additional conversation. George had danced a reel with her, then had returned her to Lady Wentworth.

He drew a line through her name on the list.

Lady Mary Morgan had been next. She was the daughter of the Earl and Lady Blackford. She'd been a giggler. He couldn't see himself married to someone who handled new situations by *giggling*. He had excused himself from her and her mama without offering to dance.

He pinched the bridge of his nose, fighting off the headache that currently threatened, and drew a line through her name too.

He'd been tempted to count Miss Susan Jennings's waltz after all, after his encounter with Lady Mary Morgan, but his blasted honor hadn't allowed it. So his final dance of the evening had been with the Honorable Jocelyn Wetheral, eldest daughter of Viscount and Lady Severn. Miss Wetheral had been well-mannered, conversation had been relatively easy, and she'd been a competent dancer. She'd also been very pretty. But George was having a difficult time envisioning himself married to her, for some unquantifiable reason.

He began to draw a line through her name but stopped. He would not be rash. He would consider the other young ladies on Henshaw's list and see how Miss Wetheral compared.

He set his pen down and sat back in his chair, then pulled out his pocket watch. Speaking of Henshaw, he should have arrived here before now. They were supposed to review a few essential items before Jennings arrived to meet with George later today.

There was a discreet knock at the door. "Come in, Henshaw," George said. "You're late."

The door opened—but it was Talbot who stepped inside, bearing a salver. "Sorry to disturb you, Your Grace," he said.

"Never mind that. Where's Henshaw?" George said.

"That is what I came to tell you," Talbot said. "Mr. Henshaw received a letter early this morning and informed me that he must leave and that I should inform you of this if he did not return in time for your scheduled meeting."

"Well, then, *you're* late," George said. His headache was getting worse.

"And for that, I beg your pardon," Talbot replied, remaining unruffled. "Henshaw was insistent that I allow you to sleep; otherwise, I would have told you earlier, and then, as it happens, I was at the main entrance receiving a letter for you when the appointed hour arrived. I would venture a guess that it's a rather important letter too." He came forward, the salver outstretched.

George took the letter from the salver, turned it over to examine it . . . and then stopped cold. It bore the seal of his Royal Highness, the Prince Regent.

Obviously, Talbot also knew from whom the letter had been sent; it would have been delivered by a courier in royal livery. That fully explained why Talbot had been tardy in informing him of Henshaw's absence—a prince took precedence over a duke at all times.

He broke the seal and read the letter. "Are you waiting to find out what the letter says out of curiosity or because you are expecting you will be needed to receive immediate instructions as a result?" George asked Talbot, who was still standing nearby. His question was ill-mannered, he knew, but blast it all, his head was beginning to throb in earnest now. This letter from the Prince Regent was the final straw. Why on *earth* did Prinny wish to see him? And by such a formal request, to boot. It didn't bode well. Not well at all.

"*Do* you have instructions for me?" Talbot asked. Thankfully, the man was acquainted with George's occasional moods.

George sighed. "Maybe a spot of that tincture Mrs. Bradley keeps on hand for headaches." His cook, Mrs. Bradley, kept willow bark in the pantry that reduced the pain when he had headaches or other ailments. It had been his saving grace when he'd been fevered during his bout with pneumonia.

"I shall go directly to her, Your Grace," Talbot said. He turned to leave.

"Thank you, Talbot," George said.

"You're entirely welcome, Your Grace," Talbot replied.

When Talbot was gone, George read the letter again.

To the Duke of Aylesham, greetings, it began.

It has recently come to our attention that you have done a great work for the Crown, insisting upon no recognition of your own whilst doing said work, and for this we are most grateful. We wish to honor you for this service and bestow upon you a gift that demonstrates our gratitude. To this end, we will receive you at Carlton House on Friday afternoon, the twenty-second of April, at two o'clock. Yours, George PR.

Friday was the day after tomorrow.

There was another discreet knock at the door.

"Enter," George said.

Talbot entered again holding a tray with the tincture and a glass of water.

"Thank you, Talbot," George said. He swallowed the tincture and followed it up by drinking the entire glass of water, and then he stood. "I must speak to Evans. If Henshaw returns before I do, please notify me."

"I will, Your Grace." Talbot bowed slightly and, once again, left the room.

George stood behind his desk, hands on his hips, pondering the turn of events: Henshaw was nowhere to be found, George had received a summons to meet with the Prince Regent at court, of all things, and now he must go inform Evans to prepare his most formal attire for an unexpected appearance at Carlton House.

How would a young lady who was too afraid to speak or a young lady who *giggled* cope in such a circumstance?

He shook his head and went to find Evans.

"Oh, *good*, you're awake now," Lady Walmsley said, setting her teacup down on its dish and dabbing at her lips with her napkin. "I wanted to allow you to rest for as long as you needed since you were so kind to allow me to drag you to Lady Bledsoe's ball last evening—after just arriving in town, no less." She waved at the side table. "I asked Mrs. Drake to prepare a hearty breakfast. I daresay you eat a hearty breakfast at home each morning—not that anyone would think such a thing by looking at you; you've a lovely figure, my dear—eggs, toast, kippers, sausage, beans. You're going to need your strength today. I sent word to Madame Veronique that we would be stopping by her shop and to prepare for a large order of gowns."

"Lady Walmsley," Susan began, "I appreciate—"

"Tut, tut, girl," Lady Walmsley said, interrupting her. "I will have my way on this. Fix yourself a plate, and quickly! I can hardly wait to see what we find for you. Madame Veronique's gowns are in high demand—she has such an eye for helping ladies look their best. She will have no trouble with you whatsoever."

"You are very kind, Lady Walmsley," Susan said. She'd already helped herself to some of the scrambled eggs and toast and now decided to add a sausage to her plate. "But you will remember that I am not coming out this year—far from it! I have had three Seasons already, and that was years ago. No, I am more interested in witnessing the celebrations being held due to Napoleon's impending defeat. It is history in the making." It was a time for hope—the wars fought against France had been difficult and protracted.

She sat next to Lady Walmsley at the table as Lady Walmsley poured her a cup of tea. "Lemon? Milk?" Lady Walmsley asked.

"Milk, please," Susan said.

"I know you are not a young bud waiting to blossom during your first Season, my dear. I am only too aware of the ups and downs life may send our way—nobody's life is the same, and we do ourselves a disservice by believing otherwise. But I have discovered a joy in doting on young women such as yourself—perhaps it's merely a motherly instinct within me that I forced to stay dormant when Walmsley and I weren't gifted with children of our own. So I hope you will indulge me by allowing me to indulge you."

Susan smiled and sipped her tea. "Very well. I shall try to behave and accept your generosity. But be warned—most likely, it will all go to naught, for if there was no gentleman who suited me all those years ago, it will be even less likely now. And if I think you are becoming excessive in your generosity, I intend to speak up."

"Duly noted," Lady Walmsley said, nodding. She took a final bite of kippers before setting her napkin aside and rising to her feet. "I shall inform Foster to call for a hackney to be here in a half hour's time, if that pleases you. Or would an hour be better?"

"A half hour will be fine," Susan said. "And, Lady Walmsley?" she added.

"Yes, my dear?"

"Thank you."

Lady Walmsley patted Susan's shoulder. "You are very welcome. This is going to be such fun! I can scarcely wait to begin."

The idea of having Lady Walmsley spend so much money on her had caused Susan's appetite to vanish, and so in no time at all she had finished breaking her fast and had joined Lady Walmsley in the parlor, where she had been awaiting the arrival of the hackney.

"Oh, there it is!" Lady Walmsley exclaimed, peering out the parlor window. "Let's be off, then!"

Susan followed as Lady Walmsley hurried out of the parlor. Foster already had the front door open for them, and soon, they were inside the hackney and on their way to Oxford Street.

"I must warn you," Lady Walmsley said, "that Madame Veronique is decidedly *not* French, as you will clearly recognize the minute you hear her accent. *But,*" she added with emphasis, "as a modiste, she is so talented that her customers do not care where she came from. She has such an eye . . ." Lady Walmsley studied Susan carefully. "I can't wait to see what she envisions for you. You are *such* a beauty."

"Hardly that," Susan replied. She knew her flawed features only too well: her thick, curly hair that refused to be tamed, with brows to match, a dab of a nose, and a mouth much bigger than the little rosebud lips she noticed on other ladies wherever she went, and eyes frequently hidden behind reading glasses because she always had her nose in a book.

The hackney turned onto Oxford Street, and Susan could see Madame Veronique's modiste shop up ahead.

"We are nearly there," Lady Walmsley said. "So, my dear Miss Jennings, allow me to offer a final word of advice before we go inside the shop. You are a clever woman—that much is obvious to everyone who meets you—your intellect fairly shines from your face at all times and cannot be mistaken for what it is. But you are doing yourself a disservice if you refuse to allow your cleverness and your beauty to coincide peacefully together within you. You do not have to be one or the other, Miss Jennings—and I suspect that is what you have been doing, perhaps for quite some time." She paused briefly. "But here I am, rattling on and on when we have shopping to do."

The hackney had come to a stop during Lady Walmsley's speech, and the driver had already opened the door and was waiting to assist them.

As Susan followed Lady Walmsley from the carriage, she pondered what her new companion had said. It hadn't really crossed her mind that she might be choosing her intellect over her appearance. She'd always taken what she thought to be appropriate consideration with her appearance. She was definitely more comfortable with her intellect, however. She had begged Papa to allow her to be included when her older brothers, Isaac and James, had been with their tutors. Papa had resisted at first, but he'd finally relented. Mama had told her it did not excuse her from learning a proper lady's skills—needlework, music, art, and the like—which had suited Susan fine, as she'd enjoyed learning those things too, except, perhaps, the needlework. She could sew if it were absolutely necessary, but she'd choose nearly anything else over needlework.

When she had initially made her come-out, Mama and Papa hadn't been able to afford the most fashionable modiste for her wardrobe. She didn't really think it had made that big of a difference—she'd had suitors, and a couple of them had hinted at marriage.

But having suitors and finding a suitable marriage partner amongst them had been a challenge for Susan, much to Mama's dismay. She could not see herself married to someone less intelligent than she, regardless of his rank or wealth. How could she live with decisions he made that affected her life if she didn't respect his ability to form those opinions and make those decisions? The answer was: she couldn't. And after what had happened with the one man who'd made a claim on her heart, it had put an end to romance, as far as she was concerned. She had no more expectations of marriage and a family of her own and had learned to be content.

Madame Veronique opened the door and threw her arms wide. She was a rather petite lady—not quite what Susan had expected, for some reason—but what she lacked in height she made up for in energy. "What have you brought to me, my lady?" Madame said in an outrageous French accent. "Ah, I see"—she tapped her chin with her forefinger—"we have a diamond in zee rough we will transform into a diamond of zee first water, yes?"

"Oh, yes!" Lady Walmsley replied enthusiastically.

They followed Madame Veronique into her shop while Susan tried not to take umbrage at being referred to as rough. She was hardly that.

She stopped briefly and considered Madame's words. *Was* that what other people thought when they saw her? Or was Madame exaggerating for effect?

Susan shrugged. She had agreed to this, so she would soon find out.

Madame Veronique's shop was an elegant establishment decorated in a style that would appeal to the ladies of the *ton*. The walls were cream, with white moldings, and dainty-looking tables and chairs clustered within the perimeters, beckoning to shoppers to sit, take tea, and peruse the fashion plates. A cabinet against one wall seemed to overflow with accessories, such as shawls and fans, and next to it, a full-length mirror allowed customers to see themselves in Madame's wares. The large window at the front of the shop currently displayed dresses for different times of the day—all done in a variety of pink fabrics: a day dress with a matching spencer, a silk gown suitable for supper at home, a velvet ball gown—

Madame clapped her hands, startling Susan from her thoughts. "Quickly, come! We have much work to do!" Madame said as three seamstresses scurried out from a back room.

Almost before Susan could blink, she was rushed into a dressing room and stripped down to her chemise. Every inch of her—she was certain it was *every* inch—was measured and then remeasured for accuracy. Susan's arms were outstretched for so long, she felt like a scarecrow. The modiste she and Mama had visited during Susan's come-out and the subsequent Seasons had been nothing like this. She felt simultaneously irritated and entertained.

Finally, Madame Veronique, who had supervised the entire process, nodded. "*C'est bien,*" she said with another nod. "Very good. You know what to do next."

The seamstresses—all but one—scurried off, and Susan glanced at Madame Veronique as the seamstress who had remained assisted Susan back into her clothing.

"*What* do they know to do next?" Susan asked warily.

"Zees eez where zee fun begins!" Madame replied.

Fun for whom? Susan thought as she dressed. And why had no one ever told Madame Veronique her accent was absurd?

When Susan returned to the showroom, Lady Walmsley was sitting on a cushioned chair, sipping tea and poring over fashion plates, oohing and aahing.

Madame Veronique crossed over to her and looked over her shoulder. "Ah, now zees one." Madame pointed at a specific fashion plate. "Very flattering, *non*? At least two day dresses for Miss Jennings from zees one. Your Miss Jennings—her complexion! So creamy, with such adorable little freckles—just enough to be enchanting. Her hair—eet eez long and thick and luscious, like a rich chocolate, although ever so curly and wild. There eez so much Madame can do. So much!"

The seamstresses returned from the back room with bolts of fabric and set them on the counter at the back of the showroom, and then Madame led Susan to the counter. "You see, Lady Walmsley, zees muslin with zee pretty flowers for zee day dress, and zees green one, too, and zees"—she pointed to a bolt of the most delicate silk Susan had ever seen—"for zee undergarments."

"My undergarments are fine," Susan said, feeling her face go red. How maddening! She was well past the blushing-young-maiden portion of her life.

"Zee lady feels most beautiful when zee clothes zat touch her skin make her feel zat way," Madame said. "Beauty begins on zee inside and continues outward."

That may be true, Susan thought, but it was going to cost a lot more of Lady Walmsley's money than she'd anticipated. "Lady Walmsley, surely there's no need," she argued. "I cannot ask you to replace my entire wardrobe in this way."

"Tut, tut," Lady Walmsley said with a wave her hand. "In for a penny, in for a pound, as the old saying goes."

Madame Veronique nodded decisively.

Susan sighed.

"Now, see," Madame said. She led Susan to the mirror and, with a seamstress's assistance, draped Susan with a variety of fabrics in an array of colors. "Zee lilac, don't you sink? And zees silk—see how eet brings out zee color of your eyes? Very pretty. What do you say, Lady Walmsley?"

"It's lovely," Lady Walmsley said. "They all are. I can scarcely wait to see them all completed. You are going to shine wherever we go, Miss Jennings."

Susan sighed again.

"I know it's asking a lot, Madame," Lady Walmsley said, "but is it at all possible to have a couple of gowns ready in the next day or two? A day dress, at least?"

Madame tapped her chin in thought. "Zee flowered muslin—I sink we can have eet ready by tomorrow—and perhaps one of zee simpler evening gowns. We are so busy zees time of year; of course, zat is no surprise to you. So busy. But we will see what we can do."

"That is all I ask," Lady Walmsley said. "Thank you, Madame Veronique. Come then, Miss Jennings, we have more shopping to do!"

Madame Veronique laid her hand on Susan's shoulder before she could reply to Lady Walmsley's words. "Allow yourself to enjoy zees, *mon chère*. You have a fairy godmother. Most young ladies are not so fortunate as you."

"Thank you; I shall try," Susan replied, forcing a smile. And then, because it was her nature to be blunt, she had to say something more. "You do know that your French accent doesn't fool anybody," she whispered.

Madame Veronique laughed. "Oh, I *do* like you!" she said, her French accent vanishing into thin air. "And you are absolutely correct. But do you think *le beau monde* would buy my clothes if I spoke to them like an English rustic? It's part of the illusion I offer them." She winked at Susan. "We shall keep my little secret, *non*?" she said, the accent now back. "Even if eet eez not so much a secret."

"*Oui*," Susan said. "*Et merci*."

"Off we go, then," Lady Walmsley said. "I can hardly wait to see what we do with that bush on your head you call hair!"

Susan winced, and Madame Veronique laughed.

"Fairy godmothers are demanding creatures, *mon chère*," Madame Veronique whispered, "but zey have our best interest at heart. Remember zat and enjoy."

"You lost nearly two stone this past winter," Evans said when George initially refused to change into his court clothing so it could be fitted. "I am not going to alter *those* particular clothes without putting them on you first. The tailoring they will require is more exacting than simply taking in a side seam here or there. You haven't regained all the weight you lost. Do it right the first time, or don't do it at all; that's what I always say."

"If you always say it, then you must do so in private, because I've never heard you say it before," George replied. "Very well, but we must be quick about it. I have important business to attend to this afternoon." He'd known he'd have to wear the court clothes, for he intended to appear at his immaculate best before the Prince Regent. The Prince Regent was known to be extravagant in many ways, one of which was his dress. George had no desire to exceed Prinny in opulence, but he intended to meet fire with fire. *This* was not a social occasion. George had attended plenty of those and had conversed frequently in such situations with Prinny. No, *this* was a *summons*, and although many of George's acquaintances thought Prinny a buffoon and spendthrift and would gossip about him behind his back, he was still His Royal Highness, the Prince Regent, and George intended to appear at court looking his most ducal and authoritative best. He donned the wretched court clothes.

"You see how much I must take it in here?" Evans said while he measured and pinned. He was currently kneeling next to George, pinning the inseam of one of the legs on his breeches. "You must eat more, Your Grace."

"I've gained some of it back. You make me sound like a sack of bones, and *you* sound like a mother hen."

"You are not a sack of bones precisely, Your Grace, but I don't believe you have recovered fully from—"

"I'm fine," George said. He stifled a cough. "Listening to you fret is making me lose my appetite, however."

"Being called a mother hen does not affect my confidence in my masculinity, you know," Evans said. "Just the other day, Mrs. Evans said—"

George waved his hand and cut Evans off. "Enough. I do not wish to hear what Mrs. Evans has to say about your masculinity."

"Very well, Your Grace," Evans replied with a twinkle in his eye.

"Hmph," George said. He would not let his valet get the upper hand, no matter how long the man had been in his service and no matter how fond George was of him.

George endured the fitting and returned to his office, but there was still no sign of Henshaw. This latest endeavor George had authorized had been a risky one. He hoped Henshaw's absence wasn't due to any complications.

He felt restless. There was work to be done this afternoon. Henshaw should have informed him before dashing out so abruptly. That, on top of Prinny's summons, had stirred up concerns that George was unable to quell. While England's coalition with the continental countries fighting Napoleon was proving successful, negotiations were still ongoing. The last correspondence George had received from Lord Castlereagh had been carefully worded; George had inferred from it that Napoleon had agreed to abdication but not on terms with which Lord C was satisfied. Shoring up the alliances with Austria and Prussia and the other countries was an ongoing and critical process.

George had opted not to attend Parliament today, telling himself that attention to his work with Henshaw was no less his duty than listening to his peers in the House of Lords pontificate, especially as he hadn't slept much last night.

Waiting for Henshaw to return, though, was accomplishing nothing.

He sat at his desk and busied himself with correspondence and tried not to think about his summons to Carlton House.

On Friday, at precisely half past one, thirty minutes early, George removed his top hat and walked through the front doors of Carlton House after presenting his card to the doorman. Evans had outdone himself; George's court attire fit perfectly and conveyed the refinement George desired while facing his monarch, whatever this meeting was about.

The footman then led him to a sitting room. "I will let His Royal Highness know you are here," he said. "Please, make yourself comfortable."

George nearly laughed aloud at that. *Comfortable*, the man had said as though it were possible to feel that way when awaiting an unanticipated meeting with the Prince Regent. After the footman left, George wandered over to a window and peered outside, then walked over to the fireplace where a small fire was crackling and looked abstractedly at the painting that hung over the mantel.

He had heard no rumors of other members of the House of Lords being received in such a formal manner by the Prince Regent, not that he generally listened to the rumor mill. Plenty of noblemen had worked in the cause of ending the war with France; it was something Parliament had spent a great deal of time discussing. Lord Castlereagh, as foreign secretary, and his contingent had traveled the breadth of the Continent, meeting with foreign leaders and had worked diligently to come to a consensus on how to defeat the French.

Prinny, however, had not actually involved himself overmuch with matters on the Continent. George considered the prince a self-indulgent wastrel who couldn't be bothered with the administration of the country, leaving the actual governing of it to the prime minister and Parliament.

That being said, it didn't do to dwell on the prince's weaknesses, which were legion. One couldn't afford to alienate oneself from the Prince Regent when there were bigger issues at hand. He was sovereign and had power and leverage that could not be ignored.

The door opened, and George turned away from the mantel. "His Royal Highness will see you now," the footman said, gesturing with his arm for George to follow.

They proceeded down a corridor George had traveled before but under less formal circumstances. He was not in Prinny's close circle of friends, nor did he care to be. But he had been in attendance at a social function or two at Carlton House in the past.

Eventually, they arrived at their destination, and George could hear murmuring behind the closed door before them. The footman opened the door and once again gestured for George to follow. It was a formal reception room, ostentatious in its scale and decor, a room George had never visited before. At the far end of the room were upholstered sofas and chairs arranged to create an area for intimate conversation. The prince was there, seated on a chair larger than the others, gilded, and covered in rich brocade. Seated around him were some of his closest associates and courtiers, amongst them Baron Lawton and the Earl of Frome, toadies and flatterers both, and the Earl of Cosgrove, a notorious rake. Apparently, the Prince Regent didn't care about that, which came as no great surprise, considering the prince had carried on several well-known affairs himself, including his long-standing relationship with Mrs. Fitzherbert.

"Your Majesty, the Duke of Aylesham," the footman announced.

All turned as one to look at George.

"Yes, yes," the prince said, flicking his hand in dismissal to the footman. "We already know who is here. Come forward, Aylesham, come, come."

The footman left. George walked the length of the room to the prince and bowed deeply.

"Tut, no need to be so formal, Aylesham," the prince said.

His Royal Highness Prince George was a man in his fifties whose indulgent lifestyle was catching up with him. He'd gained a great deal of weight over the years from excess food and drink—seated in his chair as he was with his belly resting on his lap, the buttons of his waistcoat straining, and his stockinged legs swollen, he looked older than his years.

He leaned forward. "We have heard good things about you as of late, Aylesham; nay, extraordinary things, have we not?"

The prince's courtiers nodded and murmured their agreement.

"We are most gratified in your service to the Crown and most impressed," the prince said.

George bowed his head. "Thank you, Your Majesty

"We have learned, perhaps a *trifle late*"—the prince paused for none-too-subtle emphasis—"that you have been instrumental behind the scenes amongst our allies in this ongoing battle against Napoleon, usurper that he is. But we do not wish to talk about him. We wish to talk about *you*." He leaned back and relaxed heavily into his chair, although George got the distinct impression that the prince was not relaxed at all—that, in fact, he was studying George carefully, rather like a gambler sizing up his opponent in a game of cards.

George waited for him to make the first move.

"We marvel," the prince said at last, "at your willingness to use your personal wealth to fund not one, not two, but *several* crossings to the Continent over this past year or so, assisting Castlereagh and others in negotiations, and that you yourself joined at least one of these crossings, we have heard, at the peril of your life."

The others nodded. The Earl of Frome gave George an unreadable glance.

"It was my honor to be of assistance," George said. He frowned in thought. How the prince had learned these details, George did not know; he had intended his participation to remain anonymous. Government coffers had been depleted by war, not just with France but with America as well. The Prince Regent's own excessive extravagance and debt and that of his family had put a further strain on available moneys. Times were lean, abroad and domestically. As a result, last year, George had privately told Lord Castlereagh that he wished to assist in whatever way he could to help secure the treaties with the Sixth Coalition members, the hope being to create a united front in the battle against Napoleon, finally put an end to this war, and begin solving problems at home for once.

The prince smiled. "We see by your expression that we have caught you unawares. We do have our own sources, you know. You mustn't be surprised." He sat forward again. "But are you well, Aylesham?" he asked in a voice that feigned concern. "We heard word to the effect that after your recent journey, you returned to us with a severe case of pneumonia. Is this true?"

There was no denying it when the prince had the facts. "Yes, Sir. I was ill, but as you see, I am well now." No need to elaborate on the fact that he'd nearly died.

"We are relieved to hear it."

"Thank you, Sir."

"We also understand that these journeys have aided our cause and that, God willing, victory is close at hand."

The courtiers all clapped politely.

"That is my hope, Sir," George said.

"You are too modest by half." The prince straightened in his chair and donned his most regal demeanor. "We daresay there are few amongst your noble peers who would be quite so generous as you've shown to be over the past year, Aylesham."

Several courtiers actually laughed. "Using your own money, Aylesham," Baron Lawton said with a smirk. "How *noble* you are."

"Perhaps our friends here feel too keenly the demands of familial life or had other priorities for their funds," the prince said, shooting Lawton a speaking glance, "whereas, *you* are unmarried—unattached, as it were, from such responsibilities—*not* that we believe you haven't been fully attendant to your ducal duties: your estate, et cetera, et cetera. Had you not paid heed to them, you would not have been able to be so generous in the Crown's cause now, what? Most admirable. We commend you. And now we wish to reward you."

"Thank you, but there is no need, Sir," George said emphatically. He hadn't done any of this for Prinny, if that was what he had meant by referring to "the Crown." George did not wish to receive a reward; he'd done only what he'd considered his patriotic duty. And he absolutely *loathed* the idea of being obliged to the Prince Regent in any way whatsoever; receiving a reward would undoubtedly make George beholden to the prince, which he suspected was precisely what the prince was trying to do.

There was something suspect going on; George was beginning to feel as though he was in the prince's crosshairs—

"Which is why," the prince continued, interrupting George's thoughts, "we wish to honor you with the gift of marriage to Princess Sophia Augusta of Schönberg-Nusse."

Chapter 6

George froze at the Prince Regent's words, and only decades of self-discipline kept his mouth from gaping.

"Princess Sophia Augusta of Schönberg-Nusse is the daughter of Prince Ernst Leopold of the Duchy of Schönberg-Nusse and his wife, Princess Eugenie Augusta. We met Prince Ernst several years ago—can't remember the particulars . . . seem to recall he was a likable enough fellow—and regrettably, we haven't met his wife. But our advisors tell us we can be confident that this is a good match. *Extremely* wealthy, we've heard. Excellent blood lines. Most advantageous for you, attaching yourself to royalty—and highly beneficial to the Crown through your marriage, diplomatically *and* financially.

"Such connections as you helped Castlereagh achieve will be even smoother in the future when one is dealing with them as family members. And imagine what marriage to the princess can do for our treasury, Aylesham," the prince continued. "Ours *and* yours—you will recoup your expenses in our country's behalf and come out much wealthier in the long run, we are assured. Oh, yes, the advantages to *both* yourself *and* the Crown are incalculable."

Prince Ernst Leopold of the Duchy of Schönberg-Nusse—George recognized that name but couldn't recall . . . "Sir—"

The prince held up his hand to silence George. George noticed that Baron Lawton and Lord Frome and the other courtiers were watching him closely. Frome's lip curled upward.

George had *never* liked Frome.

"Princess Sophia Augusta and her parents have agreed to the match, and they and their retinue are expected to arrive in London within a fortnight; after which, formal arrangements for the wedding will be finalized. This will be another crowning touch on the celebrations of victory we anticipate we shall have this Season, what? 'Crowning touch,' eh?" The prince chuckled to himself. "A little play on words there."

The arrangements *will be finalized*? The prince had undertaken them *without* George's knowledge? It was a *given*, then, at least to the prince, that the marriage would take place. George fought the buzzing in his brain so his thoughts could be coherent. What was he to do? The prince, despite his general negligence when it came to governing his people, was, nonetheless, George's *sovereign*. One didn't simply disobey one's sovereign. But to marry in this unexpected, wholly unwanted way—

"And we shouldn't worry too much about the Princess's surname, now either, shall we?" the prince added. "Can't be helped. Schönberg-Nusse. Sounds like 'noose,' what?" He chuckled again. So did all the courtiers. Frome's smirk turned into a grin.

George, on the other hand, was choking, desperate for air. He could feel that particular noose closing about his throat. He had demonstrated his allegiance to his country over the past year, but *this*? *This* was past his limit. After all these years of searching for the ideal wife, he wasn't about to simply marry a woman—princess or no—in this manner.

And then he remembered.

Prince Ernst Leopold von Schönberg-Nusse had hosted Napoleon Bonaparte at his palace on more than one occasion during Bonaparte's travels with his Grand Armée; he'd supported the French cause by doing so. Such actions meant Prince Ernst Leopold was an opportunist of the worst sort, if he was now willing to offer his daughter in marriage to Bonaparte's sworn enemy. Whether the Prince Regent knew of this mattered not one whit, apparently, for it was obvious his objective here was to seize the opportunity to get out of debt without going to Parliament once again.

George *would not* marry into such a family. Nor would he allow himself to become his selfish monarch's puppet, which this marriage would certainly assure.

But the Prince Regent was, nonetheless, his monarch, his sovereign.

How was he to go against the expressed will of his sovereign? It simply wasn't done. It was unheard of. George's heart pounded as he scrambled to think of a way to extricate himself from this utter nightmare.

The prince was waiting for his response.

"I am honored, Sir, truly," George said, grateful his voice sounded almost normal. "And I thank you. But surely there is someone more . . . deserving . . . of such a bestowal of trust." *Think, man, think!* His entire future depended on his ability to arrive at a viable solution, and quickly.

A tiny light went on in his head, and George sent a silent prayer skyward. The Prince Regent had several brothers, some who were still unmarried. Most of them had mistresses of long-standing, but other than the prince, who had an heir in Princess Charlotte, none of them had any legitimate children who could ascend to the throne. One would think the Crown would be more occupied with arranging marriages for *them* than one for George. "Consider that one of the unmarried royal princes deserves this honor more than I," he said at last.

The Prince Regent straightened in his seat at George's words, his regal posture back in place, his demeanor turning serious. "The marital arrangements of the royal princes are not within the scope of this discussion. As a reply to your suggestion, we shall say only that the situation there is complicated. No, at present, we are discussing *you*—an unmarried duke who has shown loyalty to his country and is capable, through this marriage, of benefiting the Crown *and your sovereign* greatly, not to mention yourself. Surely you would not refuse such a reward. Perhaps your misgivings are because you have not seen the princess who is to be your bride. You really needn't fear, if that is your problem; we are confident the princess is much fairer of face and disposition than our own Princess Caroline"—he grimaced—"and obviously there are ways to work around such an arrangement, if we may say so without being too indelicate."

Being reminded that the prince completely loathed his wife, Princess Caroline, was the final straw. The prince and princess had hated each other on sight and had barely stayed together long enough to produce a royal heir in Princess Charlotte. It was not a marriage at all, in George's opinion.

He swallowed and began to speak, still not entirely sure what he was going to say. "And yet, regrettably, I must respectfully decline." His mind was spinning like a top.

"Leave us," the prince ordered, waving his arm at his courtiers, clearly showing his impatience with George. "We wish to speak to Aylesham alone."

The others stood and began to take their leave. Lord Frome, passing close by George, leaned toward him and said, "I'd do it in a heartbeat if I weren't already leg-shackled. Same with the others. A royal title and money, to boot. You're a fool, Aylesham. Wives bring land, wealth, heirs, and connections. The rest we leave to our mistresses."

George pretended to ignore him and maintained eye contact with the prince.

The prince drummed his fingers on the arms of his chair and glared at George. When the two of them were finally alone, he spoke. "You say you must respectfully decline. *Why* would that be?" he asked in a low voice.

"Because I . . ." George was still frantically thinking. And then, miraculously, another glimmer of an idea sparked to life. "I am already due to be wed, Sir, and it would dishonor the lady to cry off." He said it but was unwilling, for the moment, to consider what the consequences of those words might mean beyond avoiding the current marriage being arranged for him.

The prince was not convinced, if his arched eyebrow was anything to go by. "*Why* did you not say so before, Aylesham?" he asked smoothly, his mouth barely moving. "We have not heard of any attachment between you and a lady. Nay, this comes as a *complete* surprise. We daresay it would be to many others as well." His Royal Highness was now getting angry, if the increased ruddiness of his face was any indication.

"My betrothed and I wished to be discreet," George said, holding firm to his lie. He *would not* become a pawn to his greedy monarch.

"*Discreet*?" The prince guffawed. "If a gentleman chooses to be *discreet,* he does so with his *mistress,* what? *Not* with his wife or wife-to-be. For some mysterious lady to have won the heart of our esteemed Duke of Aylesham, who has avoided marriage for so many years and, therefore, has been the catch of many a Season, it would be a coup she would wish to shout to the very ceilings of Almack's and beyond. *Why discreet*?"

"She does not wish it to be a *cause célèbre*. I am honoring her wish." It wasn't nearly enough, George knew, but it was all that had come to him. "I myself am not one for pomp and ceremony."

"*Surely* you can tell *your sovereign* who this mystery lady is and *where and when precisely* this wedding will occur?" the prince said sarcastically. He might be foolish, but he wasn't stupid. "For, you see, *we wish to be in attendance at this momentous occasion*—especially after the great service you have performed for us." It was clear the prince didn't believe George's betrothal story for a second.

One way or another, George was trapped.

"Pray, *tell us* who she is," the prince snapped.

George sought frantically for a name to give the Prince Regent. Ideally, it needed to be someone the prince wouldn't know so George could buy himself enough time to get out of this dilemma. She couldn't be fictitious, however, or he'd be in worse trouble than he already was when the prince found out, which he undoubtedly would.

But who? George's mind was a flurry of faces and gowns and fans and giggles and blushes and . . . "Her name is Miss Susan Jennings," he blurted.

Where the devil had *that* name *of all names* come from? George pressed a hand to his forehead, wondering if his pneumonia had relapsed. He felt fevered, and his heart raced, and his breath was short—he must surely be delirious to have said *the harpy's* name aloud. "I will not dishonor her or myself by crying off," he repeated.

"Susan Jennings, what? We do not recall a Miss Susan Jennings. Have we met her?" The prince obviously thought she was a figment of George's imagination. "And she's a *miss*?" he added. "You are choosing to wed a *miss* when we have offered you a *princess* from an *immensely wealthy* royal family?"

"Yes, Sir," George said, dropping his hand to his side, a cold sweat taking the place of what had felt like fever. "And I cannot say if you have met her or not—she prefers the country and a good library to London and Society, Sir, so she has not been in Town for several years." Perhaps, after all, she'd been the best name to offer the prince, despite George's antipathy toward her. She'd not been in London for eons, by the looks of her, and usually, the prince had a short attention span when it came to those outside the scope of his interest.

The prince shook his head, still in obvious disbelief. "Well, we *suppose* that explains the mystery, then," he said at last, after a lengthy pause. "We *aren't* convinced, but we will stop short of questioning your honor and integrity on this matter, and we are decidedly *not happy*, but we suppose we must accept your refusal. Princess Sophia Augusta and her parents will be disappointed when they learn the highly-sought-after Duke of Aylesham has found his own bride. Certainly, the Crown is disappointed. *Extremely* disappointed." The prince then gripped the arms of his chair and leaned forward. "*Know this*, though, Aylesham: *we expect* to receive an invitation to the nuptials. We wish to share this *happy occasion* with you. Furthermore, *we expect* these nuptials to take place *very soon*."

The prince hadn't asked—he'd commanded. And he'd made 'happy occasion' sound like a hanging. He wasn't far off in that regard, but at least George was still his own man for the time being. Except for the Susan Jennings part.

The prince stood. His interview had come to an end.

"We look forward to becoming acquainted with the *most fortunate* Miss Jennings," the prince said. "We understand each other in that regard, *do we not*, Aylesham?"

The prince had called George's bluff, blast it all to Hades and back.

"We do, Sir. Thank you." George bowed formally and backed out of the room as decorously—and quickly—as he could.

George instructed Bentley to drive to Doctors' Commons so he could procure a special license and then climbed into his carriage. He couldn't see a viable way out of this tangle—not after Prinny's stony insistence. He'd managed to escape the proverbial frying pan, but he'd thrown himself headlong into a blazing fire. *The harpy*, of all people! *How the devil* had *her* name been the first to escape his tongue?

Even more to the point, how was *he* ever to convince *her* that they were to wed, and *soon*, no less, and that the Prince Regent demanded to be in attendance? He wasn't sure if he should weep or laugh with hysteria. Perhaps he'd do both. But not now. He'd do it later when he was home and could drink a stiff brandy or two—or three—in the private confines of his study.

For now, there was unpleasant work to be done, and it required that he be stone-cold sober.

Lady Walmsley sat in her favorite chair in her favorite dayroom with a decidedly unladylike plop, which only endeared her to Susan that much more.

"Well!" Lady Walmsley exclaimed while Foster attempted to place a small blanket on her lap. She nudged Foster's hands away. "What are you doing, Foster? It's hardly winter, now, is it? A blanket?"

"This room tends to be on the chilly side at this time of day, if you'll recall, ma'am," Foster replied as he reluctantly folded the blanket over his arm. "I could have a fire lit, if you prefer."

"I don't prefer a fire. I'm perfectly fine! Wouldn't you say we are perfectly fine, Miss Jennings?" Lady Walmsley said, snatching up her sewing and poking at it vigorously with her needle.

Susan glanced from Lady Walmsley to Foster to Lady Walmsley. "Perfectly fine," she said, trying to sound meek for poor Foster's sake.

"Very well," Foster grumbled.

"I shall ring for you if I need you," Lady Walmsley said grumpily.

Susan bit her lip to keep from laughing while Foster bowed and left the room. Lady Walmsley continued to stab at her needlework.

Fearful that Lady Walmsley might drag her to other shops and spend even more money on her than she already had, Susan had diplomatically suggested that they stay in this afternoon. "You're too generous by half, Lady Walmsley," Susan had said while they'd been seated together at breakfast. "You'd hardly met me before you decided to spend a fortune on me. You couldn't have known if I merited such lavish gifts or not. I am exceedingly grateful, but if you truly wish to please me, I would prefer that we have a quiet afternoon in your dayroom getting better acquainted. London and the Season and the shops and museums aren't going anywhere, and I think a relaxing afternoon would be a nice respite. Don't you?"

Thankfully, it had done the trick.

"I confess that it was an excellent idea that we remain at home this afternoon and rest," Lady Walmsley said at length as she pulled her needle and thread through the fabric. "The past few days have indeed been rather busy, and I will admit I am a bit fatigued—but I shall deny it, especially if Foster gets wind of it!" Then she smiled at Susan. "You have been a good sport about all my indulgences for you. And Madame Veronique said that a gown or two would be delivered today." Lady Walmsley's sewing attempt was not quite so violent now as it had been when Foster had been in the room. "I can hardly wait to see you in them! We shall be able to retire the one you are wearing"—Lady Walmsley waved her arm in Susan's general direction—"and see you in something proper at last."

"My gown is perfectly proper," Susan said.

"It was perfectly proper a decade ago when it was in style, young lady. And I daresay you've taken care of your clothing over the years—the wear and tear hardly show."

"Thank you for that, at least," Susan said, unable to hold back a chuckle.

The chuckle got Lady Walmsley's hackles up. "You do not give yourself enough credit for the natural beauty God has bestowed upon you in abundance," she declared, pointing her finger repeatedly in Susan's direction, "and I intend to remedy that."

"So you have said," Susan replied.

"It baffles me that someone as lovely and gifted as yourself was not snatched up the minute you appeared on the scene at your come-out," Lady Walmsley said. "I have only known you for two days, and I am already greatly impressed."

Susan was touched. "Thank you, Lady Walms—"

"*And* I am taking you to the hairdressers on Monday, my dear," Lady Walmsley interrupted. "You have the most . . . well, to put it frankly, you have *the most hair* I have ever seen on one person's head in all my lifetime! And I am not young, so that is saying quite a lot."

Susan patted her head defensively, even though she'd chosen to wear a cap over her hair today. It had allowed her to braid her hair severely and put it out of sight. "You make me sound like a long-wool sheep," she exclaimed.

"Oh, no, no, no," Lady Walmsley replied. "Not at all! I'm terribly sorry if that is what you inferred from my words. No, with a little trim here and there, I think you may be surprised at what you discover your hair can do. Oh, yes, I can picture it now. And then we can get rid of that nasty cap for good. You are neither a spinster nor an old matron."

"Very well," Susan said. "I shall accede to your wishes in this matter—out of adventure and curiosity if for no other reason." She leaned toward Lady

Walmsley and patted her arm. "But I *beg* you," she said in a low but intense voice. "*Please* may we speak of something else? I would much rather learn about *you* than talk of these things. Does that agree with you?"

Lady Walmsley smiled, her dear, wrinkled face aglow. "You *are* a dear, Miss Jennings. So bright and strong and yet so modest. I doubt there is anything in my life of much interest that will amuse you, but if you're willing to listen . . ."

"Oh, indeed, Lady Walmsley! I am much interested in learning of my kind patroness. And you must call me Susan."

Susan spent a delightful afternoon with Lady Walmsley, listening to the stories of her youth, her courtship with her now-deceased husband, and the events that had led to the discovery that Lady Halford was her great-niece. Susan had been thoroughly enchanted.

Eventually, however, the dear lady yawned, covering her mouth with her hand. "Oh my!" she sighed afterward. "I can barely keep my eyes open. I believe I shall leave you for a while and allow myself a little nap."

"I completely understand," Susan replied. She had set her needlework aside long ago, too engrossed in Lady Walmsley's stories to do anything but listen.

"I hate to leave you on your own," Lady Walmsley said. "You are free, of course, to visit any room, find a book, play the pianoforte, walk in the garden."

Susan leaned forward and laid her hand atop Lady Walmsley's. "You needn't worry about me; I am perfectly comfortable on my own, and you have made me feel more than welcome here."

"You are such a dear girl," Lady Walmsley said, squeezing Susan's hand. She rose from her chair.

No sooner had she done so than there was a discreet knock on the dayroom door.

"Yes?" Lady Walmsley called out.

Foster slid into the room. "There is a caller for Miss Jennings," he said.

"Ooh! Madame Veronique's first delivery has arrived!" Lady Walmsley exclaimed. "Perhaps I shall forego the nap after all."

"You are fatigued, my lady?" Foster asked, seeming to entirely forget his reason for interrupting them. "You must assuredly rest, then. Allow me to assist you up the stairs to your—"

"I believe I am quite revived by this news, Foster," Lady Walmsley said, giving him a firm look. "I shall rest after I see what delights Madame Veronique has sent to Susan."

Susan smiled to herself. She was getting the distinct impression that Foster had more than just a soft spot for his employer—

"The caller is not Madame Veronique, my lady, or anyone from her shop," Foster said, apparently remembering his original reason for being here.

"The only person who would call upon me is James," Susan assured Lady Walmsley. "You may enjoy your nap after all."

"Very well." Lady Walmsley nodded and turned toward the stairway. "You will give my fondest regards to him, and I shall make up for my absence the next time—"

Foster cleared his throat, interrupting Lady Walmsley. "The caller is *not* Mr. Jennings."

Susan wrinkled her brow. "Who—?"

"The Duke of Aylesham is in the front parlor," Foster said.

Lady Walmsley gasped.

Susan shook her head in disbelief and denial. "There must be a mistake, Foster. The Duke of Aylesham would not be inclined to call upon me. If it truly is he, then it is Lady Walmsley who—"

Foster handed her the calling card. It was of the highest quality, she couldn't help but immediately notice, and it read: *George Kendall, Duke of Aylesham.*

She shook her head again.

"The duke specifically asked for *you*, Miss Jennings," Foster said.

"How exciting!" Lady Walmsley exclaimed, her fatigue a thing of the past once again. "Aylesham! Here to call upon *you*, Susan!"

"Lady Walmsley, you can dispel whatever romantic ideas you have. I can assure you the Duke of Aylesham would never, *ever* call upon me with such an intent."

"But you danced—"

"Out of an obligation he felt, owing to the circumstances—and not an entire dance, at that." Susan would not mention that she and the duke also had history—brief though it was—and that the history hadn't been friendly in the least.

"Oh dear," Lady Walmsley said. "Lady Bledsoe had such high hopes when the two of you arrived bearing cups of punch for us at the ball two nights ago. 'Finally,' Judith said to me after you two walked away, 'I had nearly given up on the boy—'"

Foster cleared his throat again.

"I know, I know, Foster. Here I am rambling, and now is not the time for it. We mustn't keep the Duke of Aylesham waiting," Lady Walmsley said. "Come, Susan. We shall greet the duke together, and then I shall hide myself away. You are of an age where you don't require a chaperone, after all."

"I can assure you there would be no need for a chaperone, regardless of my age," Susan replied. Why the duke had chosen to call upon her *did* pique her curiosity but not so much that she relished the idea of facing him on her own, however. "I am glad that you wish to be with me when greeting the duke."

The duke. His Loftiness. His High and Mightiness.

Susan allowed Lady Walmsley to take the lead as they made their way to the front parlor. Foster, ever the faithful butler, was in place to open the door when they arrived.

"Aylesham!" Lady Walmsley exclaimed as she entered the parlor, her arms outstretched in greeting. "What an unexpected pleasure!"

The duke, whom Susan could see had been seated by the fireplace, arose and came forward to greet Lady Walmsley. He nodded politely and took both of her hands in his for a brief moment. "Lady Walmsley, it is indeed a pleasure," he said.

He said the word *pleasure*, but there was something about his countenance that told Susan it was anything *but* pleasure that had brought him here today.

His Loftiness then turned toward her and bowed formally. "Miss Jennings."

"Your Grace," she said with a curtsy.

"Please have a seat; make yourself at home," Lady Walmsley said, gesturing to the seating area of the room. "I know you are here to call upon my dear new friend, Miss Jennings, Aylesham, so I shan't dawdle. You are a busy man. I shall take myself off and leave you two alone to converse." She gave Susan a knowing look and then trotted off, with Foster shutting the door behind her.

Leaving Susan and His Loftiness alone.

The duke hadn't taken up Lady Walmsley's offer to sit. He walked to the fireplace and then simply stood there, looking at her grimly—and it belatedly dawned on Susan that she was, once again, appearing less than her best. A relaxing afternoon without callers had not required she dress in one of her better gowns. And there was also the cap, which she'd not worn in any of their other encounters.

She lifted her chin in defiance. She would not allow His Loftiness's reaction to her appearance affect her. But it irked her to no end to have him at an advantage over her in that regard, for he was currently dressed to the nines. He couldn't look more immaculately put together if he had been intending to call upon the Prince Regent.

He was undoubtedly waiting for Susan to sit before doing so himself, so she walked over and sat.

Then waited.

He continued to remain standing by the fireplace. “Thank you for agreeing to see me,” he said at last.

Susan gave him a nod of acknowledgment. She wanted to hear what he had to say first before venturing any words of her own.

“You are no doubt wondering what my purpose is in being here,” the duke said. “And so, I will be brief: I am here to ask you to be my wife.”

Chapter 7

Susan froze. He could have told her she had sprouted wings and could fly to the moon and she wouldn't have been any more astonished. She was utterly speechless.

The Duke of Aylesham, for his part, stood there looking like he needed to wash the bitter taste from his mouth.

Suddenly, the absurdity of his words hit her, and something deep inside her bubbled and expanded upward. She snorted, and then it burst within her, and she began to laugh—she couldn't seem to help herself—throwing her hand over her mouth in a meager attempt to stifle the sound. Her eyes teared up. Shoulders heaving with laughter, she squinted to look at Aylesham.

He was watching her hysterics with a look of utter horror.

It was all too absurd for words.

"Please excuse my outburst," Susan choked out as she tried to curb her hilarity and search in the pocket of her gown for a handkerchief. Drat! Once again, she'd been caught without.

The duke huffed out an impatient sound, produced his own, and handed it to her, which only made her laugh more. She dabbed at her eyes and nose. She was going to have a complete collection of handkerchiefs embroidered with an *A* on them at the rate she was going.

"Have you gone mad?" His Loftiness asked her, still wearing that grim look of distaste on his face.

"I was going to ask you the same thing!" Susan said, still dabbing at her eyes. Her laughter now under a bit of control, she looked at him more carefully. His face seemed carved from granite; his dark eyes glittered but gave nothing away. Susan's humor fled entirely. "You were joking, weren't you?" she asked. "James put you up to this."

"Not in the slightest," he replied curtly.

"You're *serious*?" she said, aghast.

"Most assuredly."

An offer of marriage from the Duke of Aylesham was the last thing Susan had ever expected, and even more than that, the last thing she would ever consider. "I am flattered by your words, certainly . . . except that I am also confounded by them," Susan said. "Our previous encounters have not precisely been happy ones; in fact, I assumed you disliked me."

"You are not incorrect in that assumption," he replied, his gaze taking in the whole of her. She felt his eyes take in every detail of her appearance—her faded gown, her cap—and could tell he was passing further judgment on her as a result. And yet, he had spoken those words of marriage regardless.

How dare he trifle with her like this. "You dislike me, you accuse me of being an eavesdropper, and you could not even finish a waltz with me, no doubt because you consider me a clumsy, dusty spinster. Now you stand here judging me further—I can see it in your eyes. And yet, you propose marriage to me."

His Loftiness said nothing, which only made Susan's blood boil. "Well, Your Grace, we have something in common, for I dislike you as much as you dislike me," she spat. "No doubt you are of the opinion that any woman presented with a proposal of marriage from you would be ecstatic and would accept without hesitation—but *I* am not that woman."

She rose to her feet, her fists clenched at her sides. "I believe we have said all there is to say between us. You may see yourself out." She turned abruptly away from him, strode to the window, and stared out, waiting to hear the door open and close.

She waited.

Nothing happened.

She *would not* turn to address the Duke of Aylesham again. She had said her piece.

Two birds squawked at each other from a wisteria bush that stood by a small stone bench.

The duke apparently wasn't going anywhere. Her shoulders slumped in exasperation. "You are refusing to do the gentlemanly thing and leave, then?" she said at length.

"I am not leaving, no," he replied.

Susan spun around, incredulous.

He stood exactly where he'd been, still unmoving, still with features chiseled from granite. "There is more I must explain before I do," he said before Susan could utter any words of reproach. "And then, if you still refuse my offer of marriage, I shall do as you wish and leave."

Susan pondered his words. *There is more I must explain.*

Confound her blasted curiosity! Susan, despite her best intentions, wanted to hear what that explanation was. She doubted anything His Loftiness could possibly say would change her mind about marrying him, but it might make for a good story to recite to Rebecca in her next letter.

She stalked back to the chair in which she'd previously been sitting and sat again, gesturing to the chair next to it. "You have my full attention."

George wasn't a novice with the ladies and should have known better, but he belatedly realized he'd gone about this proposal in the entirely wrong way. He'd blundered badly, in point of fact. *Dear Miss Jennings, I dislike you immensely and, therefore, wish to marry you* was hardly the approach to gain the desired result. Prinny's threat had affected him more than he was willing to admit, as his approach to Miss Jennings clearly demonstrated.

He should have allowed himself a day to collect his wits and ponder the correct approach before speaking to Miss Jennings.

She had gestured to the chair next to hers, but he chose instead to stay by the fireplace. He clasped his hands behind his back and cleared his throat. "Miss Jennings, please forgive the abrupt manner of my previous words," he said.

She sat there, hands in her lap, looking unimpressed and hostile.

He tried again. "We have not gotten off on the right foot, have we, Miss Jennings? Discovering you in the library at Cantwell Hall made me angry, as you know, but, on further reflection, I can see how you may have felt similarly upon having had your solitude interrupted."

"Not exactly an apology," she said.

"Perhaps not," George replied. "In my defense, I can only say that the serious nature of the discussion being held was reflected in my reaction to discovering your presence." Miss Jennings said nothing in reply, so he continued. "As to our abbreviated waltz, you were no more inclined to dance with me than I was with you, so the fact that we ceased to dance and instead took refreshment to Lady Bledsoe and Lady Walmsley seemed preferable to us both, in my opinion."

From the look of annoyance on Miss Jennings's face, George suspected he was only digging himself into a deeper hole than he was already in. He looked toward the window where Miss Jennings had stood and then beyond, toward

Lady Walmsley's small park, at the green lawns, trimmed hedges, and *freedom*. If only he could climb through that window and disappear, leaving all the business of Prinny and Miss Jennings and marriage and the unknown Princess Sophia of Schönberg-Nusse behind.

But it was not to be.

George took a deep sigh. "Please allow me to explain myself one more time, Miss Jennings. I can see that I have chosen my words poorly thus far, but I cannot leave until I have explained things fully to you."

"So you said earlier," Miss Jennings said. "And yet, I am still waiting and have heard nothing that explains your offer or anything that would convince me to accept."

He reluctantly sat in the chair next to hers. "I am caught in a trap, Miss Jennings, and I fear I have caught you with me."

Her eyebrows furrowed. "A trap? What sort of trap?" she asked.

How much should he tell her? "I have just come from a meeting with the Prince Regent, during which he presented a plan to me that benefited him greatly, and he was convinced it would be of benefit to me as well. Unfortunately, his plan requires I marry an individual of his choosing. In my effort to extricate myself, your name may have arisen."

"*May have*?" Miss Jennings said.

"Very well, I told His Royal Highness I was already betrothed, in the hopes that it would be sufficient to dissuade him from pressing marriage to a European princess upon me."

"You told the Prince Regent that you and I were betrothed."

"Yes." After her previous outbursts, he was relieved that she was acting rationally thus far.

"And so, if I am understanding you correctly, to prevent yourself from spending your life with someone not of your choosing, you decided to place us *both* in that precise situation. A logical move if there ever was one, Your Grace." The sarcasm fairly dripped from her words.

"I cannot explain why your name of all names came to mind, Miss Jennings. In all honesty, I thought offering *any* name would satisfy the prince and dissuade him from his plan."

"But it did not," she said.

"No."

"There is more you are not telling me," she said.

George shrugged. "He expects us to wed quickly and intends to be present at the nuptials," he said.

Miss Jennings inhaled sharply, and George waited for the hysteria that was sure to follow. Instead, she clasped the arms of her chair tightly and closed her eyes. He watched her bosom rise and fall in an attempt to control her emotions.

Eventually, she opened her eyes. "There is a simple answer to this, Your Grace, at least for me," she said matter-of-factly. "I refuse your offer and leave you to contend with the Prince Regent on your own."

"True," George said, hoping it wouldn't come to that. Prinny would be incandescent with rage for having been lied to, and he would exact misery on George that could equal or surpass what marriage to Princess Sophia would create. Still, it had been worth the risk to try.

"And you have offered me nothing—beyond the formality of marriage—that would induce me to accept. No sort of *quid pro quo*, as it were," she said, again with sarcasm.

"The *quid pro quo* is implicit in the offer," George said. "You will be the Duchess of Aylesham—"

"I never aspired to be a duchess."

He ignored her and kept speaking. "You will have wealth at your disposal. Connections. Think of what you would be able to do for your family."

"Ah, but that depends largely upon the marriage settlements, does it not?"

"Which I assure you will be liberal. You seem the sensible type, so I doubt you will be frivolous in your requests."

George saw that his reply took her by surprise. "A compliment," she said dryly, although she looked rather astonished. "I thank you."

George nodded in acknowledgment.

"And yet, I have no basis upon which to trust your assurances," she continued. "You did, after all, lie to the Prince Regent about our nonexistent betrothal."

"Touché, Miss Jennings," George said. "So let me ask you this: which do you consider the worse offense? Lying to the prince about a nonexistent betrothal or marrying into a family who has ingratiated itself to Bonaparte?"

Her eyes widened at his words. "Obviously, there is much you have yet to explain," she said. "For starters, *why* would the Prince Regent require that you marry into a family that supports our sworn enemy?"

"I doubt he knows, Miss Jennings. You will simply have to trust me that I know it to be true. And I suspect our sovereign's judgment may be clouded by the opportunity the marriage offers him to acquire additional funds." He wished he hadn't had to share even that much with her.

She looked thoughtful as she considered his words. "I will concede that your motives are much clearer now. But it still doesn't tell me what *I* may expect from this." She stood and began to pace the room. "If I were to lay out my options, they would be these: firstly, to refuse you," she said. "Secondly, would be a marriage in name only, with the compensation for my agreeing to the match outlined in the marriage contracts."

It sounded unpalatable when stated so bluntly, George thought. It also brought up an issue that he must deal with immediately. The complicated business at hand was getting even more complicated. "Not entirely, Miss Jennings," he said. "I must have an heir, you see."

The color in her cheeks bloomed. "Ah," she said, trying not to look flustered. "And so you chose an older, potentially less fertile woman whom you have already claimed you dislike to be the mother of your heir," she said.

"Yes," he said. What else could he say? It was what he had done, after all.

The blush in her cheeks made her look younger, and she was biting her lip in such a way that George was suddenly drawn to that lip. "I had given up hope of ever being a mother," she said softly to herself.

And he thought he might finally have his bride—she wasn't his ideal choice, but she spared him being put firmly under Prinny's thumb.

Marriage to Miss Jennings was the lesser of two evils.

Was it worth it to agree to marry the Duke of Aylesham?

Susan was practical by nature. She wasn't overly romantic—any thoughts of romance she'd ever entertained had withered and died after her third Season. Correction: any thought she'd had of romance *for herself* had died after that Season. But here she was, her first week in London, being offered marriage to the Duke of Aylesham. She could be a duchess. She could have wealth at her disposal. The whole business was incredibly ironic.

There was a great deal of good she could do were she to accept the duke's offer. Susan could sponsor Rebecca's come-out next Season—it was long overdue and well-deserved. She could repay Lady Walmsley for her incredible generosity thus far—Susan had been here but three days and had been overwhelmed by Lady Walmsley's effusive manner and open purse strings.

If Susan were to marry the Duke of Aylesham, she could have a child of her own. Perhaps more than one. Could she be intimate with the Duke of Aylesham in that way? Close to him in *any* way? She'd barely been willing to touch him at the ball two nights before. She considered him pompous and aloof. They had nothing in common.

She studied him now as he sat there, and she searched for answers to the countless questions his offer raised in her mind. He was an attractive man, especially so today, wearing such fine garments. His dark hair was perfectly cut and styled. In fact, he was immaculate in his entire bearing, with no visible flaws at all. It was disconcerting, really. And while his dark eyes drew her into their depths, they gave her no indication of what he was thinking.

She refused to look away from him. It would be so easy to lower her eyes. But looking down would be submissive, and *that* she would not allow herself to be. Not with him.

"You've given me a lot to consider," she said

"I am aware of that," he replied.

She blocked from her mind the images of her happily married parents and those of her siblings, Thomas, Martha, and Isaac, who were all in happy unions—as well as her brother Lucas, just younger than she, who'd been married two years and now had a babe of his own. She had no assurances of such a happy union with the Duke of Aylesham. It was highly unlikely, in fact.

"I have made a decision," she said at length.

"Yes?" he said, straightening in his chair.

"While I thank you for your offer of marriage, Your Grace, I cannot give you a reply today," she said.

His countenance darkened.

"I need time to consider all you have told me," she explained. "I need time to consider all that you have *not* told me."

"Miss Jennings—"

"If you press me on this, my answer will be no," Susan said firmly. She had not asked for any of this. It mattered not to her that *he* had not asked for the dilemma he was currently facing either.

The door opened as if on cue, and Lady Walmsley bustled in, followed immediately by Foster bearing a silver tea service. "I know I said I'd leave you two alone to converse," Lady Walmsley said, "but it dawned on me that I was neglecting my duties as hostess." She crossed the room and seated herself in the settee that was at right angles to the chair in which Susan had been seated. "I shall pour. How do you take your tea, Aylesham? Milk or lemon?"

"Milk, please." The duke had risen to his feet at Lady Walmsley's entrance and reseated himself now while she poured a dash of milk into two teacups.

"I already know Susan prefers hers with sugar," Lady Walmsley said as she picked up the teapot and began to pour. She set down the pot and handed the duke his tea. "Come, Susan, join us."

"Thank you." Susan reluctantly returned to her chair and took the teacup offered by Lady Walmsley. Lady Walmsley beamed at her, and Susan had more than a sneaking suspicion that her hostess had been eavesdropping prior to her arrival in the room. She sipped her tea. "Such a coincidence you returned when you did, Lady Walmsley. The duke and I had just finished our conversation."

Lady Walmsley's expression was one of utter surprise.

Susan didn't believe it for a moment.

"And here I was, thinking that two such intelligent people as yourselves would have a great deal about which to converse," Lady Walmsley said. "And much to discover about each other too. My dear friend Judith—Lady Bledsoe, you know, Susan—was so fond of Aylesham's mother. They came out together and became bosom friends. I am a great deal older, of course, and therefore was only somewhat acquainted with the duchess. Such a beauty she was! I do remember that about her."

"Thank you, Lady Walmsley. Lady Bledsoe has said much the same to me," the duke said.

"But surely you have portraits of her, Your Grace. You must miss her—and your father—greatly. I imagine people have shared stories about them with you."

"Occasionally," he said. He abruptly began sipping his tea, implicitly saying the subject of his parents had concluded as far as he was concerned.

"Susan, on the other hand, has a rather large family, from what she's told me," Lady Walmsley said, apparently not picking up on the duke's implied message. "How many siblings was it again, Susan? Five? Six?"

"There were eight children born to my parents," Susan replied. "Including myself."

"Gracious! Can you imagine that, Your Grace? *Eight children*—of course, *you* are acquainted with her brother James; I saw you speaking to him at Lady Bledsoe's ball the other night."

"I am," the duke said.

"Clever young man. A solicitor, I understand," Lady Walmsley said. "You are much like him in that regard, Susan. Such a reader, she is, Your Grace! Not content to sit idly by, no. She has already prowled the stacks in my library, looking for this and that to read." She chuckled. "In my day, young ladies learned to sew and play pianoforte and manage a household. Imagine what young ladies now could accomplish were they educated in the same subjects as the young men!"

"Radical thoughts, Lady Walmsley," the duke said, but Susan noticed that a corner of his mouth had tipped upward just the slightest bit.

Lady Walmsley chuckled, obviously undeterred. "You are every bit as clever as your brother, Susan. Would you have cared to become a solicitor, do you suppose, had the opportunity for it existed?"

How was Susan to reply to that?

Before she could say anything in reply, the duke spoke up. "As a matter of fact, Lady Walmsley, before your arrival, I was conversing with Miss Jennings on a particular subject, and her observations were keen and to the point." He shot Susan a speaking glance.

"Ah, there, you see, Susan? Even the Duke of Aylesham agrees with me," Lady Walmsley said. "More tea, Your Grace?"

"No, thank you," he said, setting his cup and saucer on the tea tray and rising to his feet. "Miss Jennings, perhaps you would care to walk with me? A stroll through Lady Walmsley's garden, perhaps?"

"Oh, what a delightful idea! The weather is particularly cooperative today," Lady Walmsley said. "And I shall rest my eyes briefly while you are gone."

It seemed Susan was not yet rid of the His Loftiness after all. "Thank you, Your Grace. It's kind of you to offer," she said.

Whatever Lady Walmsley had going on in that scheming mind of hers, it had worked to George's advantage. He suspected she was doing her own bit of matchmaking, unaware that George had every intention of getting Miss Jennings to agree to his suit. Having Lady Walmsley as a surprise ally had saved him from leaving before he had secured Miss Jennings's acceptance.

He offered her his arm. "Miss Jennings?" he said as politely as possible. He could see that she was not feeling particularly agreeable—not that she'd been all that agreeable thus far.

She set her hand on his arm and allowed him to escort her from the room, after which her hand immediately dropped to her side. "Lady Walmsley's garden is best accessed by the french doors in the dayroom," she said.

"Lead the way," George replied.

She nodded curtly and strode down a corridor that led south from the main entrance, and George followed. No mincing steps for Miss Jennings, not at all. George could almost find her behavior humorous if there weren't so much at stake.

He matched her stride easily and opened the door for her when they reached the dayroom and then again when they arrived at the french doors. She stepped out onto the small terrace beyond and then stopped. George closed the french doors and moved to stand beside her.

"I understand you don't wish to give me an answer this afternoon, Miss Jennings," George said. "I have experienced much the same shock this afternoon as you yourself have. Unfortunately, there is little time. The Prince Regent's intended bride for me, Princess Sophia Augusta of Schönberg-Nusse, and her parents will be arriving in London within a fortnight, expecting to immediately become betrothed to me, with the marriage to follow shortly thereafter. They have already been informed that I am the designated groom." He gestured toward the terrace steps to the garden beyond. "May we?"

She nodded.

They descended the steps together, and George clasped his hands behind his back. Lady Walmsley's garden was a modest one, and other than a plot for an herb garden that appeared to be situated in the sunniest spot of ground, it was laid out in an informal manner. There was a row of yews that marked the back of Lady Walmsley's small property; to the left, near the wall that bordered the property on that side, was a wisteria and bench George had observed when peering through the window of Lady Walmsley's parlor. The garden appeared arranged in such a way as to create spots of color and interest. A stone pathway led to the wisteria.

Strolling toward it was the logical choice, then; they went in that direction.

"Miss Jennings," George said at last. "Perhaps you have had a moment now to think upon my offer and have specific questions I can answer for you."

Miss Jennings remained silent; George took that as a good sign since she had not been shy about sharing her opinions before now.

"I will take your words into consideration," Miss Jennings said at last.

"That is all I ask," George said.

They had reached the wisteria, but George was not inclined to sit at present, nor did it appear that Miss Jennings was either, so they continued down the path, which he discovered took them to the corner of the property, where there was a small, two-tiered fountain. In the late afternoon, as it was right now, it was shaded by the yew trees but would be a delightful, secluded spot earlier in the day.

They stopped and stood next to it, and George allowed the sound of the splashing water to surround him. The late afternoon sun occasionally peeked through the branches of the yews and bounced off the water, creating rainbows of color. He needed this moment, he realized. He felt as though he was taking his first breath since leaving Prinny.

Miss Jennings seated herself on the low stone wall that surrounded the fountain and then leaned over and ran her fingers through the rippling water. She looked thoughtful.

"As you can see, Miss Jennings, we are already more amiable with each other than we were but an hour ago," George said, sitting next to her atop the wall.

"Mm," she replied.

He watched her fingers trail through the water. She had elegant hands.

"What gives you the most pause in accepting my proposal? What more do you wish to know that will satisfy your immediate concerns?"

"There is *much* I wish to know," Miss Jennings answered, her gaze intent on the water and the ripples her fingers made. "Living arrangements and domestic expectations and dowries and personal philosophies regarding life and family and God, to name just a few. I am not a young miss who will merely bend to your every whim—"

"I have discerned that about you already," he said.

She turned and glared at him for a moment before relaxing into an apologetic smile. "I suppose you have."

"I recognize that there are many conversations that need to occur and that we must get to know each other further. In the meantime, I believe your brother James will vouch for my character," George said. "As Duke of Aylesham, I have endeavored to act honorably at all times, as did my granduncle before me. I recognize that my offer of marriage is unexpected. I cannot explain why it was your name that escaped my lips—"

She looked up at him, her eyes bright as quicksilver, searching his face for he knew not what, and he briefly lost his train of thought before collecting himself. "Nonetheless, it was your name I spoke. And so I ask you, what more do you need from me that will help you decide?"

Her eyes fairly blazed with something George could not define. "By merely asking that question, you have given me all I need to know," she replied enigmatically. "Now I simply need time to consider." She stood and turned as though to continue down the path, away from the fountain.

George laid his hand on her arm to stop her from leaving. "My words have disappointed you somehow," he said, letting his hand slip away from her arm when she stopped suddenly and looked at it. "I'm sorry for that. I can tell you wish me to leave now. But if I may, I shall call on you tomorrow afternoon to receive you answer. Will that be acceptable?"

She turned, and George could see that she was fighting to hide some terrible emotion. Her gray eyes were no longer bright but had gone dark as a cloudy sky. "I will give you an answer tomorrow when you call," she said.

"Thank you." He bowed formally to her and left her standing by the fountain, wondering what he could have said or done more and what had affected her so deeply at the end. Their conversation in the garden, which he thought had begun somewhat favorably, had ended poorly, and he didn't know why.

He'd apologized for his behavior in the past, he'd laid out as many of the particulars as he could in the time at hand, and he'd behaved with the upmost decorum around her. He'd treated her as a duchess should be treated.

There was nothing he could do now except wait.

That wasn't entirely true. There were other things demanding his attention, and Prinny's little scheme had taken too much time away from those things. He must address them as soon as he returned home, all the while contemplating what counterarguments he might need with Miss Jennings tomorrow, should she refuse him.

Susan wasn't sure how long she spent at the fountain after the Duke of Aylesham took his leave of her. She had seated herself on the stone wall again after he'd left and had stared at the bubbling water, sorting through her thoughts and emotions.

The Duke of Aylesham had apologized to her, true, but he was still arrogant. He was used to getting his way. She doubted he would have bothered apologizing at all had he not found himself in this dilemma. But during their conversation this afternoon, he had shown himself to be of honorable character. His reasons for not wishing to marry the princess had demonstrated that. She had believed him.

She ran her fingers through the water aimlessly. She understood some of what happened in government, but she was certainly lacking knowledge when it came to diplomatic relations between countries—especially now, while England was at war. But why didn't someone simply tell the Prince Regent that marriage between the Duke of Aylesham and the Princess Sophia Augusta was unsuitable and the reason? Susan had never been presented to the Prince Regent, or any of the royals, for that matter, during her come-out, so she wasn't entirely sure how one went about such things.

The duke had said Susan must trust him in that regard. Maybe there was more to it than he had told her. All she knew was that the duke had been intent enough to avoid that particular union as to throw *her* name forward to the prince.

It was unbelievable. It was utterly ludicrous, in fact. *Why her?* That single question plagued her more than anything else. Of all the names he could have said, why *hers*?

Lady Walmsley's personal maid, Tompkins, called her name, interrupting her thoughts. "Miss Jennings! I have been sent to find you. Such excitement!" She was hurrying in Susan's direction.

Susan had had enough excitement for this afternoon, thank you very much.

"I am to tell you that you must come to the dayroom at once! Madame Veronique *herself* has arrived with one of her seamstresses . . . and with so many boxes! Foster had to get *two* footmen to bring them all inside. I can scarcely wait to see what is in them. Do hurry, miss!"

Susan sighed. There was nothing for it, then. Madame Veronique awaited her presence. She stood, smoothed her skirt, and followed Tompkins into the house.

"There you are!" Lady Walmsley exclaimed. "But where is Aylesham? I expected to be able to at least bid him farewell when he left."

"Not to worry, Lady Walmsley," Susan said. "He plans to return tomorrow."

"*Does* he, now?" Lady Walmsley's eyes grew large and began to twinkle. "I *like* the sound of that. Indeed, I do! I had *no idea* that my young guest would beguile none other than the illustrious Duke of Aylesham. And so quickly too!"

"I don't think *beguile* is the word I would use," Susan said. In fact, there had been nothing in the duke's demeanor to suggest he'd been beguiled at all. He was offering her nothing more than a practical business arrangement, other than the caveat about bearing him an heir.

And that was what troubled her, for despite herself, Susan had begun to find herself increasingly attracted to His Loftiness, and it meant that were she to agree to marry the duke, she must guard her heart at all cost.

Chapter 8

Foster, under Lady Walmsley's direction, had led Madame Veronique, her assistant, and the footmen with their boxes to Susan's guest rooms. By the time Susan, Lady Walmsley, and Tompkins ascended the stairs to Susan's rooms, Madame Veronique and her assistant had laid out four gowns on Susan's bed.

"Madame Veronique, you and your seamstresses have been exceedingly busy," Susan said as she gazed at the lovely gowns before her. "We were expecting one, maybe two gowns today."

"I just had zees feeling about you," Madame Veronique said with a wink. "I said, 'We must do our best wis zees client, n*'est-ce pas vrai*? Eez true, yes?"

"Indeed, Miss Jennings," Madame Veronique's assistant said. "Madame said we must drop everything else and concentrate our efforts on your gowns. She said she had an inkling."

"An inkling," Susan said, raising an eyebrow at Madame Veronique.

"What can I say? Zere eez somezing about you zat tells Madame Veronique we must do our best."

Susan looked suspiciously at Lady Walmsley, who only shrugged. "I haven't had any communication with Madame since the two of us were in her shop."

Madame Veronique tapped her forefinger against her temple. "Madame Veronique knows, *oui*? Now, let us begin wis zees one"—she picked up a day dress made of light blue muslin—"but first, we must remove zat horrible cap and never see eet again. Off! Off!" She pointed repeatedly at Susan's cap as though shooing it away.

Susan reluctantly untied the bow of her cap and slipped it from her head.

"More," Madame Veronique said in a commanding tone, twirling her hand near Susan's head. "I want to see your hair as God gave eet to you."

Susan reluctantly unpinned her thick braids from her head and ran her fingers through the weaves, trying to untangle it all. She hated fussiness, and dealing with her hair had always been a nuisance.

"Oooh, la!" Madame Veronique breathed. "We see what we have here now zat eet eez free, *non*?" She took a clump of Susan's waist-long hair into her hand and began rubbing the strands between her fingers. "*Magnifique*! Mimi, come see."

Mimi hurried over and gently touched Susan's hair. It was rather odd having her head scrutinized in this way.

"Lady Walmsley," Madame Veronique said in a voice that heralded an announcement. "We must ask you to send a message to Miss Lily at once. She eez an artiste when eet comes to cutting zee hair. I would have no one else touch zees beautiful locks but Miss Lily. And when you see zee hair and zee gown together—mwah!" She kissed her fingers and flung them, as though throwing a kiss.

It was a bit dramatic for Susan's taste, but on the other hand, it *was* diverting. Or at least it would be if she weren't the subject of it all.

"Certainly, Madame!" Lady Walmsley said. "I shall see that it is sent posthaste." She promptly sat at the escritoire in Susan's room and dashed off a note. "This is all so exciting! I have heard of Miss Lily, you know, and I should have thought of her myself." She crossed to the bedroom door and went out into the corridor. "Foster," she called. "I need a footman at once, if not sooner! Foster!" Her voice faded as she hurried down the corridor.

Madame Veronique chuckled briefly, but then she turned a serious face to Susan. "Miss Jennings," she said, the French accent now gone. "You are an exceedingly clever woman, as I think you are undoubtedly aware. I consider myself one as well."

"I would agree," Susan said.

"Therefore, I shall be frank with you. Up until now, I believe you have relied on your intellect and have disregarded the natural beauty with which you have been blessed."

"I don't think—" Susan began.

"Yours is not a classic beauty, perhaps," Madame Veronique continued, holding up her hand to stop Susan from speaking. "And I suspect that may be why you have not given it much, if any, credence. I am telling you this because when your hair has been cut in a flattering style and you are wearing one of my new gowns, you are going to see yourself in a new light. I tell you this as a warning."

"A warning," Susan repeated, nearly laughing. Madame Veronique was *warning* her that new clothes and a haircut would make a new woman out of her! *Hardly.* Susan was Susan and would always be Susan.

"Yes, a warning," Madame Veronique repeated.

Susan was unconvinced. "I am completely aware that beautiful women hold some mystical power over men. I have a sister-in-law, you know, who used her beauty to bring men under her spell. Ruby Chadwick, she was called. The Darling of Drury Lane."

"Ahh! I remember Miss Chadwick well," Madame Veronique said.

"Now, *she* is an incomparable beauty," Susan said. "I have never had that effect on men—spellbound, utterly devoted." Susan had witnessed it happen. Her brother Lucas had fallen head over heels for Lavinia, which was Ruby's real given name, but gentlemen passersby still gaped at Lavinia even to this day.

"There are different kinds of beauty, Miss Jennings," Madame Veronique said. "I have seen it all in my shop. There are also different kinds of ugliness. For the outside eventually reflects what is on the inside, you see."

At that moment, Lady Walmsley burst back into the room, her face pink, her eyes shining, wisps of gray hair fluttering about her cheeks and forehead. "The note is on its way! Oh, I can *hardly wait* to see what Miss Lily does with that hair of yours, my dear!" She clasped her hands together and stopped to catch her breath. "What a great pleasure this all is for me! I am elated!" Lady Walmsley glowed with happiness at the prospect of dressing Susan, who had been a complete stranger to her just days before.

"You see what I mean?" Madame Veronique said softly to Susan.

"Yes," Susan replied. For there was no more beautiful sight right now than dear Lady Walmsley.

George sat at his desk in his study, watching Phillip Osbourne pace about the room and waiting for him to speak. James Jennings sat across from George, thumbing through a folder of documents.

"What say *you*, Jennings?" Osbourne said at last. "Never mind. It doesn't matter what you say. We nearly lost the duke last time, and I think it's a terrible idea for him to join us on this next assignment."

"Regardless of whether Osbourne wishes my opinion or not," Jennings said, still thumbing through the documents, "I will offer it all the same." He looked up directly at George. "It is readily apparent that you are not fully recovered, Aylesham."

"I'm perfectly fine," George said. "You both make me sound like an invalid. It has been well over a month since I was ill. And did we not give our word to the foreign secretary that we would do all in our power to see that the work accomplished at Chaumont would not be undone? Peace is at hand at last, gentlemen. We must see it through."

"And upon our word, Aylesham, Osbourne and I shall," Jennings said. "The documents are nearly ready, and their copies will be completed over the next several days. Our plans are set. The foundation for Bonaparte's abdication has been laid, and we are only assuring its success at this point. As to the other business, we will have it well in hand. There is no need for you to risk such a journey when you are only now returning to full health."

George was getting more and more irritated by the minute with this continued talk about his health. Were it not for the fact that these two men had stood at his side the past several months during some rigorous assignments on behalf of the Foreign Office, he would not allow them to speak to him in this way.

"Frankly, Your Grace, I died a bit inside when I thought I might be returning to London and informing Parliament that I'd failed to keep the Duke of Aylesham alive while under my protection," Osbourne said.

"I was not under—"

"He's right, you know," Jennings said, interrupting George. "Regardless of who was protecting whom at any given moment—for we know we were united in our cause—the death of one of the highest of England's most noble members would have been viewed as a victory by the French, and Osbourne and I would have borne the responsibility for it. We both held our breath and prayed when you were at your worst, you know."

Those particular days onboard George's yacht had passed in a fevered blur—and that was before the illness had progressed to his lungs.

"Truly, Aylesham, at this point, I believe Osbourne and I can manage on our own. Erring on the side of caution is the best course of action."

Despite their sensible argument, George wasn't ready to concede to them yet, especially since it would give him a few weeks to absent himself from his—hopefully—new bride. Hopefully. How odd it was to hope for a marriage while also hoping for an opportunity to be away from it. "We have a week or so yet to make a final decision. I will take your words into consideration." He knew full well he should remain here, that staying home would allow him to turn his attention to the new bride he expected to have. He also knew relations with said new bride would be as precarious as negotiations with the duchies and states of the Continent had been in forming the Sixth Coalition. He wasn't looking forward to that part with much relish.

He looked at his watch. He intended to call on Miss Jennings at the earliest hour etiquette would allow. The less time he gave her to ponder his offer, the better. He then looked at her brother, James Jennings. George trusted—indeed, *literally* trusted—Jennings with his life. George still couldn't quite see any similarity between him and his prickly sister.

He briefly considered whether he should tell Jennings he planned to wed his sister—rather like asking him for her hand in marriage since her father was not available—and then decided not to. This was better kept between Miss Jennings and himself at present. She was a mature woman who did not need her father's permission or that of a brother when contemplating marriage.

There was a discreet knock at the door, and then Talbot stepped inside. "I am to inform you that Mrs. Bradley has set up luncheon in the dining room, Your Grace."

"I hope Mrs. Bradley has prepared a sumptuous feast so that our sickly friend here may return to his former, robust self," Osbourne said, shooting a wry glance at George.

"You can be sure of that, Mr. Osbourne," Talbot replied. "It is a concerted effort on all of our parts to make sure the Duke of Aylesham eats well and rests as he should."

"I am *here*, you know, listening to every word," George said. "And I expect whatever weight I shed during the course of my unaccountable illness would find its way back onto my bones more quickly were I not fretted over every minute of every day."

"I don't believe 'fretting' is actually part of a butler's duties, Your Grace. I would never fret," Talbot replied without batting an eye.

"Thank you for your insightful words into your responsibilities, Talbot," George said. He should sack the man on the spot, insubordinate old nursemaid that he was. "Inform Mrs. Bradley that we shall make great haste to the dining room and eat like gluttons. Won't we, gentlemen?"

"Absolutely," Jennings said. "I myself am famished."

Osbourne simply laughed.

"And have Mrs. Bradley send her tincture as well, Talbot. These fools have made my head ache."

Talbot nodded in acknowledgment, trying to hide a victorious smile, the old fossil. "I shall inform Mrs. Bradley, Your Grace. Thank you, Your Grace."

George waved him off. He was completely surrounded by insubordinates. Talbot, Mrs. Bradley, his valet Evans . . . and Jennings and Osbourne, of course. Insubordinates all. And later this afternoon, he would be working to convince the prickliest, most insubordinate harpy of a woman he'd ever met to be his wife, because she was the lesser of two evils, heaven help him. "Come, gentlemen," he said. "We have coordinated our efforts and determined our actions going forward. I shall inform you soon of my decision regarding whether I shall accompany you or not. In the meantime, let us adjourn to the dining room. Perhaps Mrs. Bradley's fine cooking will make a difference. I am apparently still near death's door."

The others caught his intended sarcasm and laughed and then followed him from his study.

"What a picture you make!" Lady Walmsley exclaimed as Susan stood in front of the full-length mirror in her dressing room. 'I'm *so* glad Miss Lily was able to arrange her schedule and come by this morning. Your *hair*, Susan! It's absolutely gorgeous!"

Susan herself was pleasantly surprised by what Miss Lily had accomplished with her hair. By trimming off a mere few inches and adding layers, she'd managed to free Susan's natural curls in a way that looked, well, *curly* as opposed to simply bushy. Pinning the curls up rather than twisting her hair into a tight knot softened her features. Susan thought she looked younger than her thirty years, and perhaps she might even look—dare she say it?—pretty.

At the very least, it was an improvement, and Miss Lily had taken the time to show Susan how to style her hair.

"You have enviable hair, Miss Jennings, and I think you'll find it should be much easier to maintain with it trimmed this way. And please call on me anytime you wish assistance," she'd said before she left.

"I do like what Madame Veronique and Miss Lily have done," Susan said. "I owe that all to you, Lady Walmsley."

"Tut, child," Lady Walmsley said. "And you must cease this 'Lady Walmsley' business. I feel I've known you for an age. I'm Margaret. I should have told you to call me that from the very first."

"As I will consider you a dear friend forever, I shall be glad to do so," Susan said, "although perhaps Aunt Margaret might be more to your liking?" Out of respect, the honorary title seemed more fitting than merely using the lady's Christian name.

"As you wish, my dear. I seem to be adopting nieces left and right, and it suits me greatly. You *are* a sight though! I can hardly wait to see Aylesham's face when he lays his eyes on you today," Lady Walmsley—*Aunt Margaret*—said.

Susan briefly considered whether she should tell Aunt Margaret that Aylesham had proposed to her and was awaiting her answer. Having Aunt Margaret by her side during this—since her own mother was not here—would be a comfort.

No. It was better kept between the Duke of Aylesham and herself at present. Susan was a woman who could make her decision on her own.

And she had made her decision. For the most part.

Yesterday, when the duke had arrived and turned her entire world upside down, he had been wearing his finest clothes. It had given him an advantage over her. Today, she would have the advantage. She remembered Madame Veronique's words about appearances and power. Looking in the mirror now, Susan felt as though she'd put on a kind of armor, like a warrior before going into battle. She was going into a sort of battle against the Duke of Aylesham, and her new appearance gave her extra confidence.

She had lain awake a great deal last night, considering what she should do. She had gone over all the possibilities, both negative and positive, that marriage to the duke would bring. After hours of tossing and turning, she had finally arisen from bed, sat at the escritoire, and written a copious list of questions that had plagued her over and over again. Doing so had finally allowed her to sleep.

It had also clarified in her mind the concerns she felt were most critical to address with the duke. She wanted assurances from him. Her final decision was contingent upon his answers.

"Let's take a turn in the garden, shall we?" Aunt Margaret said. "Or are you hungry? We can inform Mrs. Drake that we'd like lunch."

Food did *not* sound like a good idea at present. "The garden would be nice, I think," she said.

Aunt Margaret looked at her knowingly. "The Duke of Aylesham has this effect on everyone, you know. I'm sure you'll be able to chat and get to know each other quite easily once you get past the awkward beginnings."

Aunt Margaret had no idea just how awkward all of Susan's *beginnings* with the Duke of Aylesham had already been. "I'm sure you're right," she replied.

"A good, hearty lunch will do you good, you know," Aunt Margaret continued as she made her way to Susan's dressing room door. "Especially as you ate so little at breakfast time. I do notice such things, you know. A brisk turn in the garden, then, just to put a bit of color in your cheeks, and then a nice luncheon will be just the thing." She opened the door. "Foster! Oh, here you are already. Please inform Mrs. Drake that Miss Jennings and I would like luncheon as soon as it can be prepared."

"I am here, your ladyship, because you and Miss Jennings have a caller," Foster said from the corridor beyond the door. "The Duke of Aylesham—"

"He's here, then! So soon! I *do* like the sound of that. Come, Susan, it appears lunch will have to wait. Foster, please inform Mrs. Drake that the Duke of Aylesham will be joining Miss Jennings and me for luncheon this afternoon. What a grand idea! Taking luncheon with him will be just the thing!"

Susan's stomach wasn't inclined to agree, but what was done was done. The battle was about to begin.

She took a deep breath and followed Aunt Margaret down the corridor toward the parlor, where the Duke of Aylesham awaited.

They were nearly there when Susan stopped in her tracks. "Wait," she said.

Aunt Margaret turned around. "What is it, dear?"

"There is something in my room I need to fetch," Susan said. "I wasn't expecting the duke to arrive so soon."

"I can't imagine what it would be that you need; oh, very well, but be quick about it! We don't like to keep the duke waiting, do we? In the meantime, I shall greet him and see that he feels welcome."

"Thank you. I shall be only a minute," Susan said. She dashed up the stairs and back to her room. The notes she'd written during the night were in the drawer of the escritoire, and she wanted them with her when she spoke with the duke. She slid the drawer open and took out the papers and then folded them so they would fit neatly in her pocket. Then—she couldn't help herself—she paused and checked her appearance in the mirror one last time.

Her day dress of pale-green muslin was a delightful concoction, with slightly puffed short sleeves and a smocked bodice that flattered her figure and somehow managed to make her appear both youthful and mature. Madame Veronique was a gifted woman.

Susan patted a curl—a *natural* curl, freed from the weight of its previous length—into place and marveled once again. Miss Lily and Madame Veronique had truly worked wonders, and Susan was beginning to understand Madame's warning to her. She felt the suggestion of a power she never had before. The reflection in the mirror told her she was more than merely presentable. Armed with that knowledge, she spoke to the new woman she saw in the mirror. "You are more than a mere viscount's daughter. More than the tomboy who played hard and fought hard with five brothers and prided herself on outsmarting them most of the time. More than a disregarded spinster."

She must hold on to this feeling of power. Madame Veronique had not issued a warning after all. She had given Susan insight, and Susan intended to use it to her advantage in her discussion with the Duke of Aylesham.

Susan took a deep breath and then nodded to the footman to open the parlor door for her. She stepped inside. The Duke of Aylesham, seated opposite Aunt Margaret, rose to his feet at her entrance. Susan watched carefully to see his reaction to her changed appearance.

His gaze began at her face and then continued downward, eventually returning to her eyes. His face remained as expressionless as if he'd just skimmed through a document. "Good afternoon, Miss Jennings. You are looking very fine today," he said at last.

At best, his words were a platitude.

After all of Madame Veronique and Miss Lily's work on her behalf, his remark was more disappointing than Susan wished to admit. Her fortitude wavered, and she discovered, much to her chagrin, that her eyes were burning as though they threatened tears.

That she would not allow.

She blinked a few times to force them back and then pasted her most cordial smile on her face. "Thank you, Your Grace," she said and strolled farther into the room.

"We were about to take luncheon," Aunt Margaret said. "Would you care to join us, Aylesham? I have already informed our cook that you are here."

"That is kind of you, but I must decline," the duke said. "I have taken lunch already, you see, and I doubt I could eat another bite. But I thank you, and I apologize if my arrival has interrupted your plans."

"Not at all!" Aunt Margaret assured the duke. "I myself had a hearty breakfast. It is Susan I'm thinking of—"

Susan hoped Aunt Margaret had stopped speaking because the dear, exasperating lady had realized she'd just said a bit too much for Susan's liking. "I believe I can go without eating for a while longer without collapsing," she said.

The duke made a small noise, but when Susan glanced at him, his face was as unreadable as ever. "It is settled, then," he said. "Lady Walmsley, perhaps I may beg your forgiveness and ask again if I may spend some time alone with Miss

Jennings. I am well aware that we abandoned you yesterday, and am deeply sorry about that. I shall make it up to you, I promise."

"Quite all right, Your Grace, quite all right." Aunt Margaret fairly bolted from her seat on the settee. "I have plenty of work with which I may busy myself in the meantime. Young people such as yourselves need time to get acquainted, is that not true? But I will not leave until I have had your opinion on my dear Susan's new dress. What an enjoyable time we had yesterday after you left us as she tried on new gowns, and then again this morning when Miss Lily arrived to trim her hair! Did we not, Susan?"

"Indeed," Susan murmured. She wished fervently that she could disappear through the floor at Aunt Margaret's flagrant request for a compliment from the duke, but as the floor seemed to be made of solid wood, she didn't put much stock in it actually happening. Who had referred to Aunt Margaret as her fairy godmother? Ah, yes, it had been James. *And* Madame Veronique. Aunt Margaret needed to study her "How to Be a Successful Fairy Godmother" instruction book—if there were such a thing—a little more closely, in Susan's humble opinion.

Thankfully, Susan wasn't typically the blushing type, which was her only saving grace at the moment, as bright pink would undoubtedly clash with her pale-green frock. Instead, she simply stared back at the duke, whose attention had turned from Aunt Margaret to *her* after Aunt Margaret's unfortunate words.

"Miss Jennings is a vision of loveliness," he said.

High praise indeed, Susan thought drolly.

"Will you join me now, Miss Jennings?" he asked her, gesturing to the settee where Aunt Margaret had been sitting.

"I shall, thank you." Susan walked over and sat where he'd indicated.

"I'll leave you two alone, then," Aunt Margaret said, looking pleased as punch. "But I believe I will have Foster send for tea, at least. You know you hardly ate any breakfast, young lady, and I will not have you wasting away while you are a guest in my home."

"Thank you, Lady Walmsley," the duke replied. "Tea will be much appreciated."

She nodded, satisfied, and left the room.

They were alone.

The duke sat back down, flipping the tails of his coat out of the way as he did so. He was not dressed so finely as he'd been yesterday, but his clothing was still of the finest quality. Susan was glad Madame and Miss Lily had visited her, despite the duke's dismissive attitude toward her just now.

"Are you wasting away, Miss Jennings?" the duke asked.

"Indeed not, Your Grace, I assure you. Are you?" If he could ask such a question, then so could she.

"Some would say I am," he replied. He paused. "No, I believe it would be more accurate to say they think I haven't put the weight I lost back on. I may have alluded to the fact that I was recently ill."

Had he? Susan didn't remember but didn't think so. "But you are recovered now?"

"Yes, for the most part," he said. "I will not be making you a dowager duchess anytime soon . . . assuming, of course, that you agree to wed me in the first place."

And there it was.

"I have many questions I wish to have answered," Susan said. "Assurances." She pulled out the notes she'd written and unfolded the pages.

"Questions indeed," he murmured.

"Yes. And my final reply will hinge upon the answers you provide."

"I think you truly must be a lawyer at heart, Miss Jennings, if your copious notes are any indication," the duke said. "And I say that as a compliment. Let the negotiations commence."

"Thank you," she said. "I will begin by pointing out that I have questions regarding the actual event and how it will take place. These are important considerations, because my family resides in Lincolnshire, and most of them are currently there, excepting James, as you know, and my younger brother, Simon." Simon, the rascal, was enjoying his young adulthood in ways young ladies were not allowed. As far as Susan knew, he was currently at a house party in the Cotswolds, but that may have changed since she had last heard. "And my youngest sister is laid up with a broken leg at present. How are they to be at nuptials that must occur sooner rather than later and must accommodate the Prince Regent?

"And speaking of my youngest sister—Rebecca is her name—this was to have been a come-out Season for her, to have been provided by the generosity of Lady Walmsley."

"There is no question that as Duchess of Aylesham, you would be able to sponsor your sister," the duke replied.

"Thank you, but these are presumptions I do not wish to make, you see. These are precisely the types of assurances I must have."

"Let me simplify this for you," His Loftiness said, twirling his quizzing glass between his fingers and beginning to look bored already. "Allow me to take your notes, and I will have my private secretary go over them. Anything you've listed of a financial nature, I'm sure we will be able to accommodate, and those that he questions, you and I will discuss later."

"I think not," Susan said. "I want you to *hear* the various and sundry ways in which your utterance of my name to the Prince Regent has affected me and my family."

"That sounds rather as though you wish I were standing in the Dock having my list of crimes read aloud to the jury," the duke said.

"You are making light of a situation I find exceedingly serious," Susan said.

"Quite the contrary," he retorted. "I find the situation as serious as death." He arose and walked to the window; his hands clenched behind his back.

Susan waited, unwilling to be the next one to speak. Finally, after a long and uncomfortable silence, he heaved a sigh and returned to his chair, closing his eyes after he did so, looking fatigued suddenly. "Please proceed with your questions," he said at last, his eyes still closed. "I will listen carefully to each one and answer to the best of my ability."

George had actually felt a glimmer of hope when he'd arrived at Lady Walmsley's house today and seen a completely different woman than the one he'd encountered in the past. Miss Jennings had taken his breath away, what with a few soft curls framing her face and a gown that flattered her exceedingly well. It was undoubtedly a superficial male reaction on his part, but he'd suddenly discovered he was attracted to her. He considered it a positive thing.

Listening to her detailed analysis of his proposal was not nearly as enjoyable, however, and Miss Jennings had only just begun going through her litany of questions. He had become impatient and had spoken harshly. It had been poorly done of him. *He* had put her in this situation, after all, and owed her the courtesy of listening to her concerns on the matter.

Perhaps his insubordinate friends and employees were correct in assessing his state of health, after all, for he felt exhausted. He must be having a relapse to feel this way, certainly. The rigors of the past few months, coupled with Prinny's machinations, had finally caught up with him. The last thing he wished to do was listen to Miss Jennings go through her copious bargaining points.

But he'd told her he'd listen, so he would.

"You're not paying attention," she said.

"I most certainly am," he said.

"Your mind has been elsewhere this entire time."

"What makes you say that?" he asked, feeling indignant.

"Your eyes."

"My eyes." He opened them a crack.

"Yes," she said, squinting her own eyes at him.

"You are concerned about your little sister and her broken leg and whether your family will be in attendance at your wedding," George said. "You wonder at my finances and assurances of my wealth and generosity toward your family members, should it be needed. You are concerned about the reaction Society will have when our betrothal is officially announced, especially as the ceremony will occur shortly thereafter, and the gossip that will proceed as a result—not that you are concerned for yourself, I would venture to say, but for your little sister's ability to be accepted by Society when she makes her eventual come-out. You wonder about your inadequacy of being a duchess and whether you will get on with my household staff and whether they will respect you. You wonder at our living arrangements and whether I will merely resume the life I have led prior to this point, leaving you to fend for yourself and find your own way. Shall I go on?"

She glared at him. "I didn't mention most of those."

"True, but I am trying to point out to you that I am *fully* aware of the complicated situation in which I have put you. For you to rehearse them all to me is a waste of precious time. I wish to get to the core of your concerns. The rest we may figure out as we go."

"You are assuming I will say yes to your offer," she said.

"Of course I am," he replied. "The very fact that you are weighing the cost and benefit to yourself and your family tells me that you are, at least, considering my proposal. You are speaking to a man who has considered the costs and benefits of marriage numerous times over the course of several years." He rose from his chair and positioned himself on the settee next to her. "I will be frank, Miss Jennings," he said. "I refuse to become one of the Prince Regent's lackeys. Marriage to you allows me to be loyal to my country and not merely to my selfish monarch. I am at your mercy, Miss Jennings, and I assure you that when it comes to your personal concerns, you have the advantage of me. I will do all in my power to support you and your family in whatever ways you deem best. I give you my word.

"That being said, there are a few caveats I must insist upon," he continued. He slid closer to her and felt with satisfaction the frisson of energy that emanated from her when he did. It was enough for the moment to know he had a physical effect on her. "I want a marriage in full, as I have already said. I want heirs."

"I cannot guarantee—"

"I know," he said. "But I want your willingness." He locked gazes with her.

"A true marriage means I must give myself to you, body and soul," she said.

"As must I," he murmured in reply.

She shook her head, her eyes searching his own. "I will be giving up *everything* if I wed, Your Grace—freedoms I currently have as an unmarried woman. My very personhood. If I am to give myself to you fully, I expect the same in return. Fidelity, for one."

"Obviously," he said.

"There is nothing obvious about it, Your Grace," she said. "Society turns a blind eye to a gentleman's indiscretions and ruins its womenfolk for much less." Her expression was serious, her face pale, the small spray of freckles along the bridge of her nose a bit more apparent as a result and adding a hint of vulnerability, her eyes large and gray and indomitable.

"You have my word, Miss Jennings," George said. "I can say nothing more, except that I must stand on my reputation in that regard. There is to be one woman in my life, and that woman will be *you*, if you agree to marry me." He cast his gaze over her features once again and decided he wanted to explore that frisson he'd felt earlier. He wanted to kiss her, wanted to see how she would respond to his touch. But if he did, would it convince her of his intent toward her or would she feel manipulated?

The blasted woman now had George overthinking things.

Enough!

He laid his hand on the curve of her jaw and lowered his mouth to hers. She reacted with surprise, so her lips were slightly parted, and he felt her breath, warm, as a gasp escaped her. And then she sighed, and George knew he had won, so he let the kiss linger and slid his fingers into the wisps of hair at the nape of her neck for one pleasurable moment.

He drew away, and when he looked into her eyes, he saw victory. "I believe we will suit, Miss Jennings, if our kiss is any indication," he murmured.

Those eyes immediately flashed silver again. "If you think for one moment that a single kiss—"

He kissed her again to silence her, but this time, he took his fill. Her hands clutched his arms and slid upward until they clung to his shoulders. Her head fell back, and he explored her lips, the column of her throat, the skin behind her ear.

"Unfair," she murmured.

He smiled inwardly and nipped at her earlobe. "What is your answer?" he whispered.

She let out a deep sigh. "No," she said.

He blinked. Had he heard her correctly? He had not expected that answer, not from her response to his kisses.

She raised her head and gazed steadily back at him. "It takes more than kisses to make a true marriage," she said softly.

"Perhaps so," he replied. "But it is a beginning."

"If I had said yes to you just now, you would have thought me weak and malleable, easily persuaded by token affection, and that I cannot allow. You have said we will have a marriage in full . . . but I fear we may have differing views on what that means. To me, it means we are one in more than just body. Be prepared for me to share my opinions openly with you, Your Grace."

"I would expect nothing less from you, Miss Jennings," he said.

"As long as you are prepared for the heated discussions that are bound to follow," she said. "As I'm sure there will be."

"So am I," he replied, heaven help him. He reached into his jacket breast pocket and removed a ring bearing a ruby stone encircled with diamonds. It had belonged to his mother. "Miss Jennings, having now considered the various reasons whether to marry or not, I ask you again, will you agree to be my wife? And if so, will you take this ring as a symbol of our betrothal?" He held it out for her to see.

"It's lovely," she said. She looked up at him, an earnest expression on her face. "Based on your assurances and your honor and with clear recognition on both our parts of the challenges that lay ahead for us, I will agree to marry you."

"Thank you," George said. He'd done it. He'd gotten her to agree. "May I?" he asked, nodding toward her hand.

"Yes," she said.

He took her left hand in his and slid the ring onto her finger. It was a near perfect fit. "It becomes you," he said.

She looked away from the ring on her hand and searched his face. He wondered what she was looking for and what she saw. He leaned toward her and gave her a gentle kiss. "May I call you Susan?" he asked.

"I suppose you must," she said.

"Thank you. And sadly, I am George," he said wryly. "Although most people call me Aylesham these days. I was Kerridge before that. In fact, I don't think anyone has ever called me George, thank heavens."

"George is a fine name," Miss Jennings said. No, she was Susan. *His* Susan. Who would have thought that a mere week ago? Certainly not he.

"I confess I don't particularly like its parallel to the current reigning monarch," he said, offering her a glib smile. "Not that I would say so to anyone—you now hold great power over me."

"Do I?" she asked.

He chose not to explore her question. "Shall we inform Lady Walmsley of our news?" he asked. "And where is that tea she said would be forthcoming?"

"She's a sly one," Susan said. "I wouldn't be at all surprised if she were eavesdropping through the door."

"I am not!" a voice called out from beyond the door just as it opened. Lady Walmsley marched into the room, head high, her butler following behind, bearing a tea tray.

Susan bit her lower lip to keep from laughing. George wanted to kiss that lip again, perhaps nip at it a bit just as she was.

He settled for taking tea with her and Lady Walmsley.

He was officially betrothed to Miss Susan Jennings, the harpy. She had accepted his proposal after all. But he wouldn't feel safely out of Prinny's clutches until the vicar had pronounced the words "man and wife."

Chapter 9

"You are *what*?" James asked, his voice crescendoing on his last word.

"Betrothed to the Duke of Aylesham," Susan said. It did sound rather incredulous, even to her. She didn't blame James at all for his reaction.

He turned and glared at the gentleman standing by the window. "What have you done, Aylesham?" he asked in an accusing tone. "You didn't even know my sister before this week. It's incomprehensible! What are you up to?"

Susan patted James's arm. One of the agreements she and the Duke of Aylesham—she couldn't quite think of him as George yet—had made was that they would put on a united front with their story: they had become acquainted the year previous, and their connection had resumed upon Susan's arrival in London. It was as close to the truth as possible. One of the duke's other caveats had been that Susan appear enthusiastic about their betrothal. "It is the only way to convince Prinny," he'd said before James had arrived. "We must appear besotted with each other—within reason, of course. If you were to be overly effusive, I doubt anyone would believe it."

"I suspect that actually applies more to you than it does to me," Susan had told him. "Society would expect a countrified spinster to swoon with happiness at the prospect of marrying a duke, whereas expecting a duke—especially *this* duke"—she'd looked pointedly at him—"to be enthralled with a countrified spinster is not nearly so believable."

At any rate, now she must attempt her first performance—informing Aunt Margaret hadn't counted as a performance because the dear lady had been too busy hugging and kissing Susan and hugging and kissing the duke, which had been less awkward than Susan had expected it to be, and exclaiming over her happiness that the two of them had found each other and how glad she was to have played a part . . . so Susan had simply smiled and nodded and shown Aunt Margaret the ruby ring and had left most of the talking to the duke.

Aunt Margaret had then proceeded to instruct Foster to tell Mrs. Drake that the duke would be dining with them that evening. Whether the duke had previous plans or not, he hadn't said; he'd simply acknowledged the invitation with thanks. Susan had then sent a note to James, inviting him to dine with them as well. If she'd known Simon's address, she would have sent a note to him too, although he was probably still in the Cotswolds with his friends.

"James," she said, still patting his arm. "Is it impossible to believe that we discovered an affection for each other?"

"Quite frankly, *yes*, Susan, to put it bluntly," he said. He stood and strode over to the duke. "I don't know what is going on, but, *by thunder,* I'm going to find out. You're my *friend*, Aylesham, or at least I believed you to be. I will not be having you abuse that friendship or take advantage of my sister."

"I'm not sure what should offend me more," the duke said in a deceptively bored tone that clearly issued a warning, "that you believe I would dishonor our friendship in such a manner as you suggest or that your low opinion of your sister's overall appeal should make me call you out in defense of her." He brushed past James and walked to Susan, taking her hand in his and raising her to her feet, and then he planted a perfectly believable kiss on her cheek.

"You see, James?" Susan said. She hoped she sounded calmer than she actually felt—his kisses seemed to have quite an effect on her. "You must simply accept that the Duke of Aylesham—George"—she smiled at the duke—"and I have come to an understanding. Perhaps it seems sudden, but we are both adults who know our own minds. We wish to marry, and quickly too—this Monday week." The haste had been another of the duke's caveats. Nine days from today—*only nine days*—but he thought it imperative they marry before the arrival of Princess Sophia Augusta and her parents.

"*What*?" James exclaimed again, crossing the room back to her; it rather seemed he couldn't stay still. "*A week Monday*? I can scarce believe what I am hearing! How are our parents and our brothers and sisters to attend on such short notice, Susan? And where will these supposed nuptials take place?"

"St. George's on Hanover Square," the duke responded smoothly. "And there is nothing 'supposed' about it. As to your family, it is my understanding that your youngest sister is currently infirm, and a sister-in-law gave birth not long ago. Susan and I are in agreement that we marry now rather than later. I do not wish to go through the Season without my bride at my side, you see, nor do I wish to impose upon your family. We shall have a small ceremony, as

I have no immediate family, and then we shall journey to Lincolnshire later in the Season to celebrate with one and all."

James narrowed his eyes at the duke. "Marry now and hold a family celebration in Lincolnshire later in the Season, you say." There were undertones in his words that Susan didn't quite understand.

"Precisely," the duke said.

"You are in full accord with this?" James asked, abruptly turning toward her.

Susan smiled as confidently as she could. "I am. And it is my hope that you will stand in for Papa and give me away, James. I am not so girlish that I need such sentimental touches, but having you there in his place would be a comfort."

"Of course, dear sister." He opened his arms to her. Susan stepped into them, and he wrapped his arms about her tightly, and she drew in as much strength from him as she could. "I only want your happiness," he murmured in her ear. "We had quite given up hope that you would ever marry, you know, especially after—well, never mind that. If you have found love at last with Aylesham—*Aylesham*, of all people—then my felicitations to you both. You have my support."

"Thank you, Jennings," the duke replied drolly from behind Susan. "I didn't realize I was as unlovable as you seem to think I am."

"I'm still suspicious," James said. "But as I love my sister, and more than that, I trust her intellect and her reason, I am suspending my suspicions for the time being and choosing to support her decision in this."

"Very generous of you," the duke said.

"Yes, it is," James replied.

"Well, that's settled, then," Susan said firmly, stepping back from James and smiling as brightly as she could. "There is much to do between now and Monday week."

"To that end," the duke said, "if I may, tomorrow I shall accompany you and Lady Walmsley to church services. You may join us if you like, Jennings. The sooner I am seen publicly with my betrothed, the better, and your brotherly support is welcome. Then first thing Monday, I shall instruct my secretary, Henshaw, to draft an announcement for the papers; afterward, he and I shall join you here, Susan, so we may outline our agenda for the week and determine what must be done and by whom."

"Excellent," Susan said. "Now, if you are both agreeable, I shall inform Lady Walmsley that we are ready to dine. I myself am famished, I understand the illustrious Duke of Aylesham is in need of increased sustenance, and my brother is always hungry." She crossed the room without waiting for their responses and tugged on the bell pull. Foster immediately opened the door.

"Please thank Lady Walmsley for her patience and inform her that we are ready to join her for supper."

"I shall, Miss—"

"Tut, Foster, I can already hear what she's saying," Lady Walmsley said. Apparently, she'd been behind Foster the entire time—probably pacing the entrance hall, Susan imagined with a smile, listening to what they were discussing and wishing she were a part of it all. But some discussions needed the illusion of privacy, and this had been one of them. "Susan, my dear, supper is ready, and Mrs. Drake has outdone herself for the occasion. But *you* must begin as you mean to go; you are to be a duchess, and that means you must dress for supper. Off, now, and be quick. Go!" She actually shooed Susan on her way.

Susan half expected to hear James and the duke laughing over Lady Walmsley's comments, but the parlor was suspiciously quiet. Her clever and intuitive brother would take more convincing than she and the Duke of Aylesham had given him.

Susan understood theoretically that arriving at church on the Duke of Aylesham's arm would attract attention from those in attendance. She had attended events in the past where one person or another had seemed to draw everyone's eye and murmurs of conversations had ensued.

For that reason, she had dressed carefully this morning, choosing one of Madame Veronique's more demure creations to wear and paying meticulous attention to her hair and its newly discovered ability to curl. She wished to appear as restrained and tasteful as possible, in a manner that wouldn't lend itself to additional talk. For there would be talk.

Understanding something in theory and experiencing its actuality were not as similar as Susan had anticipated. The duke had arrived promptly, looking elegant in a well-cut gray coat and burgundy waistcoat, his ever-present quizzing glass hanging on a gold chain around his neck. He had bowed over Aunt Margaret's hand and over Susan's, had assisted them both into his extremely fine carriage, seating himself opposite the two ladies, and then had given the coachmen the signal to drive.

The carriage had lurched forward, and so had Susan's heart and stomach.

The time was now at hand for them to be seen publicly as a couple. His countenance was serious, and even Aunt Margaret seemed to sense this was a time of reckoning, for she sat quietly on the bench next to Susan.

All too soon they were at St. George's, and the duke assisted each lady out of the carriage, whereupon he proceeded to offer an elbow to each.

Susan had scarcely slid her hand into the crook of his elbow when she heard the whispers begin. "Remember Lady Walmsley's wise words of last night," the duke murmured to her. "'You must begin as you mean to go.' You are to be my duchess. Take your cues from that."

Susan lifted her chin, took a deep breath, and smiled serenely, but it all felt like pretense. As they climbed the steps to the portico, they nodded in greeting to those they passed, but no one approached them to chat. It seemed to Susan as though the passersby were caught up in the spectacle that was the Duke of Aylesham arriving with a lady on his arm for the first time in memory rather than in offering Sunday wishes.

Aunt Margaret greeted the rector, and then it was the duke's and Susan's turns to receive the rector's welcome.

"Mr. Hodgson, I hope you will allow me to introduce Miss Susan Jennings, the daughter of Viscount and Viscountess Thurlby of Lincolnshire. Miss Jennings, Mr. Robert Hodgson," the duke said after he and the rector had shaken hands in greeting.

"Miss Jennings," the rector said in reply.

"Mr. Hodgson," Susan said with a slight curtsy.

"Miss Jennings is my betrothed," the duke added.

Susan heard gasps behind her, and the rector glanced over her shoulder before returning his gaze to her. He smiled amiably, but his eyes were much sharper. "My felicitations, Miss Jennings."

"Thank you," she managed.

The duke placed his hand at her back and guided her through the doorway into the church. "Head high," he whispered.

"If it were any higher, it would pop off my neck," she retorted under her breath.

"That's the spirit," he replied.

He led them down the aisle to a pew apparently reserved for the Duke of Aylesham and family, and the three of them took their seats.

"I remember going to church for the very first time with dear Lady Elizabeth, you know, just last year—now, *that* was a to-do!" Aunt Margaret whispered to her. "After everything her wretched father put her through, poor sweet girl. We were trying to restore her reputation, you know, and appearing at church seemed the best first step. People are going to curb their tongues in church. And it worked for the most part, I daresay."

The duke shot a discreet glance at Aunt Margaret, which Susan took to mean that conversation, even whispered, should cease.

Aunt Margaret ignored his look. "Now *this*, by comparison—*this* will create a flutter of excitement of the best kind! Ah! I see Lord and Lady Bledsoe just over there." She fluttered her handkerchief discreetly at them and then motioned to them to come over. "We can make room for them on this pew, can we not? There will still be enough room for your rogue of a brother should he decide to make an appearance."

Susan watched Lord and Lady Bledsoe weave through the worshippers toward them.

"What have we here?" Lady Bledsoe asked quietly when they arrived at the pew.

"Look what our Aylesham has done—and in such a short time too!" Aunt Margaret exclaimed in as low a whisper as an exclamation of that sort would allow while she grasped Susan's hand and thrust it in front of the poor lady.

Lady Bledsoe gasped rather too loudly upon seeing the ring on Susan's finger, and more heads turned in their direction, and others peered down from the gallery.

The duke sighed, and Susan carefully extricated her hand from Aunt Margaret's grasp.

"Oh, Aylesham," Lady Bledsoe exclaimed in the same sort of whisper as Aunt Margaret's had been. "Oh, Aylesham," she said again, her eyes welling up with tears. "How *thrilled* your dear mama would be today if she were here! Finally! A soon-to-be daughter-in-law for her, and surely grandchildren will follow!"

The murmuring increased at Lady Bledsoe's words.

The duke sighed again. "Thank you, Lady Bledsoe," he murmured and then deliberately gave a side look toward the lectern.

Which meant they *all* turned to glance at the lectern.

Which was a good thing, for the rector was taking his place at the front of the chapel. The service was about to begin.

Everyone sat, and the rector waited—rather patiently, Susan thought, all things considered—until the murmuring finally diminished and silence ensued.

Susan prided herself on her ability to concentrate, listen, and learn. She knew she was clever and always had been. Had she the opportunity to attend university as her brothers had done, she would have excelled, which was why she was entirely baffled by the fact that she wasn't retaining a single word of the church service. Somewhere in the back of her mind she knew that a sermon and scriptures and hymns were taking place and that she was even participating at the appropriate times, but other than that . . .

She was highly aware, however, of the arm of the man who sat next to her. That arm was pressed against hers, and each subtle movement he made created more awareness. She could feel the muscles in his upper arm flex against her own. She was aware of his thigh, the masculine fabric of his dark trousers so close to the delicate floral muslin of her gown. He occasionally shifted slightly, and each movement only brought the intense awareness back again.

His hands were clasped lightly in his lap. He had large, strong-looking hands, with long fingers and, of course, well-manicured fingernails. Susan studied his profile out of the corner of her eye and memorized each detail. Were she to take a university exam on the subject of the visage of the Duke of Aylesham, she suspected she would get full marks, she thought wryly.

His nose was straight and narrow, and his jawline bore an edge that spoke of resoluteness. His neckcloth was impeccably knotted beneath that jaw, and she noted that it was held in place by a ruby stickpin. She recognized his subtle ploy of matching his stickpin to her ring, one that again told others that she and he were a betrothed couple.

His complexion was not pale; it seemed the type that would tan quickly in the sun. Susan's own complexion tended to tan as well, if she wasn't careful—but more than that, it brought out her freckles, and she despised that. Here in the low chandelier light of St. George's, the duke's thick, dark hair didn't show as much of the deep burgundy hues Susan had noted on other occasions. And his brows—

He turned his head and lifted those brows at her.

He'd caught her.

Drat! What to do next? She could either retreat in guilt or face him boldly, she decided. Well, she wouldn't be Susan Jennings were she to retreat—heaven forbid!—so she lifted her brows at him in return. And then she smiled.

And an incredible thing happened: his lips twitched. It was just the slightest of twitches, but she'd seen it, all the same. And then he turned his head toward the rector once again, who was still preaching about something or other—living a life of piety?—at the lectern.

She closed her eyes and breathed in deeply through her nose, letting the air out again slowly. The duke had caught her studying him, *and his lips had twitched.*

Had the twitch indicated surprise? Humor? Irritation? Disgust? Had it been more of a smile or a smirk? It had happened so quickly that it was difficult to discern what it had meant—

A warm hand settled atop her own. Her eyes flew open.

His hand—the duke's hand—clasped hers and moved it to his lap.

He was holding her hand during church services.

It was a small action, really, Susan told herself. It made sense for him to do so. It was merely another statement of the betrothal announcement that was to come and the marriage to follow.

But Susan had watched her parents hold hands frequently over the duration of their marriage, as well as her married siblings with their spouses. It had *meant* something—affection, commitment . . .

Love.

Her mind and heart warred with each other. Everything was happening so fast regarding this marriage to the duke that it was difficult to keep up. Her heart raced in her bosom. If something as simple as this put her in such a state, how was she going to react when the actual nuptials took place?

She needed to get her emotions under control. His taking her hand like this was not a display of any affection he held for her. It was a display for the public.

This was not a marriage based on love, and here, once again, was a clear reminder that she needed to keep her feelings in check.

George stepped from his carriage and took the steps up to his front entrance two at a time. A footman opened the door, and George strode inside.

"Welcome home, Your Grace," Talbot said.

"Thank you," George said, handing over his hat and gloves. "I shall be in my study."

"Very good, Your Grace," Talbot replied.

"Is Henshaw about?" George asked. Sunday was one of Henshaw's days off work, but sometimes he remained in residence.

"I believe so. Shall I ask him to join you?" Talbot said.

"Yes, please—but only if it doesn't inconvenience him."

Talbot nodded in acknowledgment. "I shall have refreshments sent in," he said.

George wanted to snap at Talbot that he was not undernourished in any way, devil take it, but he resisted. "Thank you, Talbot," he said instead. He hoped his tone wasn't too sharp.

When he reached his study, he crossed to the side table and poured himself a small brandy before seating himself at his desk.

His betrothal to Miss Jennings was now public. Word had spread quickly through St. George's, and they had endured a veritable reception line of well-wishers from virtually all in attendance at church following the services. He and Miss Jennings had smiled and responded while all and sundry had bowed and curtsied and expressed their surprise and excitement and joy . . . It had gone on for more than an hour. Afterward, George had taken Miss Jennings and Lady Walmsley home, had politely refused Lady Walmsley's invitation for luncheon, and had left.

Frankly, Miss Jennings had looked relieved when he'd refused the invitation. *What of it?* he thought rather grumpily, fingering his quizzing glass. If she needed time to herself after they'd endured each other's company all morning, that was fine with him. He needed time to collect his thoughts and determine how to proceed anyway. At the very least, word of the betrothal would now circulate quickly through the *ton*.

"Your Grace?" Henshaw said quietly after poking his head through the door.

"Come in, Henshaw," George said. "I'm sorry to interrupt your Sabbath, but I fear there is work to be done."

Henshaw seated himself across the desk from George, looking inquisitively at him.

"I am to be married, Henshaw," George said. "In eight days."

George watched Henshaw's jaw drop before he collected himself. "Hearty congratulations, Your Grace. How may I be of assistance?"

Before George could reply, the door burst open, and James Jennings strode into the room, with Talbot following frantically behind him.

"We must talk," Jennings barked.

"Missed you at church this morning, Jennings," George said sardonically.

"I mean it, Aylesham! I expect more of an explanation than you gave me yesterday. Susan is too bright, too full of life to end up in a loveless marriage. And I highly doubt it will be anything more than that."

"Will you excuse us for a moment, Henshaw?" George said.

"Certainly, Your Grace." Henshaw hastily left, and Talbot followed him, shutting the door quietly behind them.

Jennings crossed the room, planted his hands atop George's desk, and glared at him. "I know for a fact that you only became acquainted with my sister at Lady Bledsoe's ball. *Devil take it*, man, you looked upon her with utter indifference, as she did you. *More* than indifference—contempt. And yet, four days later, you expect me to accept that the two of you are marrying *in one week's time*? I *will* have answers, Aylesham. As her elder brother, standing in place for her father, I *demand* them."

George took a sip of his brandy before replying. "You may demand answers all you like, Jennings, but what has transpired between your sister and me is our concern, not yours."

"Not good enough, Aylesham," Jennings snarled, still leaning over the desk at him. "Not good enough by half. I brought her to Town; I gave my word to our parents that I would keep her safe. She hasn't even been here a week yet!"

"Pour yourself a drink, Jennings," George said. "You're distraught."

"Do *not* toy with me, Aylesham," Jennings growled.

George sighed and took another sip of his brandy. "Very well. You are correct that your sister and I got off to a prickly start. We briefly encountered each other last year, and it wasn't a particularly congenial meeting."

"You have proven my point exactly," Jennings said. "And yet, in the four days she has been in Town, you and she have suddenly seen the light and have fallen in love?"

"Love?" George said. "She and I have reached an understanding, certainly, and I shall endeavor to ensure her happiness, but when has marriage amongst the higher ranks ever been about love?"

"Precisely!" Jennings nearly shouted. "My sister may be of the 'higher ranks,' as you call it, but she has been content to be at home with her loving family surrounding her these past several years. She got her fill of Society during the few years she was in Town for the Season. I have never gotten the impression she has missed London one whit since then. And I *will not* have her heart toyed with as it was—" He abruptly cut off his speech and went to the end table to pour himself a drink after all.

Ah.

"Who?" George asked softly.

Jennings only shook his head and set the decanter down.

"*Who*?" George asked again. If he was understanding Jennings's unspoken words correctly, someone had broken Susan Jennings's heart during her earliest years in Town.

"It matters not who the blackguard was," Jennings said. "I will not lower myself to speak his name."

"Very well," George said. He rang the bell that sat on the corner of his desk. A footman stepped inside the room. "Please inform Henshaw that he may rejoin us, and have Talbot inform Mrs. Bradley to prepare luncheon for the three of us." The footman nodded and left. George turned his attention back to Jennings. He must do his best to contain this contretemps now and not let it escalate.

"We have been through much together, my friend," George said, "and have had to trust each other in the most extreme of circumstances. Trust me now. I fully intend to wed your sister, and your support—for her and for me—would be gratefully received by us both."

"I cannot bear the thought of her marrying for anything less than love," Jennings said. "Susan is clever and strong, and that is what people see. They don't know her heart as I do. She is my little sister."

"She is a woman who knows her own mind," George replied. "If I have learned nothing else, I have learned that about her. I will be frank; I cannot afford the luxury of marrying solely for love, nor have I ever had that luxury. But marry I must, and I have delayed doing so for too long. I have proposed to your sister, and she has accepted. There has been no deception on my part with her regarding this marriage. She has agreed to be my wife with full knowledge. But if it will appease you, I shall make you a vow: I shall do all in my power to make her happy and to see that she has no regrets over this. This will have to suffice for now."

"You will be accountable to me in this, Aylesham, I guarantee it. And I shall be watching you closely."

There was a soft knock at the door, and Henshaw stepped inside.

"Come in, Henshaw," George said, watching Jennings closely. "First item of business is to go through the calendar and the various invitations that have been received thus far. This is going to be a busy week."

"Yes, Your Grace," Henshaw said, seating himself in the chair next to Jennings'.

Jennings scowled at George but said nothing, so George proceeded to go through the invitations that had arrived from all and sundry. The Season was well underway, with the hint of victory over Bonaparte on the air. It was George's plan that he and his betrothed be seen about in public a great deal this week.

He hoped that Jennings would join them as much as possible but only if he came to terms with the inevitable.

The week had been a blur thus far. Not that it had flown by—in some ways, Susan thought it had been tediously long, but so much was happening, so much was changing, that she was having trouble keeping up with it all.

On Monday morning, the duke, along with Mr. Henshaw, had arrived at Aunt Margaret's house, as promised, to meet with Susan. Aunt Margaret had joined them, and the four had outlined a schedule for the week, which had included assemblies and balls and the like, and had also made time for correspondence to be written. Aunt Margaret had informed the duke that while she had been more than willing to provide Susan with her current wardrobe—and hadn't it made a wonderful difference in her appearance?—as a soon-to-be duchess, her wardrobe needed to be increased much further.

"Aunt Margaret," Susan had tried to interject, "I really don't think—"

"Hush, child. I know of what I speak here. You may claim modesty and frugality all you like, but it will do you no good."

"She's right," the duke had said. "I shall entrust that to you, Lady Walmsley, if I may, since I have no expertise in that particular area. Have the bills forwarded to Henshaw."

Apparently, Mr. Henshaw had been tasked previously with sending an announcement of the betrothal to the paper, which he'd informed the duke had been done. Susan had written to her parents Sunday evening and had sent it off to be posted; she had asked them to inform her brothers and sisters since they all lived within a reasonable distance of each other in Lincolnshire. She had also posted a note to Simon at the last known address she had for him here in London.

Monday evening, Susan, the duke, and Aunt Margaret had attended a musicale hosted by the Earl and Countess of Iverson, which had featured a violinist, whose name Susan could not now remember, for there had been too many other people and names to try and remember instead. She wished she had been able to concentrate on the performer and the music being played, but it had become clearly obvious as soon as they'd arrived that there was to be more interest in the Duke of Aylesham and the lady at his side than in the violinist. The two of them had endured more congratulations, the duke had taken jibes about the end of his bachelorhood, and Susan had smiled and nodded and answered any questions about their courtship with brevity.

On Tuesday, Susan and Lady Walmsley had spent the entire morning with an ecstatic Madame Veronique. "I told you so, did I not, Miss Jennings? Madame Veronique, she knows zees sings," Madame had exclaimed joyfully. "'I see in Miss Jennings zee highest of quality and will make her see eet too,' I say to myself. Did I not say just zees very sing to you?"

Her seamstresses had all nodded in agreement.

Thankfully, Susan's measurements had been taken during their first visit to the shop, so Susan had only to endure being draped with velvets and satins and lace again while Aunt Margaret had pored over fashion plates and Madame Veronique had offered her opinions and waved her arms and directed her seamstresses hither and thither.

Upon leaving Madame Veronique's shop, Susan and Aunt Margaret had then proceeded to the milliner and the shoemaker before Aunt Margaret had announced they would take refreshment at Gunter's. By the time the two of them had returned home with Lady Walmsley's coach filled to the brim with dress boxes and hatboxes and glove boxes and shoe boxes, Susan had been overwhelmed and speechless—and she was *never* speechless. Or, at least, rarely. She had been more speechless in the past week than in her entire life.

And to think the receipts for all of these purchases would simply be sent on to Mr. Henshaw, and that would be the end of it! The notion of what Aylesham's wealth must actually be boggled her mind.

On Tuesday evening, Susan and the duke, again with Aunt Margaret, had gone to the Opera House, with its stage and gallery and *five* tiers of elegantly ornamented boxes. When they'd arrived at the duke's box, Susan had sworn that every eye from every box on every tier and from the entire gallery below had all turned as one and looked specifically at the two of them.

"Such a sensation you've become!" Aunt Margaret had exclaimed as she'd settled into her chair. It had been obvious to her too.

"You're not smiling," the duke had murmured to Susan.

She'd smiled.

On Wednesday, Susan and Aunt Margaret had been invited to tea by none other than the Duchess of Atherton. Aunt Margaret had casually informed Susan that the duchess was a close friend of the Marchioness of Ashworth, and Aunt Margaret had a family connection to the Ashworths. "My dear great-niece Amelia is married to Lord Halford, the Ashworths' son, you know."

Susan had known, but that hadn't made taking tea with the Duchess of Atherton—and the Duchess of Wilmington and Lady Bledsoe and Lady Melton, to name just a few—any less confounding.

She'd already known the duke's strategy behind these events: the more people, especially of the higher ranks, who acknowledged Susan as an acquaintance and the two of them as a couple, the less likely the Prince Regent would be to change his mind.

But she was coming to realize that it also meant that she would be less able to change *her* mind too. And that suddenly had become terrifying.

For Susan had gotten tired of smiling and chatting about nothing and being fawned over and whispered about and receiving sideways glances from everyone with whom she came in contact, whereas the duke had merely continued on like everything was business as usual.

She didn't like it.

So upon their return from taking tea with the Duchess of Atherton, she excused herself from Aunt Margaret, claiming the need to rest.

"I completely understand, my dear," Aunt Margaret said. "A nap will be just the thing. I believe I shall do the same. We have been *so* busy the past few days, and it has been *such* fun, but I think I understand that it must also be tiring for you. It's rather a Cinderella story, isn't it? You and Aylesham?"

More like Beatrice and Benedick than Cinderella, Susan thought joylessly, even if Aunt Margaret were her fairy godmother. She excused herself and went to her room and then sat at her escritoire and wrote a simple note to the duke:

> *G, I have concluded that our agreement is flawed, if the past few days are any indication, and I am reconsidering. Please advise. Yours, SJ*

She sealed the letter and then slipped quietly out of her room in search of Foster. She eventually found him in his office near the kitchen. "Will you see that the duke receives this?" She held out the letter to him.

Foster glanced down at the note she held and then looked her gravely. "I hope you will forgive me, miss, but I'm not sure that I should, judging by the expression on your face."

"I am merely tired, Foster," Susan said.

"That is why I'm concerned," he said kindly.

"You are a good man," she said. "Lady Walmsley is fortunate to have you at her side, and I am grateful for your concern. Nonetheless, I wish this note to be delivered to the duke this afternoon, if you please."

"If you insist," he said, although it was obvious he was reluctant.

"Thank you," she said.

She returned to her room and sat at the small escritoire, staring out the window while her mind went around and around in circles over all she'd experienced since arriving in London and dreading the anxiety that the days that lay before her would bring.

Chapter 10

Evans had just finished shaving George's face for the second time today when Talbot entered George's dressing room. "Excuse the interruption, Your Grace, but a note has arrived for you from Walmsley House."

"Hmm." George finished wiping the lather from his face and tossed the towel to Evans, who caught it adeptly. The plan for this evening was for Miss Jennings and Lady Walmsley to enjoy a quiet night in after having taken tea at the Duchess of Atherton's home while he took supper at White's. He thought it a good opportunity to give the ladies a brief respite and for him to assess how word had spread.

The delivery of a note struck a warning bell within him.

"Walmsley House, you say?"

"Yes, Your Grace."

George took the note from the salver Talbot held out while Evans set about straightening the shaving toiletries. He broke the seal and read it.

> *G, I have concluded that our agreement is flawed, if the past few days are any indication, and I am reconsidering. Please advise. Yours, SJ*

His stomach balled into a knot.

Our agreement is flawed, and I am reconsidering.

Blast the woman! At least she hadn't fled to Lincolnshire without any warning and left George high and dry. "Plans have changed, Evans," he said. "Something a bit less elegant, if you please. In fact, something considerably less elegant. Talbot, is the footman from Walmsley House awaiting a reply?"

"I requested he do so, Your Grace, just in case you wished to send one," Talbot said. "He wouldn't have remained otherwise."

"Tell him to inform Miss Jennings that she is to prepare for a visit from the Duke of Aylesham in a half hour's time," he said. "And, *by thunder,* she'd better be ready to see me," he muttered to himself. "Don't tell the footman that last part, Talbot."

"Understood, Your Grace." Talbot left.

"Are we dressing the part of a simple country gentleman, then, Your Grace?" Evans asked with mock meekness.

"It isn't funny, you know," George growled. "And the answer is yes."

"Very good, Your Grace," Evans said.

Perhaps George could salvage this. Perhaps there was a way to convince Miss Jennings to continue. For if she were to back out of their agreement now, it would be exponentially worse than had she never agreed in the first place. At least when he'd been briefly betrothed to Lady Louisa—

He waited to see if the bitter feelings returned at the thought of her, but they did not. At least she had cried off before their betrothal had been made public.

Soon enough, George was dressed and on his way to Walmsley House, his mood diminishing further the closer the carriage got to its destination. When they eventually reached Walmsley House, he bounded out of the carriage before it had even come to a full stop and rapped on the door as soon as he reached it. He stood there fuming, waiting for someone to answer.

Eventually, Lady Walmsley's ancient butler, Foster, opened the door.

"I am here to speak to Miss Jennings," George said curtly.

"Ah, Your Grace," the old man replied. "Welcome. I shall inform Miss Jennings of your arrival." He made way for George to enter the house and directed him formally to the front parlor. "Please, make yourself at home."

The old man left, shutting the door behind him and leaving George alone with his thoughts. He was too restless to sit, so he wandered over to the window, but there was nothing of interest to be seen, so he moved to the fireplace and studied the landscape painting hung above the mantel. After a few minutes, the door reopened, and George turned toward it, expecting to see Miss Jennings. Instead, it was old Foster again.

"Pardon my interruption, Your Grace, but I thought you might enjoy a small sherry." He entered the room carrying a silver tray bearing bottles and glasses and placed the collection on a side table. "Would you like me to pour one for you? Or perhaps you'd prefer a brandy."

"Neither, thank you," George said.

"Very well, Your Grace," Foster said. He turned to leave, then paused. "Is there anything else I can get for you instead? Tea? Biscuits?"

"No, Foster," George replied, feeling a bit impatient. "I am in need of nothing at present."

The old butler started on his way once more, but once again, he paused. "Forgive me for speaking out of turn, Your Grace," he said, "but I have noticed in my duties as butler that Lady Walmsley's visitor appears to be quite fatigued this afternoon, in mind as well as body."

"And you felt the need to point this out to me?" George asked, taken aback by the old servant's bravado in speaking to him in this manner. What *was* it with old servants and their inclination to speak their minds? Foster was beginning to rank right up there with Talbot and Evans.

"Well, Your Grace, I have observed you to be an exceptionally astute gentleman. But frequently, people show only what they wish for us to see, do they not?"

George had no argument whatsoever for that; he took in a deep breath and exhaled, working to get his emotions under control. "I shall keep your words in mind," he said.

"Thank you, Your Grace, that is all I ask. I do hope you'll forgive my outspokenness," Foster said meekly.

"Think nothing of it," George muttered.

Foster bowed and left the room.

Once again, George found himself alone, and once again, his mind began running in circles. *Quite fatigued in mind as well as body. Our agreement is flawed, and I am reconsidering, her note said. We wish to share this happy occasion with you. Furthermore, we expect these nuptials to take place very soon. Prinny's words.* George gripped the mantel with both hands, lowered his head, and stared blankly at the cold grate of the fireplace. He hadn't asked for any of this. One week ago, he'd been living his life as he'd seen fit, working behind the scenes to do his part in bringing this infernal war to an end. And now . . .

The door opened, and George turned to see who'd entered the room this time. Thankfully, it wasn't Foster again, here to offer more sage advice. It was Miss Jennings. Susan. She closed the door and stayed next to it, her hands clasped in front of her, a somber expression on her face.

George straightened and stepped away from the fireplace. "You requested advice," he said. "And so I am here." He gestured to the sitting arrangement in front of the fireplace. "Will you be seated?"

She crossed the room, choosing to sit on the settee that faced the fireplace, so George chose the chair that sat at a right angle to her. Her face was pale, he noticed, her smattering of freckles more visible as a result, making her solemn countenance appear . . . vulnerable?

The woman he'd considered to be a harpy, *vulnerable*? It brought Foster's words back into mind.

"One cannot anticipate all the consequences that result when one makes a particular choice," she said at last.

George waited for her to say more and willed his hands not to clench.

"I have seen my future the past few days, and I do not like what I see."

"I'm listening," George said.

"For example," she said, "I have never been bothered by idle gossip or the occasional barb disguised as flattery. I have always simply brushed them off. I am not a person easily overcome by my sensibilities. But I have also never been bombarded by it in such a manner as I have endured the past three days."

"Bombarded, you say?"

"Yes," she exclaimed. "Under siege, assailed, entrapped, surrounded—"

"I take your point," he said. "I confess, I have not observed this bombardment you describe."

"That is because you are *Aylesham*, and the crowds part like the Red Sea when you enter a room and begin bowing and scraping and licking your boots—"

"I said I take your point," he repeated with an edge in his voice.

"I'm not sure that you do," Miss Jennings snapped. "Which is precisely the reason I am reconsidering our arrangement!"

Susan wanted to shake him. Grab his shoulders and shake him until his head flopped back and forth. It was the most unladylike thing she'd ever considered doing, even considering she'd grown up with five brothers, but she didn't care. For he simply sat there wooden faced, those black eyes of his glinting back at her but giving her nothing.

"I'm listening," he said again in what sounded like a bored voice.

Certain she truly would throttle him, she abruptly stood and stepped toward the fireplace and then turned to face him. "Where shall I begin?" she said, matching his bored tone with a sarcastic one of her own. "I have endeavored to ignore the swell of murmuring. I have endured the legion of staring eyes, like a parliament of owls following our every move, at church and the opera and everywhere we have ventured to go. I have been tempted to count the number of fans that snap in front of ladies' faces whenever you and I enter a room. I am not used to such attention—I'm not used to *any* attention, for that matter—and while I confess I knew this betrothal would draw interest, I had no idea it would to the extent that it has." She stopped speaking to take a breath.

"Is that everything?" he asked.

Was he *really* that oblivious?

"*Not in the least*, Your Grace. During the past three days, I have striven to remember the names of the dozens—nay, *hundreds*—of people to whom I have been introduced and keep all of their names and faces sorted afterward."

"And?" he said.

"And?" she said in return, her voice rising. "*And*, you ask? Very well. *And* while I am doing my best to retain all of this information, I am being probed in rather clever ways by all and sundry about our connection, requiring that I be creative in my replies and careful of what I say, lest my words come back to haunt us. It is exhausting work."

"I can see how that might be somewhat rigorous," he said.

"Rigorous," Susan said, her temper nearly at its peak. "Yes, *rigorous* certainly sums it up. 'Gracious, what a *rigorous* couple of days we've had, Your Grace,'" she said, mocking him. "Oh, did I forget to mention the dozens of little comments I've heard whispered behind my back? Meant for my ears, not yours. "Let's see"—she tapped her chin in feigned thought—"'I cannot imagine what he could possibly see in her,' or, 'What sort of hold does that odious old cow have over the duke, do you think?' or—"

"Enough," the duke said, rising to his feet.

"Oh, I've just begun," Susan declared in a low voice, facing him, her anger burning like hot coals within her heart. "The eyes, the whispers, the introductions *ad nauseam*, all peppered with subtle barbs intended to sting. And they *do* sting. But that is not all." She began to pace. "Then there is the new clothing."

"I thought ladies liked—"

"I have lived modestly, Your Grace, happily so. I have had no need for an elaborate wardrobe. I was barely coming to terms with Lady Walmsley's generosity when, suddenly, I am inundated with day dresses, riding habits, evening gowns, ball gowns, gloves, slippers, bonnets—"

The duke held up his hand for her to stop, but at least he didn't say, "I get your point," or she truly might have hit him.

Susan ignored him and continued on. "I did not expect such a generous gift from Lady Walmsley, nor did I ever ask for the wardrobe she bought for me, and I have felt a great deal of guilt over receiving it."

"You needn't feel guilty about—"

"Oh, I don't feel guilty about the expense *you* incurred from the additions to my wardrobe," Susan declared hotly. "No, in that regard, what I feel is *resentment*."

Her words stopped him cold, and Susan watched as his countenance darkened with intensity. He stood and moved toward her until they were face-to-face; Susan held up her hand, forcing him to stop, and looked up at him defiantly, for she had not finished speaking her mind. "How are you any different from the Prince Regent when you set about getting what you want at the cost of another person? When you promise advantages but are entirely indifferent to the needs and desires of that person, so consumed you are by your own wants and expectations?"

Her eyes burned, but she *would not* allow tears to fall. She would not allow herself to appear weak before this man. "And then today," she continued, "an esteemed group of ladies spent the bulk of the afternoon instructing me on the responsibilities of being a duchess. They were kind, mind you, but it was apparent that they were concerned for me and for my ability to join their ranks."

"I highly doubt—"

"The words as such were never spoken, naturally," Susan said, "but while Lady Walmsley and I were taking tea with these duchesses and marchionesses and countesses—ladies with whom I have *never* been acquainted before this week—the pitying looks in their eyes convinced me that it was time to inform you of my *myriad* concerns."

"First of all—"

"I have barely scratched the surface!" she cried. "For my entire life, I have believed myself to be a strong person. But I will tell you—"

"Enough!" he exclaimed. "You have continually interrupted me thus far, and now it is *my* turn to speak." He took a deep breath and then exhaled, appearing to try to calm himself and then looked squarely at her. "I have listened to you, and I assure you that I have heard every word you have uttered. You have made it abundantly clear that the past few days have been overwhelming in a variety of ways and in manners more extreme than I had foreseen. Perhaps I should have anticipated such a response from the *beau monde*; my only excuse is that I have been under significant duress over this matter myself.

"Let us sit and discuss your concerns as two rational beings, setting aside the emotions of the past few days," he said. "For, despite your concerns, which I concede are valid, we are more entangled now than ever. We must find a way through this, Miss Jennings."

"If I were to go home to Lincolnshire, *I* would not be entangled at all," she said.

His gaze felt solid and strong, his words too reassuring, and her tears nearly escaped. If only . . .

"Is that what you wish?" he asked.

She could not say aloud what she wished. "I am willing to discuss the matter further," she said at last.

"I am glad," he said. "May I?" he asked, extending his hand palm up to her.

Susan hesitated . . . and then placed her hand in his. She assumed he'd meant *relieved* rather than *glad*. For gladness denoted joy and pleasure, and she had seen little evidence to convince her that the Duke of Aylesham truly felt any of those things when it came to her.

George was taken aback at what Miss Jennings had told him. But more than that, he was ashamed of himself, for she was essentially correct: he had been more concerned with his own predicament than in recognizing the extent of the sacrifice she was making on his behalf.

Unfortunately, they were both deep in the mire now—he more so than she, for she was also correct in that should she prefer to live the rest of her life quietly in Lincolnshire, she undoubtedly could.

He led her back to the settee and sat beside her, turning his body slightly so he could face her more directly and taking her hand in his again once they were settled. "Let us sit quietly for a while," he said. "Shall we?"

She nodded in reply, so they sat side by side, her hand in his, and he allowed the silence to surround them for a time.

As he did, he studied her closely—more closely than he ever had before. She was not in the flush of youth; her features were those of a mature woman. Her bosom rose and fell with each breath she took as she tried to contain the intense emotions he'd observed in her, and he realized that when she was animated—which she frequently was, especially when expressing her opinions, which she frequently did—she was attractive. Her hair was a cluster of loose curls arranged high on her head, with a few errant ones softening the line of her forehead and cheeks. Her brows were drawn together as she gazed down on their clasped hands. Dark fringes of eyelashes cast a small shadow on her cheeks, and he could nearly count the freckles across her nose. There weren't many, but he realized he had a fascination with each one.

He had not allowed himself to see her properly before now, having formed his opinion of her last year and having clung to that opinion.

Her full lips were drawn down into a pensive frown. He had kissed those lips. He had tasted their softness and had felt her sweet response to him. He had kissed her because he had felt something stir between them and had thought it might work in his favor.

It had worked—and it hadn't. She'd recognized his ploy and then, on her own terms, had agreed to his marriage proposal, making clear that her decision had not been made based on his kisses. He realized he wanted to kiss her again, merely for the pleasure of kissing her this time. If he were to kiss her now, however, she would surely consider it another ploy to sway her.

Since he judged it unwise to do so, he allowed her more silence and studied her further—beyond her physical attributes. He knew she was exceedingly clever and that she had even studied with her brothers as a young girl. George had considered her to be a spinster and harpy. What could he see now that might give him more insight into her person?

And *why* was it that *her name* had sprung to mind when Prinny had cornered him?

"Which of your concerns would you care to address first?" he asked her at last.

He waited for her reply.

She sighed, and George thought it a sorrowful sound. "It is much more preferable, I believe, to be alone with oneself than to feel alone in a crowd," she said at length. "I have felt very much alone these past days."

"What of Lady Walmsley?" he asked quietly.

Miss Jennings offered a tiny smile. "Lady Walmsley is a dear, and I have already grown to love her. But she is so elated at the prospect of this union that I cannot express my feelings about any of this to her."

"She would not hear them."

Miss Jennings nodded. "Exactly. There are others who have been gracious and amiable. Lady Bledsoe, for one." She glanced at George, but then, of course she knew of his mother's friendship with Lady Bledsoe.

"I know we put together a busy schedule for this week," he said. "Perhaps we can send our regrets for some of them—or even all of them, if you would like. I think we have created enough of a stir for the present. I myself can get rather annoyed by the fawning I receive from certain members of the *ton*, so I should have expected that to happen. As to the staring eyes, one simply learns to ignore them.

"I am confident that once the nuptials take place, the *ton* will move on to new gossip. The end of the war and the celebrations being planned should suffice, I think—victory over Emperor Napoleon surely outranks the marriage of a mere duke to his duchess."

She turned her gaze on him once more. She was holding something back from him, but it was there to be read in her expression, if only he could interpret it. What was he missing?

"A respite from some of the social engagements would be welcome," she said. "Thank you for understanding."

"I should have recognized the problem sooner, and for that I apologize," he said. "But I suspect you have more concerns than just those. Come, let us address those now as well."

Her expression grew soulful, and George watched as a pinkish tint bloomed in her cheeks, making her look younger than her thirty years. It intrigued him. And then he watched as the person he recognized as the harpy took over her countenance. "Very well," she said. "Tell me everything you know about me."

The Duke of Aylesham's face went blank.

"I can see by your expression that you have no idea even where to begin with that question, so I shall go first. I know that you are the Duke of Aylesham. I know that both of your parents died when you were very young. I know that you are friends with my brother James, and the two of you have worked together—in what capacity I do not know, although I intend for you to remedy that lack of information.

"I gather you have been ill lately, and that as a result, you are leaner than usual. I know you are tall; your hair is dark but gleams with burgundy hues when in the light, and you have the darkest, most piercing eyes I have ever seen. I know you are handsome and that many would call you attractive. I know that—"

"Would *you*?" he asked, interrupting her.

"Would I what?" she asked cautiously.

"Call me attractive."

"It is not gentlemanly of you to ask me that question."

"I agree," he said. His black eyes glinted.

Susan refused to react to his unnerving question and proceeded onward. "I know that you are well regarded by your peers and by Society in general, if the way they interact with you is any indication." A sudden thought hit her—he'd been Lord Kerridge before becoming the Duke of Aylesham. He'd mentioned it previously, but she'd been so overwhelmed by his offer of marriage that it had slipped her mind until just now. There had been gossip about a Lord Kerridge during her last Season, eight years earlier. A Lord Kerridge who had become briefly betrothed, although not formally announced. The rumors had claimed the young lady had cried off—

"Oh, good heavens," she murmured. "You're Kerridge. *That* Kerridge."

"I was Kerridge, yes," the Duke of Aylesham said matter-of-factly. "Do you know something of my past, then? Do you not have a past too, Miss Jennings?"

She did have a past. "That is precisely the point. We know little about each other beyond the basics." Had she not discovered what she had about Lord Frome when she had, she might now be married to a rake and a wastrel.

She had been twenty-one and in love.

"Did you love her?" Susan asked.

His face gave nothing away. "It was years ago."

"I know. Did you love her?"

"Did you love him?" he replied.

That took Susan aback. "How—?"

"*Did* you?" he asked again, interrupting her question.

Had James said something to him? He must have. "I pride myself on being an excellent judge of character," she said, "but I will concede that there was a brief moment in time when I allowed my heart to rule my head."

"You did, then," he said, "love him."

"You're confident about that, are you?" she shot back. "Go ahead, then—tell me all you know about me, since you are able to draw conclusions about my innermost thoughts so easily." She tried to pull her hand away from his, but he wouldn't let it go. He raised it to his lips instead and pressed a kiss on her fingers. *Blast* him.

"I know you are the daughter of a viscount and come from a large family that adores you, as a recent encounter with your brother demonstrated clearly," he said. "I know you are clever and have a keen desire to improve your mind, for you were sequestered in a library the first time I saw you. I know you are passionate in your opinions; I have witnessed it on multiple occasions. I believe you are a passionate person in all respects, although I think a part of that passion has been carefully hidden away."

He drew closer to her, and Susan's breath caught. His gaze coursed over her face. "I know you have gray eyes that can appear as stormy clouds or flash like swords of steel. You have a face that expresses everything you think or feel, you know—not that you are loath to speak the words that go along with the expressions."

"I do have a modicum of discretion, you know," she muttered, hardly able to think with his face so close to hers. Her fingers itched to touch his clean-shaven chin and discover how it felt.

He smiled slightly, and Susan swallowed and tried to maintain her ground in the discussion they were supposed to be having. He was distracting her from the subject, which was that they didn't know—

His free arm slipped around her shoulders, and he released her hand so he could run a forefinger along one of her eyebrows. "Your brows are furrowed again. You do that frequently, I've noticed." That same forefinger then traced its way along her forehead and began winding itself around one of her curls. She couldn't move.

His eyes were half closed as he gazed at her. "I have never seen a woman with such a glorious abundance of curls before," he said. "What a gift from God. I imagine when they are freed from their pins, they make a breathtaking sight. I cannot comprehend why you took such efforts to hide them. You hide many things, Miss Jennings."

He was but a breath away from her now, and Susan felt her defenses failing her. She could remember the sensation of his lips on hers, the giving, the taking, the yielding. She had thought herself contented to be in her world. She had still been able to refuse his proposal afterward. She had not lost her heart to him, despite his kisses.

She had told him a marriage must be built on more than kisses. And so he had come here today at her request, because of her concerns. It wasn't enough, but perhaps it was a gesture of something more.

"I know we do not know enough about each other," he said softly. "But I do know there is a fire that burns between us and that you know it as well as I do. And that fire gives me hope."

Susan knew her resolve to stay strong was weakening further. If only . . .

"Is it enough?" she asked, clinging to what resolve she had remaining.

"No," he murmured. "But it can be a beginning." And then he took her mouth with his own.

She didn't, couldn't resist. She welcomed his kisses and then gave herself permission to kiss him back. The smooth skin she'd been yearning to touch was masculine and delicious against her skin in contrast to his instructive lips that caressed hers and then explored her vulnerable throat and nipped at her earlobes. Her hands slid inside his coat to cling to his back, holding him near her, drawing him closer . . . She simply let herself feel. Time and place evaporated from existence. Her sole awareness was of him.

At length, he stroked his fingers across her cheek and raised his head to look into her eyes. He was silent; his breathing was labored, much as hers was.

"No," she gasped and hungrily pulled him back to her.

"Ahh," he sighed, chuckling before his eyes darkened with passion once again. "Yes." He took her lips with his own once more.

It was so gloriously empowering to know that she, the dusty spinster on a shelf, had this effect on him, this attractive, sought-after man. But he had power over her too, and she couldn't deny it anymore.

At length, he drew away again. "Dear Susan, I fear we will anticipate our wedding night at this rate, so I must refrain from any more of your kisses, although it grieves me sorely to say so."

Susan was unsure what to do or say next, having rarely been in this situation before. Lord Frome had—She would not think of Lord Frome and spoil this moment with George.

"What is it?" he asked, looking concerned.

She smiled. "It was nothing. Anyway, the thought has fled." She had thought of him as George, and he had called her Susan. *Dear Susan.*

He studied her closely until he appeared satisfied. "If you say so; I will trust you in that regard. Now, while we are on extraordinarily amiable terms, let us plan the remainder of the week and what needs to be done between now and our wedding day so that you may feel the happy bride."

Susan's nose began to tingle at his words, and she told herself emphatically she would not allow the tingling to progress to tears. But it was truly the first time he had directed any of these plans toward *her* happiness. She hoped he meant those words.

Hope. Hope was a beginning. He had said so himself.

Chapter 11

GEORGE SAT AT HIS DESK in his study and watched Phillip Osbourne pace about the room and waited for him to speak. James Jennings sat across from George, only instead of thumbing through a folder of documents as he had been when this same scenario had played out only days before, he alternated between glaring at Osbourne and glaring at George.

"One would think that contributing to the end of a costly, protracted war with France would be considered vastly more important than witnessing a marriage, especially when one has multiple siblings and has witnessed multiple weddings as a result," Osbourne said. He pointed at Jennings. "But this fool insists he will not leave for the Continent until this marriage between you and his sister has taken place, regardless of the fact that every day we wait is critical, and Castlereagh is waiting."

"You obviously don't have a sister," Jennings shot back. "If you think *for one moment* that I am leaving her here in London to marry this blackguard with no family present to support her, you best think again."

"There's Simon—" Osbourne began.

"I am not leaving her in the care of my prodigal baby brother, who may or may not even show his sorry face!" Jennings snapped. "If this latest mission cannot wait a day or two, then you better find someone else to step into the breach!"

"You know your legal expertise is necessary," George said, hoping he sounded calm. This current dilemma was his fault, even if Osbourne and Jennings didn't know the reason why. And for Susan's sake, he wasn't about to tell them.

"Not to mention your ability to speak French *and* German fluently," Osbourne added curtly. Jennings had a gift for languages, which was undoubtedly one of the reasons he had excelled as a lawyer. George and Osbourne were fluent enough in French but weren't nearly so in German. Jennings's ability to clearly explain the details of the treaty with the various representatives of the dukes and princes choosing to ally with the Sixth Coalition was imperative, and to find someone to replace him when the three of them knew precisely what needed to be done was a huge dilemma. George had not anticipated Jennings's insistence on remaining in Town for the wedding, although he should have.

Negotiations on the Continent were at a critical point. Would five days make a difference in the outcome of the war? It might not matter—or it might make all the difference. George didn't know the answer, but how was he to tell Jennings he must leave his sister's side when it was George who had put her in this situation in the first place?

"I cannot change the date of the nuptials. Even if my betrothed were to agree, the invitation has already been sent to the Prince Regent with a reply that he will attend."

"I am standing beside my sister," Jennings said firmly.

Osbourne threw his hands in the air in frustration. "I don't care about Prinny or his plans. We have delayed long enough already. I cannot believe that you don't see how critical it is that we leave immediately. It was enough that we decided Aylesham didn't need to accompany us, but I expected that I would *at least* have your legal expertise and German-speaking skills upon which to rely."

"That was before I knew Aylesham was going to propose marriage to my sister after having been in London less than a week!" Jennings bellowed.

This discussion was taking them nowhere, so George raised his hand to silence them. "Enough. I shall write a letter to the Foreign Office explaining your travel delay. You may deliver it in person, Osbourne, and await a reply, if you like. Will that suffice?"

"Perhaps," Osbourne grumbled. "It will depend entirely upon the answer I receive, of course." He glared back at Jennings.

"Understood." George opened the drawer of his desk and removed a sheet of paper, then took up his quill. He was about to dip it in the inkwell when there was a knock at the door. "Come," he said.

Talbot entered the room. "Pardon the interruption, Your Grace, but a letter just arrived from the Prince Regent, and I deemed it important enough to tell you as soon as possible."

This did *not* bode well.

"What does Prinny want now?" Osbourne asked impatiently.

George had the same question on his mind as he broke the seal and read the words within. "It appears I am obliged to attend a reception at Carlton

House tomorrow afternoon, celebrating the arrival of Prince Ernst Leopold of Schönberg-Nusse and his wife, Princess Eugenia Augusta, and their daughter, Princess Sophia Augusta."

Jennings and Osbourne both looked at George quizzically. "Prince Ernst Leopold of—" Osbourne began.

Talbot cleared his throat, interrupting him. "The messenger from Carlton House is awaiting a reply, Your Grace," Talbot said, shooting an apologetic look at Osbourne.

Prince Ernst and his wife and *daughter* had arrived in London ahead of schedule, had they? The Prince Regent was determined to push George and Princess Sophia into each other's orbit before George's nuptials occurred, was he? His Royal Highness was obviously determined to see George marry Princess Sophia, but George was equally if not more determined to make sure it didn't happen. "Tell the messenger that I will be there, along with my betrothed, Miss Susan Jennings."

Talbot paused for the briefest of moments. "I will see to it, Your Grace," Talbot said. He left.

"Prince Ernst Leopold of Schönberg-Nusse," Osbourne said, rubbing his chin in thought. "I recall that name, for some reason."

"His name came up during the discussions of who sided with Bonaparte and who fought against him," Jennings said. "The rumors were that he hosted Bonaparte and his generals for a time during the battles against Austria."

"That is what I thought I remembered hearing also," George said.

"If that is true, then why is our monarch holding a reception in his honor?" Osbourne asked. "Never mind. I doubt Prinny is informed enough to know."

"Osbourne, I would like you to see what you can learn about Prince Ernst Leopold while you are at the Foreign Office," George said. He set the invitation from the Prince Regent aside and quickly drafted a letter, blotting and sealing it and then handing it to Osbourne. "If Prince Ernst Leopold is indeed allied with the French, then Prince George needs to be informed as soon as possible. Be discreet when making your inquiries."

"What else would you expect?" Osbourne said with a speaking glance.

"Apologies, Osbourne. I fear I am presently not myself, owing to this invitation from Carlton House."

"I'll go with you, Osbourne," Jennings said. "We will sort out the truth more quickly if we work together."

"Well, what do you know?" Osbourne said dryly. "Jennings is finally willing to join in the effort."

"Thank you, both of you," George said. "Please let me know the minute you learn anything that will shed light on the situation."

"We shall." Jennings rose to his feet. "Come, Osbourne. You said yourself that time is of the essence."

"*Now* he's also in a hurry," Osbourne said. "Adieu, Aylesham. We shall bring you word as quickly as possible."

"Thank you," George said.

Once he was alone, he reread the invitation from the Prince Regent.

> *The Lord Chamberlain is commanded by The Prince Regent to invite The Duke of Aylesham to a Garden Party on Friday Afternoon, April 29th at 2 o'clock to have the Honor of meeting His Royal Highness Ernst Leopold of Schönberg-Nusse . . .*

It had been worded specifically so as to include only himself in the invitation. He also knew it had been done intentionally, as the prince had already responded in the affirmative to George and Susan's wedding invitation. Etiquette would have included an invitation for Susan to attend with him.

George intended to call the Prince Regent's bluff. He intended to have his betrothed at his side when he greeted the prince and his guests.

He rang for Talbot and then pulled out another sheet of paper.

"Yes, Your Grace?" Talbot asked when he eventually arrived.

George was just putting the finishing touches on the letter he'd dashed out. "Please have this sent to Miss Jennings and see that she receives it immediately. And then have my carriage readied."

"Yes, Your Grace," Talbot replied.

George wanted Susan by his side tomorrow afternoon, but he had learned by now that he could not merely presume that she would be compliant. She had already expressed her misgivings over their nuptials, and she had only just agreed to give him more time—allowing her to be out of Society's eye in order to adjust to all the changes his proposal had brought along as heavy baggage.

Now he was going to ask her to meet the Prince Regent on a day's notice and socialize with the people with whom George was most intent on avoiding.

He prayed she would agree to defy the prince and accompany George to the party. He honestly had no idea if she would.

His head ached.

"Talbot?"

"Yes, Your Grace?"

"Will you also have Mrs. Bradley send up one of her willow bark tinctures?" George asked.

"Certainly, Your Grace," Talbot replied. "And perhaps a bit of sustenance wouldn't be amiss either."

"Thank you, Talbot," George said.

He went to his dressing room to make himself presentable for his betrothed.

Susan and Aunt Margaret spent Thursday morning going through Susan's wardrobe, trying to decide which of her new gowns would be most suitable for the wedding on Monday. They had narrowed it down to two, and Susan had tried on each one so that she and Aunt Margaret could then decide together.

"What do you think?" Aunt Margaret said, looking back and forth between the two gowns currently hanging side by side. "This rose-colored silk is very pretty and would look splendid next to the Duke of Aylesham and that hair of his, but this cream one with the gold embroidery is some of Madame Veronique's finest work; I daresay you veritably glow in it. I don't believe you can go wrong with either one, so it's really up to you to make the final choice. Which one makes you feel the most like a duchess? Or like a bride?"

"I'm not sure any gown can make me feel any particular way," Susan said, fingering the fabric of the rose silk. "Especially like a duchess."

"Nonsense, girl!" Aunt Margaret said. "Clothes are not the most important consideration in life, to be sure, but clothes *do* inform others about who we are. They can boost our confidence on occasion or allow us to feel more relaxed. Recall how you felt the first time Aylesham showed up on my doorstep and you were in one of your old gowns and wearing a mobcap."

"I'm not sure I wish to recall *that* particular picture," Susan said with a smile. "And I take your point, Aunt Margaret."

"You may wish to feel like a bride, but you will also be Aylesham's duchess, and there's no getting around that fact," Aunt Margaret said. "You may as well pick the gown that informs Society that a Duchess of Aylesham has arrived and is a force to be reckoned with."

Susan sighed. "I will allow that the rose silk seems more like the gown of a duchess, but I've always thought that *if* I were ever to marry . . . I would prefer a simple gown—I don't know why. Funny, I had forgotten all about that. It's been a long time since I've held on to such girlish dreams."

"The cream one it is, then, and you'll look exquisite in it. Aylesham won't be able to take his eyes off you."

"Excuse me, milady," Mrs. Tompkins said after stepping into the room.

"What is it, Tompkins?" Aunt Margaret asked.

"Foster handed me this letter, just arrived from the Duke of Aylesham, and told me to bring it straight in to Miss Jennings."

"Thank you, Tompkins," Susan said, taking the letter from the maid. What could possibly be the matter now? Yesterday, during their conversation, George had told her he would not disturb her today so she could rest and reflect on all that had happened this past week and that he would call on her tomorrow and they would spend time truly getting to know each other better.

She broke the seal and opened the letter. Its contents were brief and to the point.

"What is it, my dear?" Aunt Margaret asked.

"The duke has informed me that there has been a new development in our nuptials, and he is calling on me—us—within the half hour to explain it in person."

"Gracious! Whatever could have happened?" Aunt Margaret exclaimed. "I say, when I invited you and your young sister to spend the Season here as my guests, I never dreamed you would bring so much excitement with you! I feel like a veritable girl again. It's quite invigorating!"

"Oh, Aunt Margaret!" Susan said, taking the older lady into her arms for a brief hug. "What a dear you are! I have known you but a week but feel as though I've known you forever. How glad I am that I've had you to rely on these past few days—more fantastical days I've never experience before in my life."

"The girl who caught a duke without even trying," Aunt Margaret said with a chuckle.

Without even wanting to, Susan added silently to herself—although his note had made her prickle with anxiety. Was he now going to end their betrothal? The idea of a new development left Susan feeling uneasy, and she realized . . .

Oh, good heavens, she didn't want her betrothal to the duke to end! She *wanted* to marry him. How could a person be so certain of something so life changing in such a short amount of time? Was her heart overruling her good sense again as it had when she had been a naive young lady and she'd become smitten with Lord Frome?

"You're woolgathering when you should be seeing to your hair," Aunt Margaret said.

"My hair—oh, yes." Susan absentmindedly patted her head. She had been pulling gowns on and off; her hair was certain to be a mess.

"Tompkins, perhaps you can assist Miss Jennings with her coiffure," Aunt Margaret said.

"No, I'll—I'm fine," Susan said. "No need; thank you, Tompkins."

"I'm happy to help," Tompkins replied. "If it sets your mind to resting."

"Very well. Thank you." Susan was usually able to remain matter-of-fact and practical, but right now, she was feeling fraught. She must rein in her emotions. She was not a quavering female who threatened the vapors at every whim.

She sat at her vanity and stared at her image in the mirror while Mrs. Tompkins saw to her coiffure. There was a new development regarding their nuptials, George had said in his letter, and he wanted to explain it to her and Aunt Margaret in person.

Her mind coursed through the various options of what that development might be and chose the worst options possible upon which to dwell. The Prince Regent had decided to push George more forcefully into marriage to Princess Sophia Augusta was one option. Or perhaps George had finally met the princess and had decided to do the bidding of the prince . . .

She shut her eyes and rubbed her temples. She thought she might be sick—what a humiliating thought! There was no use in speculating, she told herself firmly. She would know all soon enough.

Aunt Margaret came up to her and laid a hand on her shoulder. "Foster informed me that Aylesham is downstairs, my dear. Are you ready?"

She wasn't.

"Yes," she said.

George had spent altogether too much time pacing about this very parlor over the past week, yet here he was again. Pacing.

He didn't have to pace long, thank goodness, for soon the door opened, and Susan and Lady Walmsley entered the room.

"What is it?" Susan said, coming straight to him and taking his hands in hers. Her action meant a great deal to George. The Susan Jennings who had formerly despised him would not have greeted him in such a manner.

"Perhaps you would allow me to speak to Susan in private for a few minutes, Lady Walmsley," he said, still holding Susan's hands and looking straight at her.

Lady Walmsley left without a word.

"What is it?" Susan asked again.

"I scarcely know where to begin," he said.

Her eyes grew large.

"Come, sit with me." He led her to the same settee where they had sat yesterday, where he had kissed her and lost part of his heart to her. This was all becoming a farce in so many ways.

He turned to face her and kept her hand in his. "My dear Susan, I have imposed upon you so much already, usurped your free will and pressed you into undesired circumstances. And yet, here I am again, about to do the same thing." He paused, unwilling quite yet to speak the words aloud, for once he had spoken them, there was no turning back. Susan would either agree to his plan and be at his side, or she would refuse, and he would be facing great pressure from the Prince Regent once again to marry Princess Sophia Augusta.

But upon receiving this latest invitation from the prince, he had realized it wasn't fear of being under the prince's thumb or marrying a stranger from a foreign country that motivated him today. He had realized he wanted to marry Miss Susan Jennings, the spinster harpy he would have vowed he hated before this past week.

He didn't know how he could be so certain of this so soon after getting to know her—truly, he still barely knew her at all—yet, he *did* know. And he knew her intellect, her courage, and her inability to suffer fools gladly. She had put him in his place despite his being a duke, but he'd also seen her address servants as equals. He'd seen her humor and felt her passion, too, a passion for life and, he believed, for him as well. He knew her beauty without and her fire within and . . .

"I am listening," she said, watching him with concerned curiosity.

He smiled briefly at her solemn face and took up his courage. "Today I received an invitation—more of a summons, really—from the Prince Regent to attend a garden party to be held tomorrow afternoon," he said. "It was worded in such a manner as to make it clear the invitation was for me alone."

"I don't see the problem here," Susan said, her brows furrowing in that way of hers. "I have no desire to be included in such an invitation; if you are concerned such an exclusion will have hurt my feelings, I can assure you that I will be more than happy to remain here while you mingle with the Prince Regent and his guests tomorrow."

"There is more," he said. "Prince Ernst Leopold and his wife *and daughter* have arrived in London ahead of schedule. It is for them that Prinny is hosting this party. I suspect it is a last-ditch attempt to press me into marrying the princess."

"Ah," she said.

George waited for her to say more, but she was silent. She gazed at their clasped hands and said nothing. George had learned by now that she needed time to sort out new details, so he remained silent as well to let her think.

Lady Walmsley would be returning soon, though, and George had more to say to Susan before then, so he lifted her hand to his lips and kissed it. "I have come here today to ask for your help. You may refuse. I brought you into this debacle through my own arrogance and selfish expectations. I will not do so again."

"Oh, George," she said.

"Despite the wording on the invitation, it is my intention, if you are willing, to show up at Carlton House tomorrow with my soon-to-be duchess on my arm."

"*What?*" she exclaimed, her eyes now huge and flashing silver. "You wish me to show up, *uninvited*, to Carlton House to be presented to His Royal Highness the Prince Regent willy-nilly, just like that? And what happens when the doormen refuse my admittance? Do you think I have the bravado to stare them down and browbeat them into submission?"

"I do, actually, yes," he said bluntly. "And before you say anything more, I think it the finest compliment I could bestow upon you—at least the finest one that you would accept from me at present. I can think of many others."

Her eyes narrowed at him. "You are *not* trying to flatter me into agreeing to your preposterous plan, are you?" she said.

"Not in the slightest. I am allowing you to choose, even though I dearly hope you will attend with me tomorrow and be at my side. I plan to take another personal stand against Prinny's machinations, but if necessary, I will face him on my own."

"You may find that Princess Sophia Augusta is your perfect match, yet there I will be on your arm, ruining any chance you may have of securing her hand."

"I have grave doubts about the first part and high hopes for the second, which is why I desire to have you with me tomorrow afternoon."

She sighed gustily. "You may not realize this, having been schooled in such things since birth," she said, "but there is more to attending this party at Carlton House than merely outstaring a doorman. I was never presented at court, never made my curtsy to Queen Charlotte. There is much I have not learned regarding royal protocol . . . and what I did learn when I made my come-out has been long forgotten. I don't know the first thing about chatting with the Prince Regent at an afternoon party. I honestly don't see how this can work."

"Ah, but that is where Lady Walmsley comes in," he said. "May I include her in our conversation now?"

Susan looked at him for what seemed to George an eternity. Finally, she shrugged. "I suppose you may."

He rose from the settee and strode to the parlor door, where he unsurprisingly found Lady Walmsley scolding Foster about something yet again.

"I do *not* need an upholstered chair in the entry hall," she said as old Foster and a footman dragged a heavy decorative chair from one of the adjoining rooms. "If I'd wanted to sit in that chair, I would have gone into the room to sit in it!" she huffed.

"Now, Lady Walmsley," Foster began.

"Don't you 'Now, Lady Walmsley' me, you old codger. My bones can handle sitting on a wooden chair for a few minutes, for heaven's sake! If you must insist on such foolishness, a pillow would have sufficed."

"I only wished—" Foster said, trying again.

"Take that chair back immediately," she ordered. She spied George and pointed at him. "See? Aylesham is here already. You went to a lot of work for no reason. I *cannot* understand you at times." She stomped away from Foster and the footman toward George.

No wonder Susan and Lady Walmsley got along so well, he thought humorously as he smiled and gestured for Lady Walmsley to precede him into the parlor.

"Lady Walmsley," George said after said lady had sat with a disgruntled plop next to Susan. "I have been invited to an afternoon party tomorrow by the Prince Regent, and I have asked Susan to attend the affair with me. She has expressed concerns, however, over certain protocols that might be of use in mingling with the royals who will be present. I thought, perhaps, you might assist her in that regard."

"Why, there's nothing to it, my girl," Lady Walmsley said. "You already comport yourself with dignity and intelligence, your manners are what they should be, and you already have one or two gowns that will allow you to appear the duchess you will become. The rest we can address easily enough this afternoon: refreshing you on a few curtsies and addresses to get you through the first of it, introductions and the like, and then you will be fine, clever girl like you. An afternoon party is not the same as a formal dinner—not nearly so stuffy. You have nothing to worry about."

"There, you see?" he said with an encouraging smile to Susan.

She didn't smile back. "I don't believe for one moment it will be as easy as either of you claim," she said. "But I will go to the party with you."

"Thank you," George said, his chest nearly bursting in relief. "Thank you most humbly. I have every confidence in your ability to learn what Lady Walmsley deems necessary. Now, I will leave you both so you may prepare for the party with my best wishes. Thank you, Lady Walmsley," he said and bowed over her hand. "And thank you, my dear Susan," he said, taking her hand and kissing it.

"Mm," she said.

"Until tomorrow, then," he said.

"Mm," she said again.

She had not said no to him, George thought as he rode in his carriage back to Aylesham House. She had agreed to be at his side when facing Prinny and his foreign guests. He had confidence in Lady Walmsley's ability to teach Susan enough basics in courtly etiquette to get by since Prinny wasn't always a stickler about such things, especially at a garden party. Under the time constraints, it would have to do.

He wondered what Osbourne and Jennings had discovered, if anything. George needed to know as much as possible before showing up at Carlton House tomorrow.

When George arrived back at Aylesham House, he learned that Jennings was there waiting for him.

"I put him in the dayroom, Your Grace," Talbot said. "Henshaw is with him, and they are having tea while awaiting your arrival. Mrs. Bradley made a currant cake, exceptionally fine cake, as always."

"Thank you, Talbot," George said. "I shall be certain to eat a large slice so everyone will breathe a little easier." George was relieved enough that Susan had agreed to attend the party with him tomorrow that he refrained from commenting further on his servants' continued efforts to fatten him up.

"Very good, Your Grace."

"What is the news?" George asked Jennings when he entered the dayroom. He'd barely spoken the words when a footman hurried over to the table to set a place for him and prepare his tea.

"Castlereagh is in Town, just arrived last night," Jennings said before taking another bite of cake. "You really must try this, Aylesham. Your cook works magic with currants."

"Where is Osbourne?" George asked, ignoring the slice of currant cake the footman set before him.

"We stopped to get the documents from my lodgings and took them with us to the Foreign Office, which was a stroke of great luck since we were able to meet with Castlereagh himself. Napoleon rejected the Chaumont treaty, so there is more work to be done on that front, and with haste. Castlereagh informed me of the changes to be made in the drafts I wrote, and Henshaw here has agreed to help me amend them."

"With your permission, Your Grace," Henshaw added.

"Of course you have my permission," George said. "And where did you say Osbourne is?"

"Since these drafts need amending, Castlereagh has given us additional time. One week," Jennings said. "Osbourne is continuing on to the Continent without me on the other part of our errand, but since he won't need a German-speaking legal expert for that particular task, he intends to leave first thing tomorrow. He and I shall meet up later."

"I see. Excellent. Henshaw, will you write up the necessary papers for Osbourne to give to the captain of my yacht, then, and see that he gets them? It may not be required, but since I won't be there, it's best to err on the side of caution." During their travels to assist the Foreign Office, they had encountered other desperate issues that needed attention, in George's opinion. An end to the war would do wonders in correcting them, but in the meantime, he and Osbourne and Jennings had committed to doing what they could to assist in the short term.

"Osbourne also said I was to congratulate you on your nuptials Monday since he won't be in attendance," Jennings said.

"If you'll both kindly excuse me, I believe I will begin straightaway on those papers for Osbourne, et cetera." Henshaw set his napkin on the table.

"Good man, Henshaw, and thank you," George replied. Once Henshaw had left the dayroom, George leaned closer to Jennings. "And what did you learn about Prince Ernst Leopold? Anything of import?" he asked quietly.

Jennings sipped his tea and then set his cup down on its saucer. "Ah, now that part was interesting, I must say," he said in an equally low voice. "Didn't ask Castlereagh—he barely had time to speak to us as it was. But we talked to an associate of mine in the Foreign Office who happened to be there, and he knew a great deal about our Prince Ernst Leopold of Schönberg-Nusse. One of the lesser principalities, Schönberg-Nusse, and like many other minor princes and counts, Prince Ernst attempted to court Bonaparte to stay in his good graces. Apparently, Prince Ernst's exorbitant efforts didn't pay off, as his principality was eventually mediatized—annexed to the King of Bavaria. He lost all but his castle and its surrounding acreage. In that regard, he isn't much different from dozens of other princes and counts on the Continent—except that he is *here* wooing the Prince Regent with promises of wealth, should his daughter be given a choice husband."

"Hmm," George said. He could almost feel sorry for Prince Ernst had he not gotten George caught up in this mess.

Jennings looked at him enigmatically. "Interesting, wouldn't you say?"

George tensed. "Interesting that the prince should want to leave the Continent and secure his place among the members of the Coalition?" he asked, hoping to redirect the conversation away from the prince's daughter. "I see it more as a strategic move on Prince Ernst's part."

Jennings was watching him too closely. "Strategic on Prince Ernst's part—or on Prinny's? Or both?" he said. "And then there's the rumor that he comes looking for a husband for his daughter."

"It shall be amusing to see him interact with Prinny and his guests tomorrow, then, I suppose," George said with a bland smile. Jennings was getting too close to the truth for George's comfort. He stood. "If there is nothing else, I'm afraid our conversation must end. I have—"

"Been leading me on a merry chase," Jennings snapped, also rising to his feet.

The pieces had fallen into place for him, then, blast it all.

"I *knew* there was something amiss in your betrothal to Susan. The animosity was fairly reeking from the both of you when you met at Lady Bledsoe's ball. And yet within mere days, you're announcing a betrothal. All this time you have been using my sister as a means to thwart Prinny's plans to marry you off to this German princess. I am certain that's what this is all about. I should call you out right now for what you are doing to my sister!"

George raised his hands in conciliation. "I assure you I have done nothing that your sister hasn't agreed to with full knowledge," he said, hoping his words would calm Jennings. He didn't particularly want to duel with the brother of his future bride. "Consider that you might not be giving her enough credit, Jennings. She isn't a hapless creature fainting in distress over the villainous Duke of Aylesham. She is strong and clever and knows full well who she is and what she wants." And George realized with a great deal of satisfaction that his description of her was indisputable.

"If anyone knows how special Susan is, it is I," Jennings responded with vehemence. "She and I played together as children and are extremely close. She has also been hurt before, and I *will not* see her hurt again." They were nearly nose-to-nose now.

"She will *not* be hurt by me," George said. "I will stand by her, come what may. I swear it."

Jennings remained silent, scrutinizing George. He finally relaxed and moved back a step.

"The invitation to the garden reception at Carlton House was for me alone," George said at last, once he could see that Jennings had calmed down a bit. "I believe it was indeed intentional for Prinny to invite me and not include an invitation for Susan when he knows full well we are betrothed. He is still attempting to throw me in the direction of Princess Sophia."

"Even though he has already accepted your invitation to the wedding?" Jennings exclaimed.

"Yes, well, that would be Prinny, wouldn't it? He seems rather intent upon it." George said.

"What do you plan to do?" Jennings asked.

"I called upon your sister this afternoon while you were with Osbourne. I explained the situation to her and asked her if she was willing to go with me to Carlton House tomorrow."

"Without an invitation?" Jennings asked, sounding incredulous now.

"Yes," George said. "And she agreed. But I gave her the *choice*, Jennings. Had she chosen not to go with me, I would have honored her decision."

"You will be placing her in an utterly precarious situation tomorrow, arriving without an invitation, surrounded by the very elite of England, not to mention going against the very wishes of the Prince Regent. I daresay you will survive, but *she* will be cut to shreds."

"I am aware of the stakes, and so is she. But she offers me—us—the best opportunity to prevail by being at my side."

Jennings only shook his head. "You are mad—*both* of you." He rose to his feet. "I will bid you adieu now. It appears you are turning me religious, for I feel the distinct need to pray for my sister's and your souls." He pointed his finger directly at George. "But know this, *Your Grace*, should my prayers and your foolish plan fail, I will be here to collect my sister and return with her to Lincolnshire, for I will *not allow* her to remain here and become a laughingstock or, worse yet, a pariah. And I will seek justice for her. From *you*."

George stood and locked eyes with Jennings. "Know this, *my friend*, that I intend to marry your sister this Monday. Prinny or the devil himself may attempt to stop me, but they will not succeed."

"I hope for your sake you are correct," Jennings said, and then he turned on his heel and strode from the room.

Chapter 12

Susan stood in front of her dressing room mirror one last time to inspect her appearance before going downstairs to await George's arrival. Aunt Margaret was already there, ready to greet him so Susan would have all the time she needed.

She hardly believed what she saw reflected in the mirror. She saw a woman in the prime of life—not a girl and not a dusty spinster either. The rose silk gown flattered her figure, and her hair, which Miss Lily had agreed to style today, looked more elegant than Susan could have imagined after years of dealing with the unruly mop.

She tugged on her gloves and took up her shawl and reticule. As a last-minute thought, she went to her armoire and grabbed one of her new, pretty parasols. The skies weren't overcast, so an actual umbrella wouldn't be needed, but the parasol felt like a shield, and it was a comforting thought.

Then she stood in front of the mirror *one* last time.

There was nothing for it—it was time to take up the gauntlet. When she reached the head of the stairs that descended to the entry hall, George and Aunt Margaret were both standing below, waiting for her.

"There she is, my duchess," George said, then he took the stairs two at a time until he reached her. "You are a vision to behold," he whispered to her, his words making her heart flutter faster than it already had been. "Come," he then said louder. "Allow me to assist you." He offered Susan his arm, and they descended the stairs together.

"How absolutely stunning you look, my dear!" Aunt Margaret exclaimed, clasping her hands at her bosom. "What Aylesham says is the truth—you look every inch the duchess. Did I not say it would be so?"

"Thank you, Aunt Margaret," Susan said.

"Do you feel ready for this afternoon?" George asked her.

"We went over everything I could think of yesterday after you left," Aunt Margaret said. "She's a clever girl, this one, as you well know. I suspect she can act the part of a duchess nearly as well as the Duchess of Atherton herself—and I half suspect the Duchess of Atherton would agree with me. You met her, Susan, remember? Of course you do, along with the other ladies at that tea we attended."

"I do remember," Susan said. "I remember them all giving me pitying looks."

"I saw nothing at all of what you are saying," Aunt Margaret said in a softly chiding tone. "And *if* what you say is true—*if*—they would certainly see you in a different light now," she added. "The gown does not make the duchess, of course, but it *does* inform people and gives one confidence in oneself. You remember my saying those words, don't you? You can be confident today, my dear. You are every bit their equal."

"Oh, Aunt Margaret," Susan said, reaching out to take the dear lady's hands in her own and placing a kiss on her cheek. "I believe you truly are a fairy godmother."

"There is one last bit of business to attend to before we leave," George said. "Continuing along the theme of looking the part of a duchess, I have brought you this." He picked up a small case from a side table nearby. "I hope this provides the finishing touch."

He opened the case, and Susan caught her breath. Lying on a bed of black velvet was a stunning ruby necklace, similar in style to her betrothal ring.

"I will not allow the future Duchess of Aylesham to be the only unembellished lady present, although I don't believe for one moment that you need this in order to shine. It is merely pride on my part." He smiled at her. "May I?"

"Yes, thank you," Susan replied softly, still in wonder at his surprising gift. She turned her back to him, and he carefully draped the necklace around her throat and fastened the clasp.

She turned back to look at him, her fingers reaching up to touch the rubies, hardly believing they were real. But he wasn't looking at the necklace. He was looking at her.

"Perfect," he said.

"Oh," she replied.

He smiled at her. "Shall we be on our way?" he asked her, gesturing toward the door.

"Yes," she said.

She put on her small, stylish bonnet, and then he assisted her with her shawl and offered her his arm; she laid her hand on it, chiding herself that all she'd managed to say to him after such a gift and compliment was, "Oh." The man was turning her into a half-wit.

He assisted her into his carriage and then climbed inside after her, choosing to sit next to her rather than across.

It was a rather cozy fit.

They rode in silence for a while, and Susan felt every bump of the carriage over the cobblestones. Each one seemed to toss her against him, reminding her of his touches and kisses. The *last* thing she needed at this moment was to be reminded of *that*, however, when her brains were already failing her. She needed to concentrate; the task ahead of them required she have all her wits intact. She put a hand to her forehead.

"Are you unwell?" he asked her.

"No," she replied. "But I am feeling the extremity of what lies ahead, and I would be lying if I didn't say it weighs on me."

"Lady Walmsley assured me that you are well rehearsed," he said.

"As well rehearsed as one can be in a half day's time," she replied.

"And you are clothed for the part," he said. "Your gown is exquisite, by the way."

"Thank you." She suddenly realized that his waistcoat was a brocade of burgundy and rose and wondered if his valet had contacted Lady Walmsley to determine what Susan would be wearing. "You look very fine too, and—*coincidentally*, I'm sure—we appear to complement each other."

The corner of his lip twitched. "Ah, a trace of the saucy girl I met in Lord Cantwell's library a year ago just showed herself. I had feared she had vanished." He glanced out the carriage window. "It appears we are nearly to Carlton House, so we must make final preparations."

Susan was still mulling over his "saucy girl" comment. "What final preparations?" she asked.

He suddenly became serious. "If we are to succeed, I need to introduce them to the woman who cared not a whit that she was standing up to a duke and who was not afraid to put him in his place. The woman who is clever and discerning and can infer the nuances of conversation and return fire with fire when necessary. You won't know this, of course, but I referred to you as 'the harpy' after I first saw you."

"Very flattering," she said.

His face was still serious, despite her retort. "It wasn't at the time, but it is now. Or perhaps Athena is a better description. Yes, you are my Athena this afternoon—my gray-eyed goddess of reason, intelligence, peace . . . and battle strategy."

"Those are lofty words, Your Grace," she said, and then she chuckled. "I referred to you as His Loftiness when I didn't know who you were."

"Touché, my dear. You weren't wrong. And I must be at my lofty best today, with my Athena at my side, if we are to succeed." He leaned closer to her. "This is for good luck," he said, and then he gently kissed her, laying his hand on her cheek. "May we be victorious," he murmured afterward, and then he kissed her again.

The carriage rolled to a stop.

"And thus it begins," he said.

George assisted Susan from the carriage and once again offered her his arm. He watched her face as she took in the imposing façade of Prinny's residence. The place was impressive enough from a distance, but approaching the entrance on foot would be intimidating to one unaccustomed to such grandiosity.

He leaned toward Susan so he could whisper in her ear. "Do you remember the look you gave me when I accused you of eavesdropping?" he asked her. "That is the expression I would like you to assume right now."

She turned to him. "You mean *this* look?" she asked him sweetly, but her eyes bore through him like fiery darts; a single brow lifted disdainfully; her beautiful mouth formed a moue of pure haughtiness.

"It is even better than I remember," he said warmly.

"Charmer," she said.

"These doormen must believe that you and I together have every right to be here, even though the invitation bears only my name," he said. "You must put any egalitarian feelings you have behind you for now."

"Do you take me for a fool?" she asked him acidly.

Perhaps she was going to be *too* good at her role. "Trust me when I say that I would never dream of such a thing," he said. "And well done, by the way."

She smiled at him.

"One last word of advice," he whispered as he caught her eyes wandering to the grand columns of the entrance portico. "Do *not* gape."

"I'm not gaping," she said.

"You may be inclined to once we get inside. No matter what, do *not* act impressed. You must appear blasé. Indifferent."

"I *know* what 'blasé' means," she said.

As they approached the doors, George reached into his breast pocket and retrieved his invitation, then handed it to the livery-clad doorman. "The Duke of Aylesham and his betrothed, the Honorable Miss Susan Jennings," he stated firmly in his most ducal manner.

The doorman looked at the invitation and then at George and then at Susan and then back at the invitation.

"Did you not hear me clearly?" George asked, assuming a bored attitude this time and raising his quizzing glass halfway to his eye. "Do you need to borrow my glass to read what it says?" He twiddled the quizzing glass in the doorman's direction.

"Begging your pardon, Your Grace, but—"

"*Really*, Aylesham," Susan interrupted, sounding just as bored as George had, "I *told* you Prinny would get the details wrong, with so much excitement going on. You *should* have cleared up the little inaccuracy on the invitation *before* we had to become a *burden* on this *important person's time*."

The doorman's face went a deep shade of red.

George shrugged at him as if to suggest the two of them were subject to the demands of their womenfolk and what was a fellow to do? "Sorry, my good man, but I really *am* offended that *you* would think my bride-to-be would not be welcome. Would you care to go confer with Prince George or the Lord Chamberlain right now so we may sort out this matter quickly?" Out of the corner of his eye, George noticed another carriage pulling up to the entrance portico and another carriage behind it. "You seem familiar. Has this post been yours for a while?"

"About a year, Your Grace," the doorman replied.

"*Such* a responsibility, assuring that only those properly invited are allowed to enter," Susan said, making George cringe—how did she think they were going to succeed if she was pointing out to the man precisely what they were doing?

"A year," George echoed, hoping to distract the doorman from Susan's words. "I thought I'd seen you. I was here not a week past. No wonder you look so familiar."

"I—" the doorman began.

"What *was* it I was going to discuss with the Princess Sophia Augusta?" Susan asked rhetorically.

George looked at her in alarm, not knowing what she intended.

"Oh, that's right: *Maibaum* traditions," she said emphatically. "That's *maypole* for us, here in England," she explained to the doorman. "Quite a thing where she comes from, apparently. I *am* curious, now that I remember."

"Ah," George said, unsure what else to add. Out of the corner of his eye, he could see the other recently arrived guests approaching. "What say you, man? Is my bride-to-be to be allowed to pass?"

"It's not a problem, Your Grace," the doorman said at last. "Please, enter."

"Thank you, Sir," Susan said, and George swore her words would have melted butter. He merely nodded at the doorman as they walked past and through the doors into the familiar Hall of Entrance. They were successfully past the first obstacle.

"Don't gape," he whispered to her.

Her mouth closed.

"And well done," he added.

A footman approached them, welcoming them once again, and gestured for them to follow.

"I'm *so glad* the weather decided to cooperate this afternoon," Susan said in her own version of a bored tone. Good girl.

"Indeed," George replied with the same amount of ennui. "How *dreadful* it would have been to welcome such *illustrious* guests and then not allow them to see London at her finest."

"I agree *entirely*, my dear duke," Susan replied.

They kept up the verbal nonsense until they reached the doors that led to the garden. The footman bowed and left them to return to his post. Through the windows, George could see a fairly large group of people already assembled, and he tried to discern who was in attendance and who was located where so he could strategize. He could see already that mixed in with the prince's usual dilettantes and minions, there was a surprising number of government officials and members of Parliament, although there was no one of any great influence, like Castlereagh or Lord Liverpool, the prime minister.

George eventually spied Prinny mingling with his guests, and next to him was an unfamiliar trio—a tall, robust man with full, gray sideburns who looked to be in his fifties, a solidly built, middle-aged woman with reddish hair who was nearly as tall as the man, and a young lady who was really quite beautiful and was as tall as the other two—the trio must certainly be Prince Ernst Leopold and his wife and daughter.

"I propose we go straight to Prinny and get it over with," George said. "I see no need to mingle with the other guests or stay any particular length of time."

Susan gazed out the window. George expected the guests who had arrived after them to show up behind them at any minute. "There are so few people here I know," she murmured.

"That is just as well," George said, "for many of them presume to be the cream of Society but are, in fact, rather poor examples. Lord Alvanley, for one"—George pointed discreetly at the man in question who was currently laughing with a pair of other dandies—"is rich in witticisms but lacking in judgment and is living well beyond his means. And he is not alone." He glanced at Prinny.

"Nonetheless, this is a great deal more intimidating now that I'm here," Susan said. "It is quite one thing to envision something and quite another to face it in truth, as I have recently learned. The doorman was nothing compared to what I see here."

"That may be so. But remember, we succeeded with the doorman *and* the footman. Take courage from those successes," he said. "You are the future Duchess of Aylesham. Allow them to see *her,* and we shall succeed again. I am sure of it."

Susan looked out the window at the crowd, trying to gather her courage. All too soon, on George's signal, the footman posted outside the french doors would open them to allow them to step outside. *Outside*, where the Prince Regent and all of his guests would see her with him and recognize her for the fraud she was. Why, oh, why had she ever agreed to this? She could be safely back in Lincolnshire right now, sitting next to Rebecca, reading aloud to her, sharing anecdotes of the past week. It had been a choice she could have made. She had told George that very thing.

Now he was waiting for her to choose again—choose to go through those doors and face her monarch and his friends or to leave. If she were to tell him she wanted to leave, he would oblige her; she knew he would. But he believed in her too. *You are the future Duchess of Aylesham. Allow them to see her, and we shall succeed again.*

She nodded her consent, the footman swung the doors open, and she stepped outside. George followed. Surprisingly, while a few heads turned in their direction, the world didn't come crashing to an end. At least not yet.

She opened her parasol, and together they crossed the lawn to greet their host.

"Ah, Aylesham," the Prince Regent said. "Glad you could make it to our little party. Prince Ernst, Princess Augusta, Princess Sophia, allow us to introduce the gentleman we were telling you about earlier, George Kendall, the Duke of Aylesham. Aylesham, we are pleased to have you meet His Royal Highness Prince Ernst Leopold of Schönberg-Nusse and his wife, Princess Eugenia Augusta, and *their daughter*, Princess Sophia Augusta." The Prince Regent ignored Susan's presence altogether, making his intentions perfectly clear.

Everyone made their perfect bows and curtsies and followed the Prince Regent's lead while Susan stood uncomfortably at George's side. Lady Walmsley's instructions on the protocols of conversing with royalty coursed through her head: *One does not take the liberty of introducing oneself to those of higher rank; one is invited to do so.* It was one of the cardinal rules. George could not introduce her without some sort of overture from the royals that would allow it.

But George had told her he wanted the harpy at his side—no, *his Athena*. His goddess of battle strategies, among other things.

Athena would not be invisible, nor would George's future duchess.

Susan straightened her spine once again, lifted her chin, and smiled as though she possessed all that lay before her. Prince Ernst, despite himself, looked directly at her with a questioning expression on his face. It was all the opening they needed.

George cleared his throat. "Your Royal Highnesses, allow me to present the Honorable Miss Susan Jennings, daughter of the Viscount Thurlby of Lincolnshire. She is my bet—"

"Miss Jennings," Prinny said with the slightest of nods, interrupting George before he could finish uttering the word *betrothed*. "Aylesham, Princess Sophia has expressed an interest in viewing the garden and learning more about the sights of London. Perhaps you would be so kind as to show her and provide some insights."

Susan could see George's jaw go rigid. She needed to do something. "What a *lovely* idea, Aylesham," she said. "After such long travels, I'm sure Princess Sophia would enjoy stretching her legs and having a chance to mingle with the other guests."

"Certainly, *my dear*," George said, surprising Susan with the endearment, although it would serve to make their relationship obvious to the others. "Shall we?" he said to the princess, offering his arm to her.

"How kind of you," she said and placed her arm on George's sleeve. Susan watched as they walked away together. Princess Sophia was tall and exotically beautiful, Susan thought begrudgingly, with auburn hair and a creamy complexion and large, blue eyes that tilted upward and added to her allure.

"Prince Ernst, Princess Eugenia, we believe we see Lord Alvanley engaging in some lighthearted banter. Let us go see what is so amusing." The Prince Regent gestured toward the gentleman, who must be Lord Alvanley, and then led the others in that direction, ignoring Susan and leaving her entirely alone.

George and the princess were nowhere to be seen.

Susan wracked her brain, trying to remember if Lady Walmsley had instructed her on what to do when one had been introduced to virtually no one and had no acquaintance at hand who could perform the introductions. She would be seen as having no manners whatsoever were she to walk up to total strangers, especially ones of higher rank than she, and brashly introduce herself. She doubted even Athena would do that if she found herself amongst the *beau monde* here at Carlton House.

Unsure what to do with herself, she shifted her parasol slightly to conceal her face a bit, her bravado having taken a bruising after the Prince Regent's cut direct, and began to make her way through the various clusters of guests in the hope of finding a discreet spot where she could be alone until George returned with Princess Sophia.

The utterly breathtaking Princess Sophia.

Susan shook her head, mentally chiding herself. It would do her no good to allow herself such thoughts at present. Additionally, she told herself, it wouldn't do her or George any good if she were to make herself too scarce. There was a difference between being discreet and being cowardly.

Once again, she straightened her spine and—

"It appears I have stumbled upon a fair lady who is on her own," a male voice said behind her. "We cannot allow that, now, can we?"

Susan froze. It was a voice she knew only too well, even if it had been eight years since she'd last heard it. Albert Sutton, the Earl of Frome—and the one person in all of England she'd hoped never to see again.

Thankfully, Susan's parasol had been concealing most of her face from Lord Frome, so she had the briefest of moments to collect her wits before facing him, but there could be no avoiding the situation. She turned fully toward him now. "Lord Frome," she said and then watched as his face paled.

"Miss Jennings," he said. Susan doubted he had ever expected to see her again either, if the look on his face was anything to go by. He recovered his composure quickly. "Such a pleasure to see you again after so many years," he said in a congenial tone Susan didn't believe for a moment. "Would you care to take a stroll with me? The flowers just over there are at their most beautiful. I believe you would enjoy seeing them."

"I will, thank you," she replied.

He bowed in acknowledgment and then offered Susan his arm. She ignored him and clasped her parasol with both hands.

His feigned agreeable demeanor vanished. "Ah, I see how it is," he said as they strolled toward the flowers in question. "You haven't changed a bit, have you?"

"Nor have you," she replied. "How is your wife, by the way?"

"I wouldn't know," he said. "She prefers the country, and I prefer her in the country. We are very much in agreement in that regard." The Earl of Frome had always been a handsome man—tall, his dark hair closely cropped, his features fine—and he still was, but he was beginning to show the effects of his dissolute ways. His hair was graying at the temples, and lines were forming near his eyes and bracketing his mouth. He caught her studying his face. "Are you impressed to see your former suitor associating with such esteemed company or gloating to yourself that he has fallen in your expectations?" he asked.

"Neither," Susan replied. "I feel sorry for your wife."

"The wife *you* chose not to be," he said. He stepped closer to her until they were face-to-face. "We loved each other, you and I," he said in a low voice, his face near hers again after so many years, the essence of his familiar cologne filling her thoughts with memories long past. "You said the words to me as I did you. I bared my soul to you and asked for your hand—but you refused me. Tsk-tsk." He placed a hand over his heart as though it had broken anew. "All because of a few minor indulgences," he added.

"A dalliance with an actress is not a minor indulgence in my opinion," she said. "Nor is an obvious penchant for high-stakes gambling and drinking to excess."

"I was young," he said, shrugging. "It is what young gentlemen do. It is what young ladies forgive them for doing."

"You are not young now," she said softly.

He laughed mockingly. "Ah, still the same Susan, I see—so clever, so self-righteous—and full of so much passion that, sadly, is still locked away deep inside you, unless it has withered into nothing more than dust, that is." He took her by the elbow and led her farther away from the crowd of mingling guests. "Such a waste of a passionate woman," he whispered in her ear, "hidden away these past years on a lonely, old shelf, all but forgotten."

Susan turned to face him and stared at him coldly.

He stared back at her for a moment and then shook his head. "Ah well. The past is the past. Broken hearts do heal in one form or another, don't they?"

Susan said nothing.

"Changing the subject, I cannot deny the surprise at seeing you here this afternoon," he said. "I didn't figure you for the type to fawn over Prinny. How did you come to be here?" he asked.

"I am not here to fawn over the prince," Susan said.

"But you did not arrive on your own, I daresay. Not Saint Susan, the patroness of all things virtuous. Not to a party at Carlton House, if she could help it."

She didn't wish to speak to Lord Frome any further, and were she anywhere *but* Carlton House, she would leave him abruptly, but her mind was a tumult of etiquette rules pressed upon her by Lady Walmsley, a heap of discomfort at being here in the first place, and an overabundance of shock at seeing Lord Frome again. "I am here as a guest of the Duke of Aylesham," she said at last.

"Aylesham, eh? What a strange coincidence!" Lord Frome exclaimed sarcastically. "Prinny wished to reward Aylesham for service to Crown and country, the reward being the lovely Princess Sophia Augusta as his bride, and there is quite a purse involved as well, I understand, but somehow, rather than accept the generosity of his monarch, he managed to slip the noose, as they say . . ." He inhaled a breath as though a thought had struck him. "*You* are the excuse Aylesham gave Prinny! Oh, that's rich! *You*, of all people. I daresay you don't even *know* Aylesham, as you've been cloistered away in Lincolnshire all these years, and yet, here you are, lying to the Prince Regent about having an attachment to the man. What a little hypocrite you are."

"I am betrothed to the Duke of Aylesham," Susan said firmly. She wanted Lord Frome to leave. She didn't care if there was proper etiquette to maintain or if she would be alone once again. It had taken her years to get over the pain she'd felt in learning of his betrayal and her mistrust of her own judgment when it came to love. Today his words were bitter and cruel. But she wasn't a hypocrite.

She also didn't owe Lord Frome the dignity of an explanation.

"I am betrothed to the Duke of Aylesham," she repeated. "And we are planning to wed this Monday." And then she smiled at Lord Frome as she hoped the goddess Athena would smile.

"We shall see," he said. "Won't we?"

"Thank you for the conversation, Lord Frome," she said. "It has been most enlightening." Then she placed the canopy of the parasol between herself and him and walked away from her past.

"You are not vat I expected," Princess Sophia Augusta said in her thick German accent to George after they had left Prinny and her parents—and Susan—at Prinny's not-so-subtle urging. He wanted to glance back to see if Susan was all right, praying she hadn't been further snubbed by Prinny, but he refrained. He must show no sign of weakness to Prinny or his royal guests. This afternoon was going to require subtlety.

"What did you expect?" George asked as he nodded at a few acquaintances.

"Someone older. Fatter." She shrugged. "It is vat happens, you know. These marriages."

"Ah," George replied. It confirmed George's suspicions that Prinny hadn't told Prince Ernst that George was already betrothed—not when they'd arrived before George's actual wedding to Susan had occurred. "Have you been to London before?" he asked, trying to keep some semblance of conversation going.

"*Nein*," she said. "No. It is not so pretty as Schönberg-Nusse, from vat I have seen so far. Although the prince's house, Carlton House—not a palace, you know, but a house—is very fine. I vas surprised to see it vas so. The gardens here are pleasant. The city, not so much."

"England's countryside might be more to your liking," George said, wondering how long he must remain with the princess before extricating himself from her company. "Or, perhaps, the pleasure gardens at Vauxhall."

"I hope it is as you say, if I am to spend so much of my time here," she replied. "I vould prefer to live in Schönberg-Nusse, but Papa says it is not possible. Not at first. So I vill adapt."

"Your English is very good—much better than my German," George said and then immediately regretted his comment, for it made it sound like they were working out their compatibility with each other. He discreetly looked about but couldn't see Susan anywhere.

"Thank you," the princess said. They strolled on in silence for a few minutes. Without any warning, Princess Sophia moved her hand into the crook of his arm, bringing them closer together, and then, even though she was nearly as tall as George, she tipped her head in such a way as to appear to be gazing up at him demurely. She batted her eyelashes slowly, leaving George wondering what the equivalent German word for *coquette* was.

It was also clear that Prinny and her parents had sent her on a mission to secure her quarry.

"You are a young man and handsome," she said. "I have seen portraits of the princes of England, and I vas not happy. But now that vee are here and I see you for myself, I approve. You vill do."

"Princess Sophia," George began. "Before you say any more, you must allow me to speak. I'm afraid you have been misinformed, for, despite the assurances you and your parents were given, I never agreed to this marriage."

"Vat?" she exclaimed, any remains of the coquette he'd witnessed before vanishing in an instant. She turned to face him fully, and her grip on his arm tightened. "I do not believe you!"

"It's the truth, nonetheless."

"You cannot say that! Vee have come all this vay, on a dreadful journey, leaving my beautiful Schönberg-Nusse and friends and my—" she stopped abruptly, leaving George wondering what—or whom—she'd nearly mentioned. "I vould never have agreed to any of this, but Papa insisted; he said he must have the assurance from the English that his home, my home, vill be safe from the vile, little Frenchman. It must happen! It is the only option. That fool you call your prince promised. Papa promised. It must be so!" Her eyes welled up, much to George's chagrin.

Dealing with a crying woman was not his favorite activity during the best of times, but he was completely helpless knowing how to deal with a crying German princess. He was suddenly grateful Susan wasn't prone to crying, although he suspected all females were inclined to weep a bit at times. "Forgive me, Princess Sophia," he said in as soothing a voice as he could muster. "I do not wish to cause you any distress, and I suspect that you are as much a pawn in all of this as I, but I am firm in my refusal. I cannot and will not be moved. I'm sorry."

"You do not understand," she cried, tears streaming down her face now. She let go of his arm and, instead, gripped both of his hands in her own. Tightly. "It must vork," she said with intensity. "I vill give you an heir. Two, if you like. And then you are free; you understand? You are not old and disgusting. I vill do that for you. And then you are free, and I can be free too. You can be vith the voman you brought today, or you can choose another. I do not care! But vee must marry! Vee must!"

"Princess—" George said.

"What a cad you are, Aylesham, causing our lovely foreign princess to cry so. Lord Cosgrove at you service, Your Highness." Lord Cosgrove, a terrible rake whom George could barely abide, walked over and bowed to the two of them.

Princess Sophia quickly dropped George's hands and dashed away her tears before turning to face Cosgrove, her expression regal and lovely, even as a few tears still streaked down her face.

Cosgrove took her hand in his and placed a lingering kiss upon it. "We met yesterday, Princess Sophia, if you'll recall."

"I remember you, of course, Lord Cosgrove," she said.

"I'm glad to hear it," he said with a too-charming smile. He handed her his handkerchief. "I know *I* remember *you* very well. I see you have captured our fair country's *most illustrious* bachelor, and so quickly too. I commend you."

"Vat is this '*illustrious*?" she asked, dabbing at her eyes.

"Notable, esteemed, exalted—" Cosgrove began.

"Pursued, ensnared," George murmured to himself, fingering his quizzing glass.

Cosgrove shot a sly glance at him. "Aylesham, I believe I see a gentleman over there beckoning to you." He nodded, gesturing to an area behind George, but George wouldn't give him the satisfaction of turning around. "I wonder if you should see what he wants. And while you are thus occupied, perhaps Princess Sophia would allow me to show her more of the garden? Perhaps I may have more success lifting her spirits than it appears you have."

"Aylesham vas to tell me of the sights of London. Perhaps there are some that might interest me; I do not know. I am beginning to doubt it very much." She glanced accusingly at George before shrugging at Cosgrove.

"Get yourself a drink, Aylesham, and see what that gentleman wants. In the meantime, I will discuss the *attractions* of London with Princess Sophia." He offered her his elbow, and she slid her hand into its crook.

"Thank you for speaking to me," Princess Sophia said to George, blinking back the few tears that remained, her face blank as she spoke the words. "I expect vee shall speak again."

George watched as vile Lord Cosgrove and Princess Sophia disappeared into the crowd. He didn't need to look for a gentleman behind him beckoning to him. Cosgrove had used the weakest of ruses.

George needed but a moment to collect his thoughts now that he'd been freed of Princess's Sophia's company. He needed to find Susan and see how she had been faring on her own.

He searched the crowd for her but couldn't see her. He spied Prince Ernst and Princess Eugenia—they had progressed farther into the garden and were now in conversation with some of Prinny's other guests. Prinny wasn't with them, and that made the knot in George's stomach tighten.

Where the devil was Susan?

Susan had barely walked away from Lord Frome when she encountered the Prince Regent. "Ah, you're still here are you? Miss—?" He waited for her to say her name, pointing out once again that she had not been included when everyone had been formally introduced to each other, and her presence had barely been acknowledged.

"Jennings," she said. "Miss Susan Jennings."

"Oh, that's right," the Prince Regent said with a succinct nod. "An acquaintance of Aylesham, apparently."

"Yes," she said. Having never conversed with royalty before today, she had only Lady Walmsley's instructions to go by. Better to start small and get a feel for the conversation, she decided, even though the Prince Regent knew very well that she and George were betrothed.

"Walk with us, won't you, Miss Jennings?" the prince said.

It was a command disguised as an invitation. Susan swallowed. "Certainly, Your Royal Highness."

He clasped his hands behind him, and they headed in the opposite direction of the one George and Princess Sophia had taken.

"Such an honorable gentleman, Aylesham," the prince mused aloud. "So generous of his time and talents—and coffers—for his monarch and country."

"Yes," Susan said.

"Such an honest, loyal, and generous nobleman, what? You must be as proud of him as we are," the prince said.

"I am," Susan replied.

"We're *sure* you are." The prince nodded at her, his eyes huge and innocent looking. The prince didn't know that Susan had five brothers and recognized that look instantly. "Why, we were just saying to someone the other day—Aylesham has accomplished *so much* in our behalf. We must certainly reward him."

"He doesn't do anything for his country expecting to receive a reward," Susan said. She realized the minute the words left her lips that they were true.

"Oh, we agree with you *entirely*," the Prince Regent exclaimed. "And where are you from, pray, Miss Jennings?" he asked, changing the subject. "We do not recall seeing you, let alone meeting you before today."

"Lincolnshire, Sir," Susan said. "My father, Viscount Thurlby's, family seat is called Alderwood."

"Alderwood, hm." The Prince Regent tapped his chin in thought. "Alderwood. Can't recall it. But Lincolnshire, you say? That's a far cry from Aylesham's own family estate. How *did* the two of you meet?"

And there it was.

"We first became acquainted last year at the wedding of the Earl of Cantwell and Lady Elizabeth Spaulding," she said.

"Hm," the prince said again, obviously unhappy with her answer, as it implied a relationship longer than the one they'd actually had and hobbled the prince's theory. "And have you been in Town long, Miss Jennings?"

Susan drew upon Athena, needing the qualities George had described. "Long enough," she said. She gave the prince the wide-eyed look he'd given her previously.

The Prince Regent's nostrils flared. "You are very self-assured," he said in an uncomplimentary way. "We would remind you to whom you are speaking, lest you become too familiar in your tone. Additionally, if we are not mistaken, and we *know for a fact* that we are not, Aylesham's invitation was for him alone, and yet you are here. Thus far, we have extended a welcome to you"—he looked her up and down with obvious disgust—"regardless of the fact that we could have you escorted from the property."

This was not a veiled threat. The Prince Regent was extremely displeased by her presence here, but then, she and George had known this would be the case. "I understand, Sir, and I thank you for your hospitality," she said as meekly as she could and then waited to see if the prince would call for footmen to usher her from the premises.

"We hope you are of a sound constitution, Miss Jennings, for we fear you will be facing quite a disappointment this afternoon. We expect to make an announcement that will, sadly, change the plans we know you have for Monday—and for your future as well. Good afternoon." He gave a slight nod of his head, which Susan belatedly remembered was a sign of dismissal, so she curtsied deeply. It was a bit tricky with her parasol, but she managed it, nonetheless.

The prince sauntered off.

She turned her parasol so the canopy kept her face shielded from the majority of the guests and then skirted along the perimeter of the area where the guests were mingling. She had thought her encounter with Lord Frome bad enough, but after her conversation with the Prince Regent, she needed a few minutes alone to regain her composure. Lady Walmsley hadn't precisely covered the topics of "Encountering the Man Who Broke Your Heart" or "Finding Yourself Threatened by Your Monarch" during their tutorial yesterday.

After watching George leave with Princess Sophia and having walked the opposite direction with Lord Frome and an entirely different direction with the Prince Regent, there was only one direction left, so that was the one she took. She began to hear the faint notes of a string quartet she hadn't heard before and followed the sound, eventually eyeing the musicians. There was a buffet table of refreshments not far from their location, and she thought getting a drink of punch might allow her to appear to have a purpose rather than merely wandering aimlessly about on her own.

No one seemed to pay any heed to her, which was precisely what she wanted, and her parasol helped further in that regard. She had years of experience in making herself invisible—it had been a way to leave and find a quiet place to be alone, like the time she'd met George—and it worked for her this afternoon too. At least for the present, while she pondered her conversations with Lord Frome and the Prince Regent.

The pastries at the refreshment table looked delicious, and although she wasn't particularly hungry after the negative encounters she'd had, she doubted she'd ever be at Carlton House again, so she decided to indulge. She picked up a small plate and selected a lemon tart and a small slice of shortbread, took a cup of punch from the serving girl stationed near the punchbowl, and then located a small table on the farthest side of the grounds where she could sit alone and eat in relative peace, with her back once again discreetly turned toward the guests.

She had just taken her first bite of the lemon tart when she heard a conversation between a man and a woman behind her. Their words gradually grew louder, so she assumed the couple speaking was moving closer to her table. And as they were speaking German, it was easy to narrow down the possibilities of who the man and woman were.

In an ironic turn, Prince Ernst and Princess Eugenia seated themselves at the table next to Susan's. She adjusted the canopy of her parasol to hide herself further and then took another bite of lemon tart. The prince and princess were not having a pleasant conversation, to say the least, if the tone of their words was any indication.

Susan lowered her head and sipped from her cup. To be sitting so close to the guests of honor and to witness their heated conversation would turn awkward if they realized they were seated near the woman who was interfering with their daughter's marriage to George.

She could only pick at her shortbread, her appetite having fled at the arrival of the prince and princess. Perhaps it might be best if she left to go search for George . . . but then she decided to stay where she was and not draw attention to herself for the time being, especially after the conversation she'd just had with the Prince Regent. She kept nibbling on her shortbread to look busy in case anyone noticed her seated here—although she doubted that would happen—while Prince Ernst and Princess Eugenia's conversation in German droned on.

By the time she'd finished her tart and shortbread, the Germans' conversation had begun to subside, so Susan took a final sip of her punch and rose to her feet, hoping to slip away unnoticed from her table.

Unfortunately, her exit wasn't going to occur the way she'd hoped. Prince Ernst recognized her at last and nodded at her with a smile that didn't quite reach his eyes. She hadn't been fully and properly introduced to them, so she supposed the prince's condescending nod was more than she'd expected.

Princess Eugenia only looked at her with puckered lips, as though she'd just eaten something sour, then said something in German under her breath.

Prince Ernst smirked.

Susan offered a slight curtsy to him and then to Princess Eugenia. Then, adjusting her parasol so that it would shield her face from their Royal Highnesses—her own little cut direct toward the German royals—she went in search of George. There was much she needed to tell him.

Chapter 13

Despite his best efforts to find Susan, George kept being pulled into conversations with others with whom he was acquainted. He hardly remembered with whom he had spoken or what had been said—just the usual drivel common at these types of gatherings.

That is, until he encountered the Earl of Iverson. George and Susan and Lady Walmsley had attended a musicale at Iverson's home earlier in the week.

"Aylesham," Iverson said when he encountered George. "Well met."

"Good afternoon, Iverson," George said. Iverson was a decent chap, and although they weren't close friends, George respected him. He knew the man to be a friend of the Earl of Cantwell, and that went a long way, in George's estimation, of approving of the man.

"You appear to be in rather a hurry," Iverson said. "Care if I join you while you walk?"

"Not at all," George said.

They walked in the direction George had last seen Susan. "Quite a fine thing, this business with Bonaparte on the verge of victory at last," Iverson said. "It certainly has been a long time in coming."

"Agreed," George replied. "There is still much more to be done though."

"Assuredly," Iverson said. "Case in point—our royal friends from the Continent who are the prince's special guests," he added, lowering his voice. "Would they be here if they didn't think allying themselves with England would benefit them now and in the future?"

George didn't reply.

"I have it on good authority that you, specifically, are the alliance they are looking to broker with Prinny," Iverson said.

"So I have been led to believe," George said, fingering his quizzing glass.

"In addition, there is more to it than a mere alliance," Iverson whispered. "I do not know what precisely that is, but in some way, it all hinges on *you*, my good fellow. I would beware, if I were you."

"Thank you for the warning, Iverson," George replied softly. "Your words affirm my own suspicions."

A liveried footman approached them at that moment. "The Prince Regent wishes to speak with you, Your Grace," the footman said, directing his words to George. "He is expecting you under the canopy on the south side of the garden. If you will follow me, Your Grace."

"Duty beckons," George said with a slight shrug.

"My best regards," Iverson said.

"Thank you, Iverson." George then followed the footman to a luxuriously arrayed canopy. In the distance, he could faintly hear a string quartet providing the music for the afternoon, and it appeared that a few couples might be dancing in the direction from which the music was coming. He still couldn't see Susan.

On the other hand, Prinny was more than visible. He was sprawled in a plush chair atop a low dais, legs splayed in a relaxed manner, fanning himself and tapping his foot along with the music. Apparently, he'd given up mingling with his guests for the moment.

The footman bowed and left.

George stepped under the canopy.

"Come, join us, Aylesham," Prinny said, pointing to a chair next to the dais. "We see you've already abandoned your duties. Where is Princess Sophia?"

"She preferred the company of Lord Cosgrove to me, Sir," George said.

"Cosgrove?" Prinny exclaimed. "We told *you* to escort Princess Sophia. Poorly done, Aylesham. We can't have Cosgrove sniffing about the princess, now, can we, what? Another one of those apple tarts, girl," he called to the serving girl who stood just outside the canopy. "In fact, make it two."

The girl dashed off, and Prinny kept on fanning himself. With his free hand, he gestured toward the guests outside the canopy. "Everyone wants something, Aylesham. All of those people. You. Prince Ernst. Cosgrove. Even *we* want certain things—like an apple tart at present. Ah, thank you, girl," he said as the serving girl returned with not only two apple tarts but a lemon tart and some shortbread biscuits as well and set the plate on the small table next to Prinny's chair on the dais. "Well done. We will see you are rewarded."

She blushed and curtsied and scampered out of the way.

"You see, Aylesham? Even that serving girl wants something, for if you think she was providing us with more than we asked for out of some sort of inward generosity, you would be mistaken. Have a tart." Prinny set his fan aside and picked up one of the apple tarts, taking a large bite that left barely half the tart remaining.

George picked up the lemon tart and took a bite, though not as big as the one Prinny had taken.

"Mmm," Prinny said. "Cook has truly outdone herself today. Excellent. Very tasty."

"Indeed," George said. It was the truth anyway.

Prinny polished off the rest of the tart and selected a shortbread biscuit. "You know, Aylesham," he said after chewing and swallowing, "we had our man run a brief errand for us the other day. What with the early arrival of Prince Ernst Leopold and Princess Eugenia Augusta and their *enchanting* daughter Princess Sophia Augusta—well, we thought to do you a favor, what?"

"And what favor would that have been, Sir, as I have already informed you of my imminent marriage, to which you have agreed to attend?" George asked, feigning innocence but knowing full well where Prinny was headed with this.

"Come, man! You've seen the chit with your own eyes now!" Prinny exclaimed. "A German princess of the highest quality and everything a duke could want. We chose to give you every opportunity to receive the reward your prince and monarch wished to bestow upon you before you made a rash and unfortunate decision." He gave George his most benevolent monarch look—a look George had seen as recently as last week and didn't believe for one second now either.

"However," Prinny continued, taking a moment to brush shortbread crumbs from his waistcoat, "our man was unsuccessful in his errand." Now he looked up and directly at George, one eyebrow raised in accusation. "We sent him to obtain a special license in yours and the Princess Sophia's names, you see, but he was informed it would not be possible, as a special license had *already* been issued to the Duke of Aylesham—that would be *you*, of course—and a Miss Susan Jennings on the *previous Friday afternoon*." He leaned forward imperiously in his chair, and George tried to ignore the dab of apple custard on his regal chin. "That would be the afternoon you were meeting with *us*, *here* at Carlton House, declaring yourself betrothed, *what*?"

His Royal Highness was decidedly *not* happy, but George refused to allow himself to get caught in Prinny's trap so easily, despite his monarch's steely look. "You know as well as I that a man can be betrothed and not have acquired a special license to wed yet," he said with equanimity, hoping it would be enough to appease Prinny for the moment. "The options are varied: banns, common licenses—"

"The *very afternoon* following our meeting," Prinny repeated. "*Immediately following* our meeting. *Directly following* our meeting. And yet you had assured us that you were *already betrothed* to Miss Jennings, *what*? And while *we were not convinced*, we allowed that we would not judge you to be dishonest and dishonorable to us. Your sovereign. Do you recall *that part* of our conversation?"

"Yes, Sir," George said.

"And so, *once again*, we will ask you: fully aware now that Miss Jennings is only recently arrived in London after spending *years* in Lincolnshire, *when* did the two of you form this tender regard for one another?" His eyes bored into George.

George stared back at Prinny, trying to find the words that would call his monarch's bluff. He *refused* to lose the battle now. He refused to marry Princess Sophia, especially now that he'd discovered that marriage to Susan was *precisely* what he wanted. After all his years of disappointment, he simply *knew* it to be true. "Miss Jennings and I met last summer at the wedding of the Earl of Cantwell and Lady Elizabeth Spaulding. Our time together was insightful and passionate, and our connection has grown since then. In truth, I love her. I am not a young cub—I have searched the marriage mart for years, and I know my mind in this matter."

Prinny's countenance took on a gray tinge. "How delightful," he said, sounding as though he were growling from the back of his throat. "You say you know your mind. Despite your claim in this regard, Aylesham, *it is our wish* that you become acquainted with Princess Sophia Augusta. *There are benefits to us all* from an alliance with her. Do you understand us?"

"I fail to see where it benefits me when I love another lady," George said.

"The money!" Prinny exclaimed. "The family connection to royalty, the status amongst the other royals on the Continent, the governing alliances that can be formed, the land . . . Need I go on?"

"What if I care not a whit for those things?" George asked. He suddenly remembered Susan's reply to him when he'd tried this very tactic on her at the beginning of all of this: *I never aspired to be a duchess*. He was struck by the insight the thought now gave him into his own vanity and arrogance.

"Become acquainted with the princess, and look to the benefits that can be afforded to all of us! We *command* you!" Prinny nearly yelled, pounding his fist on the table and making the plate of tarts jump, his complexion having gone from gray to florid. "We hoped you would be pleased with your reward and cannot understand how you can choose a . . . a . . ." He waved his hand back and forth as if trying to grasp the right word out of the air. "A *presumptuous spinster* who can barely be considered of any rank: *Miss* Jennings, daughter of a lowly viscount who's been absent forever—*and who shows up at our house uninvited*."

One couldn't go about picking fights with one's monarch, unfortunately, or George would be sorely tempted to plant a facer on His Royal Highness for his insulting characterization of Susan. He clenched his fists at his side instead.

"It was *I* who invited Miss Jennings to accompany me," George said as politely as he could through teeth clenched as tightly as his fists, "as I concluded that, after your *having insisted upon attending our nuptials*, it must surely have been an *oversight* on your part to exclude her." He would *not* allow Susan to be blamed for her presence here.

"Miss Jennings this! Miss Jennings that!" The voice of Prince Ernst Leopold cut through the conversation. George turned abruptly and watched the prince and princess storm their way under the canopy to join them. "Ve vere assured that our daughter vould be married to England's most eligible duke—but ven ve arrive, ve find no such thing! Vee are appalled at the deceit! *And vhere is our daughter*?"

Susan had wound her way through the various groups of guests who were mingling amongst each other and had covered a great deal of garden but had been unsuccessful locating George thus far—how a lazy, self-indulgent monarch could have so many people willing to bow and scrape to him, she didn't know—and then, finally, she noticed that an unusually large group of guests had begun congregating near an opulent canopy on the opposite side of the garden. Clearly, something was happening to create such interest, and Susan suspected it had to do with the Prince Regent's royal visitors, and that had to mean that George was nearby. She hurried off in that direction.

The number of people near the canopy had multiplied further by the time she got there, which meant it was going to be difficult maneuvering through the crowd. She closed her parasol and began discreetly—or not so discreetly—pushing her way closer to the canopy, as the words *marriage* and *duke* and *fraud* swirled about her and people shushed each other so they could hear better.

Lord Frome materialized at her side. "Curious to see the results of your little mutiny against Prinny?" he murmured in her ear. "I fear you may have caused an international incident."

"Don't be absurd," she answered, even though his words echoed her own concerns precisely and made her insides constrict. She might very well be complicit in this uproar by having agreed to accompany George here today. She should have refused when George had asked, but she had been unable to say no to him, moved by his encouragement that she be the woman who had shown such bravado when she'd first met him.

The difference, of course, was that she hadn't known he was the Duke of Aylesham when they'd first met. He'd merely been an arrogant gentleman in her mind. Here, now, Susan knew full well she was defying the ruling monarch of her country. She was interfering with visiting royalty.

She belatedly wondered if such things could be construed as acts of treason . . . Could they? She didn't think so, but what a time for that thought to occur to her!

She glanced at Frome, who was eyeing her with the satisfied look of someone who'd just witnessed his opponent's comeuppance. "I'm so glad I didn't marry you," she said and pushed past him.

As she got closer to the canopy, she could make out some of Prince Ernst's angry words and the Prince Regent's impassioned replies. She finally broke through the crowd.

"George," she exclaimed in relief and hurried to his side. He drew her next to him and placed his arm around her shoulder, but his attention was fixed on the exchange occurring between the two princes.

Prince Ernst was fairly vibrating with fury. "Vee travel all this vay, assured of promises by *you*"—he pointed at the Prince Regent—"at risk of battles and soldiers and all kinds of danger only to arrive and find our assurances are vorth"—he snapped his finger—"nothing!"

"Now, Ernst, as we have explained to Aylesham here—" the Prince Regent began.

"My daughter is a princess! Her blood is royal! How dare he"—he now pointed at George—"refuse her and disobey his monarch!"

"Papa!" Princess Sophia suddenly pushed through the crowd and under the canopy to join them, pulling a smug-looking gentleman with her. "Do not vorry. It is all going to be fine after all! I *do not need* to marry Aylesham!"

"Vat are you talking about, Sophia?" Prince Ernst exclaimed.

"I can marry the Earl of Cosgrove," she said. "Vee are agreed on this."

The final puzzle piece fell into place for Susan.

The Earl of Cosgrove, which was apparently the name of the smug-looking gentleman with the princess, bowed deeply to Prince Ernst and Princess Eugenia and then bowed to the Prince Regent. "It is as she says, Your Royal Highnesses," he said. "I have offered for Princess Sophia Augusta, and she has accepted."

"Cosgrove," the Prince Regent said in a warning voice. "You are meddling in matters that do not concern you."

"He is but an *earl*, Sophia!" Princess Eugenia, who had been silent up to this point, cried out. "That is but a *count* back home! Almost a *nothing*!"

"An *earl*, bah! *No*!" Prince Ernst spat. "Not vhen vee vere promised a duke of the highest privilege and vealth."

Cosgrove's smug expression faded a bit.

Susan glanced at George. He seemed willing to merely watch as the others did the talking. "George," she whispered; there were things she needed to tell him, and the sooner the better.

He glanced at her but returned his attention to the dramatic tableau before them.

"But, Mama, Papa!" Princess Sophia cried. "I *do not like* the duke. He is . . . vhat is the vord? *Hochnäsig*. Haughty, that's it. Boring. I only meet him today, and already, I can tell. But Cosgrove, I meet yesterday; he is charming and fun, and *I think I can learn to love him*. It is good!"

Susan watched George's eyebrows rise at Princess Sophia's insults, but he didn't seem particularly upset by them. Cosgrove's smug expression brightened. It was then that Susan observed that Princess Sophia's lips were pinker and more swollen than they had been earlier, and her hair was a bit disheveled.

Ah.

"Love!" Prince Ernst spat. "Vhen has marriage ever been about *love*?" he said, earning an angry glower from Princess Eugenia.

"Here, here," the Prince Regent chimed in at Prince Ernst's remarks, and Susan bit her lip. She knew full well the prince's marriage to Princess Caroline of Brunswick was a complete disaster. The two of them loathed each other and had from the very start.

"George!" Susan repeated, a touch louder this time.

"Yes?" he asked, still keeping an eye on the royals.

"There is something I must tell you," she said.

"Can't it wait?" he asked. "Things are a bit tenuous at the moment."

"No, it can't. In fact, it's rather urgent."

"Vhat are you two talking about?" Prince Ernst snapped, directing his attention away from his errant daughter and Lord Cosgrove to George and Susan. "You have tried my patience enough today! And vhy is that vile . . . person . . . still here?" he asked, pointing accusingly at Susan. "You vere not invited; you are not velcome. Vere ve in Schönberg-Nusse I vould have you banished for your brazen actions toward your ruler!" He glared at the Prince Regent. "You should do something. But no, you sit there and vait for someone else to deal vith the problem."

Susan stood completely still after Prince Ernst's verbal thrashing. She dared not speak. And yet, she had to talk to George. *Urgently.*

"How do you respond to Prince Ernst, Aylesham?" a clearly offended Prince Regent asked.

Silence hung heavy in the air.

Prinny snapped his fingers.

A footman materialized at his side. "Fetch two of the strongest doormen," he said, his eyes boring into Susan.

It was time to act.

"How dare—" George began before Susan could do anything.

She placed her hand on George and gave him an apologetic glance. "It seems Athena is going to speak without giving you forewarning," she murmured quickly. She took a step forward. "Allow me to apologize, Your Royal Highness, for the high-handed manner in which I included myself in today's festivities. But before I am escorted from the premises, I would ask that you allow me to share something with you"—she gestured around her—"and the others present."

When the prince didn't immediately cut her off, she continued. "You see, Sir, I overheard a conversation," she said, doing her best to ignore Prince Ernst, although she could feel his heated glare. "It began like this: '*Ihre Tochter ist mit diesem faulen Schwein weggegangen*, Cosgrove.' 'Your daughter has gone off with that lazy swine, Cosgrove,'" she translated for those who may not speak German.

"*What*?" the Prince Regent exclaimed, staring at her incredulously.

"I take offense to that," Cosgrove said, looking aggrieved.

"*Ach*," Princess Sophia crooned to Cosgrove. "Do not fret. She knows nothing."

"There is more that was said." Susan herself had barely believed what she had overheard Prince Ernst and Princess Eugenia say. Her German wasn't as proficient as her French, but it was still excellent enough to understand that she had needed to pay attention. Eavesdrop, as it were.

"Speak up, Miss Jennings," the Prince Regent said impatiently. "We are most curious about what you overheard."

The murmur of the crowd beyond the canopy grew louder.

"Perhaps we should take this conversation inside," George suggested.

"We agree," the Prince Regent replied, the scowl on his florid face deepening. "And *then* we want a full accounting from *you*, Miss Jennings, after which you will leave Carlton House, and we will decide what consequences await you." He looked smugly at Prince Ernst in an apparent show of regal strength.

Susan replied with a curtsy. She'd said enough for now.

The Prince Regent hoisted himself from his chair and stomped down the dais and out from under the canopy, leading the way for the others, the crowds beyond parting as he did so. Prince Ernst and Princess Eugenia followed. As they passed George and Susan, Prince Ernst grabbed Susan's arm. "Opportunist. Eavesdropper," he hissed.

"You will remove your hand from my betrothed," George said threateningly.

"Or *vhat*?" Prince Ernst shot back, but he dropped Susan's arm. He and the princess stormed off.

"Papa, vait!" Princess Sophia cried, hurrying after him, with Cosgrove trailing after her.

George took Susan's hand in his and gently rubbed her arm where Prince Ernst had gripped it. "Well, Athena, you certainly have a gift for overhearing private conversations. Shall we?"

Susan sighed. "I fear we must."

They followed the others into Carlton House.

George held Susan's hand as they walked into Carlton House, confused by the words he'd just heard. He had little time to sort out their implications before Susan faced Prinny's questions. He needed to be prepared to think on his feet and support her any way he could. He sorely wished he'd paid closer attention to her when she'd said she had something urgent to tell him. At the time, it had seemed to him he was already witnessing something that had a sense of urgency.

Once inside, George glanced at Susan. She wore a dignified expression, tinged with what George perceived as worry.

They followed Prinny into the library off to the right of the lower vestibule, and a footman nearby closed the door behind them with an echoing thud. Prinny immediately swung around and faced Susan. George squeezed her hand before letting go, hoping it would give her the encouragement she would need for what was to follow.

"Miss Jennings," Prinny said in his most princely tone, "we wish to hear from your own lips precisely *where* you were, *what* you were doing, and the *exact words* you overheard. Do you understand us?"

"I do," she replied.

"Well?" he said, frowning. "What are you waiting for?"

George stepped closer to her and rested his hand on her back.

Susan took a deep breath. "I was taking refreshment alone," she said, and George was already proud of her for the calmness of her tone and demeanor. Not a small feat one's first time facing royalty. He doubted the mute or the giggler could manage this with the same level of composure. "Shortly thereafter, Prince Ernst and Princess Eugenia seated themselves at the table next to mine. They didn't realize I was there." She paused.

"Yes, yes, you were taking refreshment," Prinny said, gesturing with his hand to pick up the pace. "We want to know what you overheard. Get on with it. We are running out of patience."

George felt Susan straighten her back and watched her lift her chin. "You said you wanted to know where we were and what we were doing. I am only trying to be thorough, Sir, for your benefit."

"So we did," Prinny said crossly. "Thank you for pointing that out to us. Continue with your explanation."

"As I told you outside," she said, "I heard Prince Ernst inform Princess Eugenia that Princess Sophia had gone off with Lord Cosgrove."

"You phrased it more colorfully the first time, Miss Jennings," Prinny said. "Were you using hyperbole?"

"Not at all, Sir," Susan said. "Do you wish me to quote the conversation exactly?"

"What do *you* think?" Prinny snapped.

"Very well," Susan replied with a slight nod of her head. "As I mentioned before, I heard Prince Ernst say, '*Ihre Tochter ist mit diesem faulen Schwein weggegangen*, Cosgrove.' '*Your daughter has gone off with that lazy swine, Cosgrove.*' Princess Eugenia replied to him, saying, '*Sie ist auch deine Tochter. Sie weiß, dass sie ihre Verlobung mit dem Herzog sicherstellen soll. Dumme Gans.*' '*She is your daughter too. She knows she's supposed to ensure her betrothal to the duke. Stupid goose.*'"

"Mama!" Princess Sophia gasped.

George watched in fascination as Princess Eugenia glared at her daughter. Cosgrove, in the meantime, looked unnerved and sidled slightly away from Princess Sophia.

"You are going to listen to this desperate woman? *Die Drache*?" Prince Ernst exclaimed, pointing at Susan.

Susan—George's own Athena—looked directly at Prince Ernst. "I am not desperate in the least," she said in a commanding, wonderfully powerful voice. "And referring to me by an insulting name like dragon only makes you look small."

"How dare you speak to me that vay! She lies!" Prince Ernst roared, first at Susan and then at Prinny. "You vill *not* break our agreement over the lies of a *pathetic nobody! An interloper*!"

"We suggest you remain quiet for now, Ernst," Prinny hissed, his florid features tense. "We wish to hear what the lady has to say to us, and then we will respond accordingly." George noted with interest that Prinny had referred to Susan as a lady, which could be an implied step upward in Prinny's estimation of her—or, most likely, was merely a tactic to use against Prince Ernst.

Susan, seemingly unfazed, returned her attention to Prinny. "Prince Ernst then said, *'Nur der Herzog hat genügend Geld, um uns zu bezahlen, was wir versprochen hatten, den fetten englischen Prinzen zu bezahlen.'* 'Only the duke has sufficient funds to pay us what we promised we would give the fat English prince.'"

"You needn't have translated *that bit* for us; we *know* what it means!" the Prince Regent snapped. "We speak German *fluently*!"

George feared his monarch might have a heart seizure at any moment, so purple was his face.

"I'm sorry. I did not know," Susan said calmly.

"It would appear our guests made the same mistake about *you*," Prinny said with a huff. "You seem to have been underestimated in everyone's eyes. Is there more? We wish to hear everything our *esteemed royal guests* had to say about *their gracious host*."

"They said nothing more about you, Sir," Susan said.

"Ah," Prinny said sarcastically. "Well, we see everything quite clearly now. Quite clearly indeed. But we get the feeling there is more you are not telling us, and we wish to hear everything that was said. What is it?"

"Nothing of consequence," she said.

"What is it?" Prinny asked again, punctuating each word, his voice crescendoing.

George watched Susan's face pale, but she stood firmly. "Very well, I will tell you." She took another deep breath. "*'Sie müssen sie finden, bevor es zu spät ist,'* she said, still looking squarely at Prinny. *"Bevor diese alte Kuh ihn für sich sichert.'"* George wished he knew what she was saying. Blast him for not learning German. French and Latin had seemed plenty to him as a youth.

She swallowed and looked at Prinny. Prinny glanced at George and then back at Susan. "Pray, continue, Miss Jennings," he sneered.

Apparently, Prinny wanted George and the others to hear the translation from Susan's own lips.

"'*You must find her before it is too late. Before that old cow secures him for herself,*'" Susan said.

That was the final straw; George had heard enough. His selfish and vindictive monarch had made Susan say aloud those insulting words about herself because he'd failed in his royal marriage machinations. He was punishing her for the selfishness of himself and the others.

But before he could speak up, Susan continued. "In summary, Sir, based on what I overheard and what has been said since and setting any resulting political connections aside, *you* were expecting a great lot of money from Prince Ernst and Princess Eugenia for procuring a suitable husband of wealth and rank for their daughter, money they did not have. And *they* were expecting a great lot of money from the Duke of Aylesham in the form of an overly generous marriage settlement, owing to the fact that they were offering him a princess, whom they deemed valuable, money they would then use to pay what they had promised you and that would also provide them with the ability to continue living in the manner to which they were accustomed.

"So, in 'rewarding' the Duke of Aylesham with the so-called gift of a bride and the enticement of more wealth, you and Prince Ernst were actually expecting to receive more from the duke than he has already generously given in the service of the Crown and his country." Her tone was clear and firm, and all eyes were upon her. "There was no reward for him in any of this. Shame on you."

Oh, but she was magnificent, his Athena.

"Lest there be any confusion," George said to Prinny, "I *do not* intend to marry Princess Sophia, nor do I intend to bestow a gift of money or of any other sort on the prince of Schönberg-Nusse"—George refused to say the wretch's name—"as part of any marriage settlements—intended, imagined, or otherwise. I am marrying Miss Susan Jennings in three days' time, and that is the end of it."

"This is all your fault, Ernst! You gave me assurances!" Prinny bellowed at Prince Ernst.

"You gave me assurances too!" Prince Ernst bellowed back. "And I have dragged *meine Frauen* on a long journey at great expense. For nothing!"

"Cosgrove, vhere are you going?" Princess Sophia whispered a bit too loudly. They all turned at her words to see what was happening and spotted Cosgrove near the door, having been caught trying to make his escape.

"I, uh, perhaps this is not the time—"

"You aren't leaving me, are you?" she cried. "Vee vere to get a—what you call?—special license. *Die Heiratsurkunde.* It is what you said!"

"My apologies, dear princess, but I fear your attractions were much more . . . tempting, shall we say . . . when they included a dowry. It would appear now that there is none. And so, I will bid you adieu. You are better off without me." He shrugged.

"Cosgrove!" Princess Sophia cried, dashing after him as he slipped out the door. She stopped short of leaving, though, and turned to face the others in the room. "He has left, and I blame you all! He vas charming and funny and much more exciting than anyone back home, except my Friedrich. If I cannot marry Cosgrove and the boring, rich duke prefers his cow to a princess, I might as vell marry Count Friedrich." She flounced over to a chair and sat down in a huff.

Princess Eugenia hurried over to her daughter's side. "Now, now, *meine geliebte Tochter,* my darling one, these Englishmen—they are not for you. Vee see that now, don't vee, Ernst? Vhat a vaste of a journey. Did I not tell you it vould be so?" She shot daggers at her husband before turning her attention back to the princess. "Vee vill find someone for you. But not Friedrich!" She shuddered. "He is only a count, and he is so . . . so . . . vell, vee vill not say. But *not* Count Friedrich."

The door opened once again, and two large and extremely serious-looking doormen entered the room with the footman who'd been sent to fetch them following behind. Neither doorman was the one George and Susan had encountered at the entrance to Carlton House.

"Finally!" Prinny exclaimed under his breath. He gestured toward George and Susan. "The Duke of Aylesham and the *person* standing with him are leaving now. We wish you to assure us that they are gone afterward. Are we clear?"

"Yes, Your Royal Highness," one of the doormen said in reply, who, despite his elegant livery, looked like he could earn a nice living by prize fighting. The two of them approached, each taking a position on either side of George and Susan, and then waited. How two people could look both polite and menacing, George didn't know, but these two managed it.

And then his glorious Athena spoke. "We do not need an escort of any kind to leave, Sir," Susan said in a firm but respectful tone. "You may rest assured that the Duke of Aylesham and I will leave now. You have a garden full of guests to attend to, who are, no doubt, wondering why you have disappeared from your own party. I imagine they must wish to associate with your royal guests.

"Thank you for your hospitality this afternoon, Sir. It is my hope that you can set aside your disappointment from the events of this afternoon. I suspect that, with time, it will seem small in comparison to the other great worries that must come with responsibilities you bear as sovereign. At least, that is my hope." And then she fell into a deep curtsy.

It was a brief but elegant speech, George thought, after her eloquent summary of the circumstances—respectful but to the point. He decided it was a good time to leave the royals to themselves to resolve their regal problems.

"With your permission, Sir, Miss Jennings and I will excuse ourselves." He waited for Prinny to respond. He could feel the massive doorman breathing down his neck.

Prinny only nodded slightly.

George turned to Susan in a formal manner, bowed, and offered her his hand. "Allow me, my dear."

"Thank you, Your Grace." She placed her hand on his arm, and together they walked away, the two doormen following behind, regardless of Susan's earlier words.

They maintained their decorum, walked sedately up the grand staircase and through the great hall, and exited out the north front doors. The two doormen followed them outside and then stood watching them as they crossed the grounds to the street beyond.

"I hope you looked your fill," George whispered to Susan. "I highly doubt either of us will be invited to step foot in here again."

Susan chuckled, and George delighted in the sound. "I think I've had enough of Carlton House to last a lifetime," she replied.

"Shall we make a run for it, then?" he asked her.

She looked at him, startled. And then she laughed.

They didn't actually run—it would have been too unseemly for a duke and a future duchess to behave in such a manner near the royal residence, especially with the doormen as witnesses—but they did speed up their steps. As far as George was concerned, they couldn't get to his carriage fast enough.

"Once around the park, Bentley," George said to his coachman as he quickly assisted Susan into his carriage. "And then to Lady Walmsley's address."

"Very good, Your Grace," Bentley said.

And then they were on their way.

To freedom, at last.

Chapter 14

"We did it! I can scarcely believe we were successful!" Susan exclaimed as George set his hat on the opposite seat of the carriage and ran his fingers through his hair.

"You know, I think I may be able to breathe again. I don't think I've taken a real breath in days," he said. He toyed with his quizzing glass in a fanciful manner and then held it up to his eye and looked at her through it. "You, my dearest Susan, were magnificent, by the way. My Athena." He chuckled and let his quizzing glass drop. "Why didn't you ever tell me you spoke German?"

"You never asked," she replied drolly.

He laughed outright. "Here, allow me to get that out of the way." He reached for her parasol and leaned it up against his side of the carriage. "And let's rid you of that little bonnet too, shall we? Although, I will say it becomes you very well."

She reached up to remove the hatpins from her bonnet, but he gently moved her hands aside, kissing each one as he did so.

"Allow me," he said. He quickly dispatched the pins and settled the tiny bonnet on the seat next to his own hat. Susan thought it was lovely to see them side by side in that way.

George then settled back into the carriage seat and closed his eyes. "I'm free," he said, letting out a deep sigh. "What an amazing feeling it is to know I am actually *free* of Prinny's schemes. I doubt even Prinny can justify a scenario in which, one, I pay Prince Ernst for the so-called privilege of marrying his daughter so that, two, Prince Ernst can pay Prinny for the so-called privilege of having his daughter marry an English duke so that, three, Prince Ernst is in a position to pay Prinny *and me* some grand amount, supposedly benefiting us both greatly, which was what Prinny originally promised me. Essentially, I would be paying everyone, including myself. Saying it out loud makes it even more nonsensical." He ran his hand through his hair again, chuckling and shaking his head.

Susan smiled at him. She'd never seen the distinguished Duke of Aylesham look so relaxed, so entirely comfortable in his own skin as he did right now. She loved hearing him laugh and watching the tension leave his face.

She twisted the ruby ring on her finger. She could free him entirely right now if she chose.

"And the look on Prince Ernst and Princess Eugenia's faces when you began spouting German at them!" George laughed again. "It was brilliant! I shall remember that moment for the rest of my life. I suppose I should have at least suspected that as James Jennings's sister, the possibility existed that you might speak some German—" He stopped himself midsentence. "No, that's not true," he said. "I believe you are the first woman I have met without family connections to the German states to speak it. Now, *French* is another matter—*all* the young ladies speak a bit of French, of course."

"James and I studied languages together in our youth," Susan said. "He is the true linguist, not I . . . but I would never let him believe it and studied hard to best him. I even succeeded a time or two."

"I imagine you did, at that."

"Which reminds me," she said. "You never did tell me what your connection to my brother James is all about." She'd been so utterly preoccupied, it had slipped her mind until now.

"You never let anything get past you, do you?" George said.

She stared at him with as straight a face as she could.

He laughed. "Very well. For now, however, I am simply going to say that the war has made allies and friends of many whose paths may not have crossed otherwise. He and I—and Phillip Osbourne, as you'll recall from our memorable encounter last year—have been working together primarily for the Foreign Office."

"I'm sure there's more to it than that."

"There is, of course. Much more. But if I were to assure you that we shall wade into the subject more deeply at a later date, would you allow us to simply celebrate our victory over Prinny this afternoon?"

"Poor Prinny," she said, trying to hold back an unladylike grin.

"Such a disappointment this all turned out for him." George chuckled. "You know, he waxed philosophical this afternoon, telling me that everyone wants *something*. I'm certain he and Prince Ernst wanted easy fortunes. I suspect that was Cosgrove's motive too."

"What did the women want?" Susan asked.

"Hm, now *that* is more of a challenge, I confess, for I have little experience delving into the minds of females. Were I to guess, I would say that Princess Eugenia wanted what Prince Ernst wanted—the security and prestige that comes with wealth and connections. And I think Princess Sophia wanted anyone who wasn't the Duke of Aylesham. What is your opinion?"

Susan pondered his question. "I think Prinny is probably correct—everyone wants *something*. But I think sometimes the *heart* wants things it can't quite articulate, and we innately pursue what we *think* will satisfy that implicit want."

"I'm intrigued," George said. "Enlighten me."

"For instance," she said, "Prince Ernst wants to restore his wealth and status amid the chaos on the Continent, so *he thinks* he wants his only child to marry status and money and establish a personal alliance with England. I won't venture a comment on the Prince Regent."

"I can do that," George said. "Prinny wants everything, thinks he deserves everything, and wants it easily. Ergo, *he thought* he wanted me to marry Princess Sophia so he could obtain money for his debts without having to grovel to Parliament once again."

"I shall never repeat your words, Your Grace," Susan said with a smile, placing a finger over her lips. "I shouldn't want you on worse terms with the Prince Regent than you undoubtedly already are."

"Thank you," he said. "It is comforting to know I have your support."

"You will always have my support," she said softly.

Her words brought an air of unease into their conversation, and Susan decided it was best to get right to the point. She twisted the ruby ring again. "George," she said, "what *you* were wanting was freedom—from Prinny and from unwanted obligations. So what you pursued was a betrothal that would—"

"No," he interrupted. "Not a betrothal. A marriage."

"A *reason,"* she said, continuing, "to avoid the Prince Regent's trap. And now you have that freedom. I was merely a device to achieve that end." She slid the ring from her finger and looked at it. The ruby glowed with deep-red hues, looking nearly alive as the carriage wound its way through the streets to Lady Walmsley's, and the light from the carriage windows struck it from varying angles. The stone reminded her of her own heart right now, alive again after so long a time. "Now that you are free, it is only right and fitting that I release you from the betrothal. You are completely free." She handed him the ring.

He took it from her and studied it just as she had done. "My clever Susan," he said at last. "You think you know what *I wanted*, and I will concede that you are partly correct. I *wanted* to be free of Prinny. I *wanted* to be able to choose my own wife.

"When I was confronted by him less than a fortnight ago—it seems like eons now—I had but the merest moment to give him the name of my bride. And the name that came to me was Susan Jennings." He took her hand in his and kissed it. "And I believe what you described earlier is the truth: that my heart recognized what it wanted before it could articulate it, when I only saw an impertinent woman."

"Harpy, you mean," Susan said with a wry smile.

"True." He chuckled. "But back then, I was His Loftiness, wasn't I? I hope I am not quite that in your eyes anymore."

He drew Susan even closer and wrapped his arm about her shoulders, and she pressed against him, savoring the feel of him, the rise and fall of his breathing, and immersed herself in her love for him.

"My dear, clever Susan," he said. "I have been aware of my need to marry for years now and have spent a good deal of time looking for the woman who could be not only *a* duchess, but *my* duchess. I believe my heart recognized that woman before I could see her clearly for myself. And so, although we have known each other but a short time, I am completely certain that *you* are *my* duchess."

"Oh, George," Susan said on a sigh.

"When I proposed to you the first time, I made the arrogant assumption that you would consider yourself grateful to receive such an offer. My dearest Susan, this is not the time or place I ever envisioned myself proposing—a carriage ride certainly lacks the pomp and decorum such an occasion should warrant—and yet, in a way, that makes it the *most* appropriate place of all, utterly without pretense, for I do not wish another moment to go by without asking you if you will agree to be my wife—freely, of your own choosing."

"Oh, George," she repeated, laying her hand on his cheek. "I have not held on to girlish romantic dreams—they shattered for me years earlier. I came to the conclusion that such would not be my lot in life. But I have watched those dearest to me experience love, so I know it exists. And I have discovered, quite unexpectedly, that I love you, that my heart recognized what it longed for when my mind would not accept it."

"You love me?" George asked.

"You aren't content having heard my declaration already?" Susan asked. "You must hear it again? Very well. I love—"

"I love you too," he said, interrupting her. "Is it not strange? Despite our short acquaintance, which should seem problematic, I have no qualms whatsoever about expressing my ardent feelings to you and marrying you—if you will have me, that is. Will you?"

"I will," she said. "And gladly. I'm usually so practical, and this seems wildly impractical. And yet, I am absolutely confident in my answer."

"You don't need a day to mull it over? You have needed a day twice before, you know," he teased, a twinkle in his eye.

The Duke of Aylesham had a twinkle in his eye—and Susan loved him all the more for it. "Not at all," she replied. "I accept your proposal wholeheartedly."

"Then allow me," he said. He slid the ruby ring back on her finger. "There. That looks much better. I know how much you want to have your family present for the wedding, and I will honor your desires in this matter, although my preference would be to carry on as planned and marry this Monday."

"Oh, George," Susan said and then paused. "I keep saying that, don't I?"

"Yes, you do," he said. "You know, I never have liked my given name. But as everyone has always referred to me by my titles, it has never been a problem."

"Would you prefer—" Susan said.

"In fact," he continued, shifting on the seat a bit so they could nestle together more comfortably. "I think you are the only person who has ever used it. But when you say it, it feels right."

"Oh, George," she said again.

"Oh, Susan," he replied with a teasing grin, then his lips descended to hers, and she wrapped her arms around him and held him close and savored his lips and the fact that he was truly hers. The carriage gently rocked to and fro as it reached Lady Walmsley's house and came to a halt.

"Oh, *George*," she murmured.

No more words needed to be spoken.

A warning knock from Bentley on the roof of the carriage alerted George, and he raised his head to see what was going on.

"What's happening?" Susan murmured as she straightened up.

The door of Lady Walmsley's house was open, and a couple of unfamiliar people were at the bottom of the stairs with Lady Walmsley, Foster close behind, and appeared to be headed straight for his carriage. "We're under attack, it would seem," George said.

Susan peered around him. "It's Mama and Papa!" she cried. She began to scramble around him to get to the carriage door.

"Wait a moment, my dear," George said, setting his hand on her shoulder to gently hold her back. "Perhaps I may assist you with your hair first and put your bonnet back on."

"Oh, yes, of course," she replied, turning a shade of pink that George wanted to kiss into full bloom. Instead, he quickly smoothed a few wild curls and pinned her little bonnet into place, right before Bentley opened the carriage door and the group arrived.

George exited first, donning his hat and bracing himself for the introductions to come, and then offered his hand to Susan to assist her from the carriage.

She took his hand in hers before doing so. "George," she said in a tone much calmer than he'd expected, considering her state just a moment before, "please allow me to present my father, the Viscount Thurlby, and my mother, the Viscountess Thurlby." Her father, a tall, lanky fellow with astute eyes, bowed formally, and her mother, a lovely woman of middle years, curtsied deeply. "Papa, Mama, this is *my betrothed*, the Duke of Aylesham."

Her words now held new meaning for George and gave him a hope he'd never imagined before.

He offered a congenial bow to each of them. "I'm sure you have many questions," he said, "which I am only too happy to answer."

"Well then," Lady Walmsley said, clapping her hands together, "we shall have Mrs. Drake prepare a most excellent tea for us all. Foster—"

"I shall see that Mrs. Drake is informed," Foster replied. He retreated inside the house.

"Your parents have only just arrived," Lady Walmsley said as the rest of them headed back to the house. "I informed them that you and Aylesham were at a garden party at Carlton House with the Prince Regent and it would be a while before you returned. We were just about to settle in the parlor and get acquainted when we noticed the carriage through the window."

"What was it like, Susan?" her mother asked, linking her arm with Susan's. "Carlton House! And the Prince Regent too. How exciting!"

"A bit more exciting than we'd planned," Susan said, shooting a wry look at George.

"Indeed?" Lady Thurlby studied her daughter's face and then studied George. "I should like to hear all about it."

"And you shall," Susan said. "There is much to tell. Oh, but I am *so glad* you and Papa are here!"

"If you are amenable, Lord Thurlby, I would like to have a private word with you," George said. "Whenever it's convenient."

Before responding, Lord Thurlby, whose intense look hadn't lessened, glanced at his daughter. Susan smiled and nodded at him. His face lightened, much to George's relief. "I believe that can be arranged," Lord Thurlby said.

"Thank you," George said.

They all gathered in Lady Walmsley's parlor, with George seated quietly next to Susan on the small settee as he allowed her and her parents and Lady Walmsley to converse. Susan was interested in hearing about her siblings back home in Lincolnshire, especially Rebecca.

"Her leg is healing quite well thus far," Lady Thurlby told her. "No complications that the doctor can see, thank goodness. She misses you and sends her love, of course. I think she would be bored to tears by now were it not for that young man who found her and brought her home to us."

"I remember him," Susan said.

"I believe he feels a bit responsible for her well-being since he was the one who found her," Lord Thurlby said. "Decent fellow, I must say."

"He drops by regularly to check on her," Lady Thurlby added. "They converse a bit, and he reads to her. I do think she'd rather be here in London with you, Susan, but we must take what life hands us on occasion."

"Ah, here's tea," Lady Walmsley said as a maid entered the room with a large tray. Foster followed her.

"Anything more I can do for your guests, Lady Walmsley?" he asked.

Lady Walmsley glanced at each of her guests to get their reactions. "I think not, Foster. As long as Lord and Lady Thurlby's rooms are sufficiently prepared, we are fine."

He bowed and left the room.

Lady Walmsley began pouring tea for everyone.

"Do tell us about Carlton House, Susan," Lady Thurlby said. "Milk only, thank you, Lady Walmsley. We have read somewhat of the details leading up to today in the few letters you have sent us this past fortnight, and I am exceedingly curious to know everything that has happened since."

"Perhaps not every detail, Alice," Lord Thurlby said. "Or I suspect we'll be here until dawn. Although I will say I was exceedingly surprised to learn that my clever and sensible daughter had gotten herself betrothed after being in London less than a week."

"Did you ever stop to consider, Papa, that it is *precisely* because I *am* clever and sensible that I am betrothed?" Susan asked, reaching for the teacup Lady Walmsley was offering her and taking a sip. "Thank you, Aunt Margaret, it's perfect, as always."

George noted that Lady Thurlby's eyebrow rose nearly to her hairline when Susan referred to Lady Walmsley as Aunt Margaret.

"And you prefer milk, if I'm remembering correctly," Lady Walmsley said to George, oblivious to Lady Thurlby's surprised reaction.

"Yes, thank you," he responded, trying to keep his expression neutral. He was sorely tempted to laugh at Susan's question to her father. How magnificent she was!

"And you, Lord Thurlby?" Lady Walmsley asked.

"Milk and two lumps, thank you," Lord Thurlby said. "I'm waiting, and I'm all ears, daughter. Please explain."

"I have been quiet up until now," George said before Susan could speak. "But I feel I must speak. I will not pride myself in claiming to be either particularly clever or sensible these past several days, but I will wholeheartedly claim to be the *most fortunate* of men to be betrothed to your daughter. She is my other half. We still wish to marry this Monday and are grateful you are here to celebrate the joyous occasion with us and give us your blessing." He glanced at Susan. She was beaming at him.

"Well," Lord Thurlby said, "I believe there are particulars I am still interested in hearing first. But for now, that being said"—he raised his teacup in the air—"I will make a toast: to my beloved daughter and my soon-to-be son-in-law, should he pass my inspection. And assuming he does, may this Monday bring them a long and happy life together, full of love and respect . . . and may it provide me with more grandchildren."

"Papa!" Susan exclaimed.

"I'll drink to that," George said, clinking his teacup against Lord Thurlby's. "I do need an heir and a spare, at the very least." He took a sip of tea and watched in satisfaction as Susan's face turned bright red.

"Susan comes from fine, fertile stock, you know," Lord Thurlby said.

George nearly choked on his tea as he burst out laughing.

"Thomas, really," Lady Thurlby said with a chiding look. "Lady Walmsley and the Duke of Aylesham will think we have no propriety at all!"

"Not in the least, Lady Thurlby, I assure you," George said. He had never had a family. He had only vague memories of his father, and portraits of his mother and father hung at his county estate and at other properties, but he'd essentially had no relatives until this new heir apparent had been located in Van Diemen's Land. It was fascinating to watch Susan and her parents interact with each other, for he was seeing it all from a new perspective.

As of Monday, George would be married. He would have a wife and a family of his own. It would take some getting used to, but he expected he would adjust fairly easily, considering how congenial Susan's family was being, under the circumstances. He found he liked them already. He smiled to himself and took another sip of tea.

"I understand that he's a duke, and he's certainly handsome," Mama said after George and Papa had left the room to converse separately. "But, Susan! You've known him barely more than a week, and it would seem that most of that time your relationship with him was contentious rather than anything remotely romantic."

"That is true, Mama," Susan replied. "And yet, I couldn't be more certain. Of the *man*, Mama. If he were a duke or a dustman, it would make no difference to me."

"That is quite a declaration," Mama said. "But I will need more convincing to be at peace with what seems to me to be a rash decision."

"Perhaps I may shed some light on the matter," Aunt Margaret said. "I have known the Duke of Aylesham since he was a lad. My dear friend Lady Bledsoe came out with his mama, you see, and grieved terribly when her dear friend died in childbirth. She took a special interest in the boy and even more so after the death of his father. To lose both parents, and so young, too, well, it fairly breaks one's heart."

"I have heard of Lady Bledsoe," Mama said. "Although, I have never met her."

"She has been genuinely kind to me, Mama," Susan said. "As has everyone. I truly think if the Duke of Aylesham were known to have a bad reputation, any one of the fine ladies I've met thus far would have warned me." Susan realized as she said the words that they were true. "I know my own mind, Mama. I am completely at peace with the decision to marry the Duke of Aylesham on Monday, and I hope you and Papa will be too."

"Well," Mama said with a sigh, "if it were anyone but *you*, Susan, I would consider this marriage impulsive and of questionable judgment. But as it *is* you telling me all of this, and I can hear the conviction in your voice, I'm inclined to trust you, heaven help me."

"I'm so delighted!" Aunt Margaret exclaimed. "We have waited a long time for Aylesham to find the wife he deserves. And I believe wholeheartedly Susan is that person."

"I rather care more that *he* is the husband *Susan* deserves," Mama said.

"Oh, Mama!" Susan said. She set her teacup down and knelt next to Mama, throwing her arms around her. "How glad I am that you and Papa are here! How I love you both!"

"I couldn't agree with you more, Lady Thurlby," Aunt Margaret said. "It is so satisfying to see two young people discover the bloom of new love, is it not? And to think I was able to be a part of it all fills my heart to bursting!"

"Lady Walmsley has been like a fairy godmother to me, Mama," Susan said, squeezing Mama's hands in reassurance. "And you know I was never one to believe in fairy tales."

"There is nothing fairy-like about me," Aunt Margaret said. "It is love that creates the magic." She picked up the teapot. "More tea, Lady Thurlby?" she asked.

"Thank you, Lady Walmsley," Mama said. "I believe I am content for now."

And Susan got the impression Mama was talking about more than merely tea.

"I don't know whether to knock you flat on your back or shake your hand," Lord Thurlby said to George. "But as I'm not a violent man by nature, I'll choose the second option."

George and Susan had explained the events of the past week to everyone, and George had watched Susan's parents' eyes grow wide with incredulity as they'd listened. Afterward, George and Lord Thurlby had excused themselves from the ladies, and Foster had directed them to a quiet room in which they could further discuss the past week and George's proposals—plural—to Susan.

"Thank you kindly, Lord Thurlby," George said, relieved that as he had just finished sharing the details of his own version of events, he wouldn't have to remain still and take a blow to the face from his betrothed's father.

They shook hands amiably, and Lord Thurlby also gave George a few slaps on the back of the hearty—not hostile—variety.

"None of this would have happened had our greedy monarch not tried to manipulate me into marriage with a German princess for his own personal ends," George said. "I would not have Susan at my side otherwise, so I must be grateful to him now—although I won't be sharing *that* particular detail with him, for he will crow and congratulate himself on what a fine deed he did, and he will never let me forget it."

Lord Thurlby chuckled and shook his head. "That is one of the reasons I prefer to stay quietly in the country. Perhaps it is selfish of me, but I am a blunt and simple man; the parsing of words was never my strength."

"And yet," George said, "your children, the ones with whom I am personally acquainted, are two of the most clever and well-educated persons I know. I would suspect they get much of their cleverness from their father, from what I've been able to glean thus far."

"Don't let their mother hear that!" Lord Thurlby exclaimed with a chuckle. "Lady Thurlby may appear the effusive country matron, but she is a force to be reckoned with, as I know only too well."

Lord Thurlby's words recalled to mind Lady Thurlby's intense study of her daughter and George when they'd first exited the carriage. "Duly noted," George said.

"And thank you for the compliment regarding my children, by the way," Lord Thurlby added. "We were blessed with eight healthy babes, and they've been a blessing ever since. A true blessing." His face clouded slightly. "Still waiting to see how one or two of them fare as they forge their way into adulthood, but I have faith, and I did and always do my best by them."

George fiddled with his quizzing glass and said nothing in reply; he rarely thought of his own parents, except in passing. Discussing Susan's siblings with her father felt . . . more personal than George had anticipated, as though he were imposing on something intimate.

"Your Grace?" Lord Thurlby said, pulling George from his thoughts. "A penny for them?"

"It's nothing," George said. "I barely remember my father, you see, and have no memories of my mother. I have no brothers or sisters. So, to hear you speak of your family in this manner, I have no context in which to frame your words. Forgive me."

"Oh, my son—for on Monday, you *shall* be my son," Lord Thurlby said, "we must and *will* strive to help you feel a part of our expanding family. I can assure you that Lady Thurlby will make it her personal mission—"

"Oh, she needn't, really—"

"She wouldn't be the woman I married otherwise," Lord Thurlby said. "We're as varied as a family can be, as you will soon discover. In the meantime, let's see to the demands of Monday, shall we?"

Monday, when he would marry his Susan. "Agreed," George said. He would take one day at a time. If he could fall in love with last year's harpy of a woman, he could undoubtedly learn to feel a part of her seemingly eclectic family too. He thought he would actually enjoy it.

"I wish you would have accepted Lady Walmsley's invitation to supper," Susan said as she watched George take his hat from Foster.

"Thank you, Foster," George said as the butler nodded and then disappeared from sight. "Good man, that," he said to Susan.

"Yes," Susan said. "I believe he is secretly in love with Lady Walmsley."

"You mean Aunt Margaret," George said with a soft smile. "Do you really think so?"

"Yes," Susan said. "I believe I'm beginning to see love everywhere I go."

"Only here, now," George corrected her. "If you'll recall, there was very little love going around at Carlton House earlier today."

"That's true," she conceded.

He bent close to her and kissed her gently . . . and too briefly for Susan's preference.

"It has been quite a day, and I want you to have time with your parents. If we are to travel to Lincolnshire sooner rather than later in the spring, as we discussed, then I have business to attend to. I hope you will have a quiet evening and an enjoyable day tomorrow. I shall collect you all for church on Sunday, if I may. And then Monday"—he kissed her again—"Monday, you shall become my duchess. My wife."

"Mm," Susan said, which, somewhere in the back of her mind was an agreement to his plan. Except—She drew back. "I won't be seeing you tomorrow?" And then she cringed. Good heavens, she sounded like a delicate flower near to wilting! "Forget I said that," she muttered.

George laughed. He laughed! "If the indomitable Athena herself is made vulnerable by her affection for me," George said with much hyperbole, "then I am forever the victorious conqueror."

She snorted and then covered her mouth with her hand and laughed until the tears rolled from her eyes, while he watched her, a look of smug humor on his face, before he laughed with her.

He wrapped his arms around her, drew his handkerchief from his pocket, and began dabbing at her cheeks. "Tsk-tsk. Once again, I find you without a handkerchief when you need one. I hardly know how you managed from day to day without my being at your side. Thank goodness that is about to change." He dabbed the end of her nose with it and followed it with a kiss on her lips, soft and caressing, which turned into two kisses and then three, and then Susan stopped counting and simply breathed and tasted and savored.

His beautiful eyes were filled with emotion, and Susan's heart swelled with recognition. "Have a quiet night with your parents and a peaceful day tomorrow, my love," George whispered.

She watched him while he descended the stairs and entered his carriage and continued watching until his carriage was no longer in sight before returning to the parlor and the others.

On Saturday morning, George called his entire staff together. "As most of you already know," he began, "I am to be married this Monday, and for the first time in thirty-five years, there will be a Duchess of Aylesham."

To his great surprise, a few of them began to clap and then more and more until they all were clapping and cheering.

He looked at them all as a group and then individually. Henshaw, with whom he had a meeting scheduled for later in the afternoon; Talbot and Mrs. Birch and Mrs. Bradley, even Bentley, his coachman, was there, along with the maids of all work and the footmen. And good old Evans, his ever-faithful valet, the person who had been like a father to him. His entire staff.

They were his family, George realized as they then broke out in song. He shook hands with each one, except for the women, of course; he bowed over their hands as though they were the highest ladies in the land while all around him the words, "For he's a jolly good fellow, and so say all of us" rang out.

He shook Evans's hand last. "Evans," he said as the singing began to wind down, "I would be humbled if you would agree to be my best man."

"I—" Evans, probably for the first time in his life, seemed at a loss for words. "Why, thank you, Your Grace! I'm deeply honored by your request." He paused and searched George's face carefully. "Are you absolutely certain, Your Grace?"

"Most assuredly," George said. "As long as you make certain I am fitted out for the day in perfect finery first."

Evans laughed and then became completely sober. "Your father would be proud to see the fine gentleman you have become. Proud, as I am proud of you."

"Thank you, Evans," George said, touched. "You are all invited to the wedding, of course," George added before the tone in the room turned maudlin, "which means we must make hasty preparations, for I wish to invite those who are attending the ceremony to a banquet afterward. Do you think we can manage it?"

"Indeed, Your Grace!" Talbot said, looking quickly at Mrs. Birch, who nodded her assent.

"Absolutely, Your Grace," Mrs. Birch said.

"And you, Mrs. Bradley? What say you?" he asked his cook.

"I have been waiting for this day for years, Your Grace," she said, "if you'll beg my pardon for saying so. You shall have the finest feast London will see this Season; you mark my words!"

"Thank you all for your dedicated service and your enthusiasm at my good news," George said. "I am grateful beyond words. I am also completely confident I will be bringing my duchess into the best-run house in London. What say you?"

They cheered as one again. It was jolly nice to hear it too. In fact, after all of these years of thinking himself a solitary being, it felt blasted good to be a part of this unity. "Carry on," he said. "And thank you all again for your well-wishes." Then he left to his library and allowed them to do what they all did best.

"Efforts to have the final agreements in place with all of the parties involved are proceeding fairly well," Jennings told George once the two of them, along with Henshaw, were settled in George's study. "You've had your hands full dealing with Prinny—and my sister," he added with a smirk, "so I took it upon myself to visit the Foreign Office this morning. The documents are nearly ready, and I should be able to leave for the Continent the day after you and Susan are wed. They've already heard from Osbourne, by the way, and I suspect if they've received correspondence from him, you should be receiving a letter from him shortly too."

"Excellent," George said.

"I shall go see if the post has arrived," Henshaw said, rising to his feet.

"Ask Talbot to have luncheon sent in to us while you're at it," George said. He was already feeling hungry again, despite eating a large breakfast this morning. Perhaps his body was finally in the mood to fully recover from his illness and he'd start to find all that weight he'd lost. It was a good omen.

"I shall, Your Grace," Henshaw said.

Once he'd left the room, Jennings leaned forward to George. "I have it on good authority that Prince Ernst was entirely effusive and financially supportive of

Bonaparte and his army—until the prince's own little principality of Schönberg-Nusse was mediatized, at which point he severed ties with the French. So the information we heard previously regarding his being a Bonapartist wasn't far from the truth. Apparently, he's now decided he bet on the wrong horse, for despite the failed marriage attempt between you and his daughter, he intends to remain in England for a while."

"Interesting," George said. He was relieved to know he hadn't put Susan through all of this based upon a faulty presumption.

"I have been instructed by my terrifying mother that after our meeting concludes, I am to hunt down my ne'er-do-well baby brother so he is there in attendance at the wedding, since we have it on good authority that he and his friends have returned to Town."

"Susan will appreciate that." George paused as an errant thought struck him. "Why did you never tell me your sister spoke German?"

Jennings shrugged. "You never asked. She's quite fluent, actually."

"Yes," George said with a touch of irony. "I know that now." He then proceeded to relate the events of the previous afternoon.

"Leave it to Susan to be in the wrong place at the entirely right time," Jennings said with a laugh. "As children, she always knew when my brothers and I had something devious planned. I don't know how she managed it to this day. It always came with an ultimatum: allow her to join us in our escapades or she'd go directly to Papa."

"So she joined you, naturally," George said.

"Naturally," Jennings replied with a shrug.

Henshaw returned at that moment, holding a small stack of letters. "Talbot says to expect luncheon shortly," he said as he seated himself. He quickly thumbed through the letters. "There isn't anything that requires urgent attention, Your Grace," Henshaw said. "Wait." He pulled one letter out. "Although, it appears you have another piece of correspondence from the Prince Regent."

"What can Prinny possibly want *now*," George grumbled as he took the letter from Henshaw. He broke the seal and opened the letter, which was written in Prinny's own flowery script. He read it and read it again and set it on his desk.

"Well?" Jennings asked. "Are you going to tell us what it says?"

George shook his head in disbelief. "I'm beginning to think I've been living in a Shakespearean comedy the past fortnight." He chuckled to himself. "Look around you. Is Shakespeare's ghost lurking somewhere about? Are there fairies hiding beneath the bookshelves or sorcerers weaving their spells from behind the window curtains?"

"What are you talking about?" Henshaw said. "Shakespeare?"

"The letter will make it much clearer," George said. He picked up the letter again and shook it out dramatically. "I will not bore you with the precise wording, but in summary, it would seem that His Royal Highness, the Prince Regent, cannot, after all, attend my nuptials this Monday, as he will be busy entertaining Prince Ernst of Schönberg-Nusse at his seaside pavilion in Brighton while the princesses remain here in London. He says they subsequently bonded—I would presume aided by several decanters of brandy—over their shared aggravation at their financial circumstances and their wives, and decided some distance from the females in their lives was the answer." He laughed. "It is as though, to Prinny, the past two weeks simply vanished in a puff of smoke."

"Sometimes, I cannot believe the country continues to function as well as it does with such a man as our ruler. But I have other questions at present. More specifically, does this change your plans? What do you intend to do?" Jennings asked.

"I intend to marry your sister," George answered. "If anything good came from all of this, it is that I found my bride. That fact doesn't change merely because of a foolish and fickle monarch."

"I suppose all's well that ends well, then," Henshaw said thoughtfully.

George laughed again. "My good man, you have hit the nail squarely on the head," George said. He rose and went to his side table to pour three small brandies, and then he handed one to each of them before he raised his glass. "Here's to all's well that ends well and much ado about nothing." They each drank. "Now, enough of Shakespeare, Prinny, and German princesses," George said. "Here's to the prize I was fortunate to find through the machinations of others. To my love, Susan."

"To Susan," Jennings and Henshaw said, raising their glasses again.

The course of love never did run smooth, George couldn't help but think as he set his glass down.

Epilogue

Monday morning arrived at last, along with low clouds and the threat of rain, which meant that Susan's hair was curlier and more temperamental than usual, even with her recent trim. The extra humidity didn't dampen Susan spirits though.

"What an extraordinary head of hair you have," Aunt Margaret said, not for the first time, as she reviewed Susan's most recent attempt to tame it. "How I wish my own hair were half as lush as yours."

"She gets it from her father's side of the family," Mama said. "Maternal great-grandmother. My side produces hair as straight as a poker."

"It has a mind of its own most days, you know," Susan said, trying to hide her amused smile. "Even after the trim it received from the talented Miss Lily."

"Much like the person who possesses it," Mama said.

"Perhaps I shall simply let it fall freely," Susan said, turning her head from side to side as she viewed her reflection in the mirror. "I'm not sure it can be tamed today, of all days."

Mama and Aunt Margaret gasped in unison.

"To *church*, Susan?" Mama exclaimed, her hand flying to her mouth in horror. "People will think you're a *wanton*."

"At the very least, they may think you are being rather too bold for London Society," Aunt Margaret added. "*Do* remember that Lord and Lady Bledsoe and, well, *others* will be there, even if St. George's isn't full to the rafters, as it should be for such an event. You want to make a good first impression as Duchess of Aylesham, do you not?"

There was a knock on the door of Susan's dressing room. "Yes?" Susan asked. "Who is it?"

"Miss Lily here to see you, Miss Jennings," a female voice replied through the door.

Susan shot a feigned look of exasperation at Aunt Margaret, although, truly, she was glad Miss Lily was here to help her look her best on her wedding day. "Come in, Miss Lily," she said.

Aunt Margaret gave a dramatic shrug as Miss Lily quietly entered the dressing room and began to assess Susan's hair in its present condition. "Well? I knew you would never ask me to engage her services, even though Aylesham would certainly have footed the bill, although I wouldn't have sent him the bill anyway, as it would be a gift on my part, now, wouldn't it?"

"Gracious!" Mama exclaimed. "Thurlby and I will pay for this woman's services. There is no need to—"

"Hush now, Lady Thurlby," Aunt Margaret said. "I suppose it was vulgar on my part to mention money. But you are *not* to worry one single bit. You are the mother of the bride, and I asked Miss Lily to assist you in looking your very best too."

"I deem it an honor and privilege, my lady," Miss Lily said. "Although you already look very elegant."

"Thank you," Mama said, patting her hair in a self-conscious manner. "Perhaps I could do with a few more curls about my ears."

Miss Lily deftly styled Susan's hair and then proceeded to work her magic on Mama. God bless Aunt Margaret for sending for Miss Lily, and God bless Miss Lily for her talents. It was quite remarkable to see how easily she managed to make Susan's hair behave.

"Now for your gown," Aunt Margaret said. She had asked Tompkins to assist Susan today, and Susan would be wearing her favorite gown of the many Madame Veronique had created—the deep-cream silk with a touch of gold embroidery at the neckline and around the sleeves.

"Oh, that's lovely, Susan," Mama said. "You look absolutely stunning."

"Thank you, Mama," Susan said.

"And the final touch. Allow me," Aunt Margaret said, picking up the ruby necklace that lay on the vanity. Aunt Margaret carefully placed it around Susan's neck and fastened the clasp. "Perfect."

Susan could scarcely believe that the image she saw in the mirror was really her. "I truly wonder if you simply keep your magic wand hidden, Aunt Margaret. But magic or no, I thank you with my whole heart. For everything."

"Now, dear, let's not get all teary-eyed when we must save those tears for the actual ceremony," Aunt Margaret said, pulling out her handkerchief she had tucked into her sleeve and dabbing at her eyes.

Susan and Mama both laughed, but Mama dabbed at her own eyes also.

"We need to go now, my dear," Aunt Margaret said, sniffing once and tucking her handkerchief away. "It's time to make you a duchess."

Susan collected her shawl and bonnet and followed Mama and Aunt Margaret out the door. She was going to become a duchess today, true, but more importantly, she was going to become a wife. George's wife.

There were two carriages waiting out front when they arrived—Lady Walmsley's and George's. Papa stood nearby, waiting for them. Susan could scarcely remember a time when her hardworking papa had looked so dashing and dignified, dressed to the nines as he was this morning in a gray coat with a silver brocade waistcoat and perfectly knotted neckcloth.

"How splendid you ladies look!" he exclaimed. "My own lovely bride, our new, dear friend, and my beautiful, clever daughter. Now, off you go to the church, Alice," he said to Mama, kissing her cheek and offering a cordial bow over Aunt Margaret's hand. "Susan and I shall follow in Aylesham's carriage."

"Oh, my darling girl!" Mama exclaimed, throwing her arms around Susan. "How happy I am for you, although I shall miss your companionship at home, as I have already missed you the past weeks."

"I shall miss you all too, Mama," Susan said. "But you don't need to miss me yet. We're all traveling to Lincolnshire in a few days, you know, and we shall celebrate together with everyone." She was so grateful George had agreed to meeting her brothers and sisters sooner rather than later.

"When next we speak, I will be addressing the Duchess of Aylesham," Mama said. "What a wonder that is!"

"No, Mama," Susan said firmly but with love. "You will be speaking to your naughty Susan, as you always have." She kissed Mama on the cheek. "I love you, you know."

"Oh dear," Mama said, searching for her handkerchief. "I didn't intend to start with the tears until the actual service began, and yet, here I am, once again, feeling the urge to weep. I love you too, Susan. With all my heart. What an honor it is and always has been to be your mama all these years."

Susan was close to tears herself now, so she began to feel around inside her pocket for her own handkerchief—

Mama quickly dabbed at Susan's eyes and smiled brightly. It was just as well that Mama had her own handkerchief, for once again, Susan had discovered that she was without.

"There we are; you never have been known to have a handkerchief when you need one. All better. Adieu, my darling!" And then, with one last, brief hug, she hurried off to the carriage, where Susan could see Aunt Margaret poking her head around the carriage door, waiting for Mama to arrive so they could be on their way.

"Shall we, then, my dear, clever daughter?" Papa asked, gesturing to George's carriage. "Are you ready to proceed?"

"Yes, Papa," she answered confidently. "I'm ready."

He assisted her into the carriage, the coachman, Bentley, tipped his hat to her in greeting, and once they were settled, Papa gave the signal, and they were on their way to St. George's Hanover Square Church.

George had never really thought much about the details of a wedding. He'd never spent time imagining what his would be like. He'd attended several over the years but had considered them only in the abstract. There was a bride, a groom, a clergyman. Words were said.

He had felt pangs of hurt and embarrassment when Lady Louisa Hargreaves had broken off their betrothal and married Lord Farleigh nine long years ago. And he'd felt the wistfulness of an opportunity lost when Lady Elizabeth Spaulding had married Lord Cantwell last year. Beyond that, he'd had no real emotional connection to the weddings he'd attended, except for an expected sort of congeniality, even if all around him people were crying and laughing and embracing.

Today, however . . .

He sat at the front of the church next to Evans, who was dressed as impeccably as George himself was—but then, considering Evans was his valet, George expected nothing less and would have told the man he was fired if he hadn't appeared thusly.

He'd already made Evans check his pocket a half dozen times for the wedding band he held in safekeeping for the appropriate moment during the service. Evans would think his employer had lost his wits if George wasn't careful.

He'd expected very few guests. He'd invited his staff to be here, of course, and Susan's mother was seated next to Lady Walmsley, and James was seated next to her, as was a young rake of a fellow George presumed was the youngest Jennings brother, Simon.

But his heart leaped within him as he glanced around the chapel, surprised by how many other people were here.

It appeared that Lady Walmsley had also invited a good share of her staff. Foster was seated behind her and, gracious, Susan might very well be correct about the old fellow's attachment to Lady Walmsley, if the look in his eyes at present was anything to go by.

He'd invited Lord and Lady Bledsoe to attend, and they were here, as he'd hoped and expected, but so were the Duke and Duchess of Wilmington and the Duke and Duchess of Atherton and Lord and Lady Melton. The ladies were the ones with whom Susan had taken tea.

Word must have spread, for even more people poured through the doors until the church was quite near capacity. George's first inclination was that some were here for the spectacle about which they could gossip with their associates later. It should annoy him, but he didn't care. Let them observe his happy moment.

Let them witness the marriage of the Duke of Aylesham, bachelor of long-standing, to his chosen bride.

He sensed a commotion that drew his attention to the front of the chapel once again. The Reverend Mr. Hodgson was moving to take his place. Finally, it was time.

George and Evans stood as the organist commenced playing processional music, and the congregation rose to their feet.

George—indeed, the entire congregation—turned to look at the back of the church. There, on her father's arm, was the most radiant woman George had ever seen. How he hadn't initially seen her in this light baffled him.

She looked straight ahead at the rector and wore a serious expression as she and her father proceeded up the center aisle of the church. And then—

And then her head moved slightly, and her eyes caught George's own, and he could feel her warmth and humor and, yes, her love all the way across the church. He'd never believed such romantic talk before, but he did now. Her eyes never left his own.

He felt something in his eye and brushed it away, then realized it was a tear. Good heavens! He wanted none of that now, not with everyone watching. Of course, they were really watching his beautiful bride as she walked toward him.

Susan's face had softened further when he'd dashed the solitary tear away. His single tear might have left her feeling sentimental right now, but she wouldn't ever let him forget that he'd teared up at their wedding. Oh, yes, he knew the woman he was marrying. And, oh, how he loved her!

She embraced her father, who then placed her hand in George's, and they together approached Mr. Hodgson.

"Dearly beloved," Mr. Hodgson began.

Strangely enough, Susan had never entered Aylesham House before today. Now it was to be her home.

She and George were greeted at the door by a dignified butler Susan realized she'd seen at the wedding.

"A hearty congratulations to you, and welcome to Aylesham House, Your Grace," he said to her with a deep, formal bow. She spotted a twinkle in his eye when he straightened. "We shall do all in our power to make you comfortable in your new home."

"This ne'er-do-well is our butler, Talbot, my dear," George said.

"At your service, Your Grace," Talbot said with another bow.

"I am pleased to make your acquaintance, Talbot," she replied.

Inside the house, the entire household was lined up at attention, albeit wearing their finest Sunday best, waiting to be introduced to and inspected by their new duchess.

"Mrs. Birch, housekeeper, Your Grace," a woman of middle years said with a polite curtsy. She had graying hair styled in a no-nonsense manner, and her clothing matched in efficiency, and despite her age, her back was ramrod straight. She looked every inch the sort of housekeeper one would expect to maintain a duke's household.

"I expect we shall rub along well together, Mrs. Birch, since I am completely aware that the duke doesn't tolerate fools. I gather you—all of you"—she gestured at the line of individuals still waiting to greet her—"are experts at your jobs." Susan had no doubt that his homes were well run, and there was no reason, in her opinion, to fix something that wasn't broken.

"Thank you, Your Grace," Mrs. Birch replied with another succinct curtsy.

It was going to take Susan a while to get used to all the curtsying and bowing that went along with her new title.

Susan met Mr. Oliver Dutton, Esquire, the long-standing family solicitor; Mr. Henshaw, George's personal secretary; and Mrs. Bradley, the hearty, red-cheeked cook.

"And I shall tell you all of the duke's favorite dishes," Mrs. Bradley said after curtsying. "So you will know how to placate him should he ever be in a bad mood, although I have yet to see—"

"*Thank you*, Mrs. Bradley," George interrupted mildly.

Mrs. Bradley's cheeks went even redder, and she curtsied once again.

"I shall be delighted to learn your culinary secrets, Mrs. Bradley," Susan said, smiling. "I daresay they will come in handy." She shot George a cheeky look.

George shot her a similar look in return. "And this is Evans, my valet," he said. "The man has been with me since I was a boy in leading strings."

Susan immediately recognized him as the person who had been George's best man at the wedding. What an insightful discovery that was! "That is an accomplishment on many levels, Evans," Susan said, responding to George's comment.

The valet bowed, but Susan saw him grin before he hid it by lowering his face. When he raised his head, his formal countenance was back in place.

She met a handful of footmen and maids of all work. It wasn't a large staff, but then, George had been a single man, a man Susan had already surmised had not been keen on entertaining Society within his home. She attempted to remember all of their names, for she felt it was crucial that these servants be recognized as individuals and were to be respected in their various responsibilities.

She had also seen clearly that these servants were devoted to George. She suspected a few of them had been the only family he'd ever known.

Oh, George.

They would always be part of his family, Susan knew, but *she* was his true family now. He was her husband.

And she intended to give him his own family of flesh and blood.

"Mrs. Birch, it has recently come to my attention that my duchess has no personal maid. We must address that particular situation posthaste," George said.

"I shall see to it immediately," Mrs. Birch said.

"Perhaps not immediately, Mrs. Birch," Susan said. "For I have gone these many years without a personal maid, and today is a day my husband has gifted to all of you so you may enjoy the celebration and luncheon that awaits." George had authorized the hiring of temporary servants for the day in order to give his full-time staff the chance to celebrate with them. "Another day will not matter."

"Very good, Your Grace," Mrs. Birch said with a curtsy.

Through the entry hall windows, she could see the guests who'd been invited to dine with them beginning to arrive. Mama and Papa and Lady Walmsley, James and—oh my goodness!—*Simon*. And no sooner than one carriage had emptied itself of its occupants and driven off than another took its place.

"Come, Duchess," George said, offering his arm to her. "It is time to welcome our guests to our home."

Susan was acutely aware of the fact that this was her wedding night. *Their* wedding night.

After a wonderful afternoon of food and conversation and music and dancing, they had bidden farewell to their guests, and Susan had hugged Aunt Margaret and Mama and had kissed Papa and James and *Simon,* to whom she'd also given a lecture about avoiding the family for too long.

Simon had looked at her sheepishly. "I shall try to do better, Suzie," he'd said. He was the only person who'd ever gotten away with calling her by that awful nickname, but as she'd been so glad to see him, she'd ignored it. She hoped beyond hopes he meant his words. She had missed her baby brother.

Now Susan and George were alone.

"Allow me to take you on a small tour of your new London home," George said after he and Susan had enjoyed a late supper together. He offered Susan his hand, which she gladly took.

He led her down one corridor after another, showing her the elegant ballroom where they'd held their luncheon, then a music room, his study, and a rather fine library, which drew her particular interest. There was also a conservatory, and near it was a charming dayroom where french doors opened onto a porch that led out into a garden with mature trees and benches and shrubbery bearing blooms.

"I don't expect you to have the entire layout of the house memorized in one quick tour," George said, "but I wanted you to feel comfortable enough to explore—" He broke off speaking. "I take that back."

Susan looked at him. "What do you mean you take it back?" she said.

"I suspect *my Susan* would already feel comfortable enough to explore," he replied, smiling indulgently at her.

She arched a saucy eyebrow at him. "I see you *do* understand the woman you have married after all," she said.

"Utterly and completely," he said. And then the Duke of Aylesham, *her* Duke of Aylesham, grinned at her.

And Susan fell in love with him all over again.

His glittering, dark eyes got darker still.

"There is another room I wish to show you," George said, and Susan's heart began to race. She knew what that room would be, and sure enough, he led her to the wing where the private suite of rooms intended for the family's use was located. Undoubtedly, there was a room for the duke and one for the duchess.